D1195575

IMPERIAL KELLY

IMPERIAL KELLY

Peter Bowen

Crown Publishers, Inc.
New York

Published by Crown Publishers, Inc., 201 East 50th Street, New York, New York 10022. Member of the Crown Publishing Group.

CROWN is a trademark of Crown Publishers, Inc.

Manufactured in the United States of America

Library of Congress Cataloging-in-Publication Data

Bowen, Peter, 1945–
Imperial Kelly / Peter Bowen. — 1st ed.
p. cm.
1. Spanish-American War, 1898—Fiction. 2. South African War, 1899–1902—Fiction. I. Title.
PS3552.0866I48 1992
813'54—dc20 92-14569
CIP

ISBN 0-517-58285-6

10 9 8 7 6 5 4 3 2 1

First Edition

For Crinoline

IMPERIAL KELLY

1

I could have shot Theodore Roosevelt any number of times. I could have sawed through ropes he was hanging on to, I could have let a couple grizzlies chaw him to death. I didn't take any of the chances I had. Just folding my arms or pulling a trigger or not pulling a trigger would have saved tens of thousands of lives and me several attacks of gout and them wim-wams you get when you are sliding down the front wave of history in a very small boat.

Someone should have shot him long ago, anyway, and I suppose I was waiting for someone even more exasperated than I to shoot him, but they never showed up and there I was, waffling like the stripe-ass poltroon I am. Well, it's a job.

I did try to brain him with one of his damned Indian clubs—he used to exercise with them, shattering busts of the dignified dead and ship's models in his office. He was Assistant Secretary of the Navy and a rising young sawlog of presidential timber, a clear danger to all about him.

America had imperial ambitions—all done for the moral improvement of whoever's land we wanted, mind you—and so it seemed that Cuba and the Philippines was in need of us. We were in a hot fighting mood and the poor sorry Spaniards was about all we could bully into going to war with us. The *Maine* had been blowed up in Havana harbor and fingers were pointing at the sneaky Dons, but my experience with the military had been such I thought it likeliest that an admiral had been inspecting the magazines by matchlight. I could name several admirals.

My luck is as sour as a Baptist's love life, always has been, and so of course I was right there with Teethadore when he commenced in playing with the fleet like a damn kid in a bathtub.

'Twas a Friday forenoon and I had stopped off to see my good old friend Gen. Nelson Miles, who had found out somehow I was in the city. I hate Washington, D.C., even more than most cities. I was there because I had been *ordered* to be there by Gen. Nelson A. Miles.

"So good to see you again, Kelly," says Miles, twinkling. If I'm near, there is always a hope in the bastard's manly breast that he'll finally have the happy job of hanging me. We go back a lot of years, and we know far too much about each other.

Miles wanted to know what I thought of the Spaniards invading Alaska. I told him it was a fine idea, they'd just vanish into the place, where the Alaskan mosquitoes would finish them off in jig time. We jawed back and forth for a while and then Miles threw me out of his office, like he always does, and some little snip of a naval lieutenant caught me the second bounce from the door and allowed as how the Assistant Secretary of the Navy Theodore Roosevelt would very much like to see me.

"Tell that four-eyed barnacle-brained socialite," I began, warming up to be unpleasant. The lieutenant was waving his hand at me.

"If you're too rushed, the Assistant Secretary understands and will merely have you clapped in irons in the basement until *he* finds time to see you."

I nodded. The little shit. I got far, far too many friends.

The War Department was overheated to the point of folks wheezing when they breathed. The pup lieutenant was soaked clear through his dress uniform and pale as a fish's belly. He ushered me through some corridors and up a flight of stairs and into Teethadore's squat presence. Teddy and I shook hands warmly and the lieutenant fell on his face, making a wet sound as he laid upon the grizzly bear–skin rug Teethadore had spread out in front of his hand-carved desk.

"Zounds!" said Teddy, leaping from his chair onto and over the desk. He commenced helping the poor kid breathe with terrible thrusts of his powerful hands against the lower part of the back. I thought the kid's lungs and kidneys would come out his mouth.

"Call the guard," bellered Teddy.

I went out in the hall and called the guard.

They come on the run—bayonets fixed and six of them at that, all firebellied in case the sneaky Spaniards decided to assassinate Teethadore. They made a circle, bayonets out, around Teethadore and the prone pup in the gold braid. Made me think of musk ox when they smell wolves. I leaned back on the doorjamb, chuckling at the sheer dignity of it all. Teddy, with his collar awry, the soldiers, the passed-out navy kid. If the might of America responded this way to a fainting spell, why, whatever would it do in war?

A shadow fell upon me and the shadow had a seegar sticking out of the top end of it.

"John Long, Secretary of the Navy," said the gent, holding out a paw. I shook it. "Kelly," I said.

The passed-out lieutenant sat up before Teddy crushed his chest flat and coughed becomingly. The soldiers jumped to attention—they was Marines, actually—only slightly damaging a few of the game heads with which Teethadore had adorned every flat vertical surface. Teddy had fogged up his glasses with the heat and exertion and was grinning blind and waving his hand out.

"God's libeled balls," said Long. "What on earth are you doing *now,* Theodore?"

"Oh, oh, oh, oh," said Teddy. He grabbed for a handkerchief to wipe his glasses with and settled for the lieutenant's sash.

"I will leave this all to you," said Long. "I'm off for a week to my country place. Can you manage *not* to start a war in my absence?"

Teddy allowed as how he could easy manage that.

My scalp began to prickle uncomfortable-like.

"Things are extremely . . . . . . ah . . . . . . um . . . . . . delicate in the matter of the Spanish," said Long. "They are trying wildly to avoid war."

"Just like them," said Teddy. He looked like a kid with a baseball glove on staring out at the rain.

"And who in the hell *are* you, anyway," says Long, eyeing me up and down.

"Luther Kelly," I says.

"Well," says Long, "you are damn near as preposterous in person as you are in them damned dime novels my children liked more than saltwater taffy," he snorted. "I always find *something* in here with Theodore. Last time it was some red Indian smelled like eight wet rams."

The naval boy twitched to his feet and staggered toward the door, ripping his sleeve on a bayonet. The Marine's port-arms was a little low on account of he'd fetched up with a couple inches of elk antler in his right ear, interfering with his uprightness.

"God," said the Secretary of the Navy, sensibly follering his seegar down the hall. Well, I gathered that Theodore's present lofty state was not Long's idea.

"Return to your posts," said Theodore. He finally found a handkerchief and commenced rubbing his glasses. In a moment we was alone, except for the mounted heads and rugs and such.

Teddy put on his glasses and blinked at the bright new world around him. He went to a big wall map—the kind that has Greenland on it bigger than Africa. He looked hard at some little pins with heads like warships on them. He poked a fat finger at the belly of Asia.

"Jolly good!" said Teddy, still in his English-period voice which he had come back from a safari with, along with all manner of strange dead critters.

Teddy fiddled with his watch chain, humming. I didn't like it, the humming I mean. Meant he was thinking. Teddy thinking was dangerous to the human race in general and me in particular.

"Well, " I said, "I'd admire going back to my hotel and taking a bath. I got a dinner date in Bismarck, North Dakota."

"Sad is the man who sees opportunity and grasps it not," said Teddy. I knew just what he meant.

"Nice seeing you," I says, sidling and grasping my prize opportunity.

"Major Kelly," says Theodore, reminding me of my rank and the scaffold could go with it any time." I think we need a brisk walk."

My guts were doing a rapid fandango and my gout was sounding Charge!

"I'm awful tired," I whined, "and I got no sleep last week and my gout . . ."

"Pity," said Teddy, fishing a red wig out of a handy elephant-foot cane stand. He stood in front of a mirror adjusting the thing. Nothing helped. It still looked like a tomcat run over by a dray.

"I'm hungry, too," I moaned. "I ain't et today . . ."

"A shame," says Teddy, eyeing a linen duster. He slipped off his frock coat.

"My foot hurts to hell aready," I groaned. I did not like any of this *at all.*

"Besides, I was to meet a friend to dinner," I said. Hoping that this display of good manners would have an effect.

"I saw that Gussie was here in town and I believe that a walk would do you some good before you slink off to entertain your animal lusts."

"Animal lusts, is it?" I roared. "I at least don't haul their damn heads back and clutter the walls with 'em."

"Come along, Luther," says Teethadore, all rigged in red wig, duster, and cane.

"Animal lusts," I grumbled. And went along like a cut sheep.

Preceded by the Assistant Secretary of the Navy, in disguise, I walked down the long hallway and followed him down a stairwell built for skinny folks running from fire. We come out behind a hedge which Teddy peered through, holding up one hand to halt me. It warn't necessary; I couldn't get out of the door without kicking his ass out of the way.

"There he is," hissed Teethadore. I peered over the top of the greenery and spied Long getting into a carriage.

"You insane four-eyed son-of-a-bitch," I snarled. "This is nonsense. Long said that he was leaving and he is leaving. Like he said."

"Sneaked back and caught me the last time," said Teethadore. "I would never trust such a man myself for high public office."

There wasn't much I could say to that. Here was one retired Injun scout and general-purpose scoundrel standing in the winter privet looking at sanity departing for the train station. I should have brained this blind sawed-off lunatic I was sharing the hedge with. We could have had less history. Always a good idea, life's best when nothing out of the ordinary happens, you will agree.

Them bicycles with the huge front wheels had become sort of dated and TR had some fancy Frog bicycle hid in the shrubs; he hopped on and pedaled off, wig flapping, looking for all the world like some escapee from an insane asylum. Well, it fit.

My curiosity had me by now so I went back up to Teddy's office and contemplated the heads on the walls and the hides on the floor and the nice collection of tusks from elephants he'd shot and the passenger pigeon stuffed and mounted that sat on his desk next to the inkwells. (It turned out to be the *last* passenger pigeon ever seen out-of-doors by anyone. Teethadore was an ornithologist and naturalist of note, so he identified it, shot it, had it stuffed, and staked his claim. Bully bully.)

I could have done with a decent glass of whiskey but Teddy was a teetotaler. A lot of his uncles died of drink, and he had an older brother, Elliott, who was to do the same. (The family had a farm in the Adirondacks where they sent their whiskeybills when they was having the DT's and lassooing green snakes with pink ones.) Anyway, Teethadore never touched a drop, another thing that failed to recommend him to me. It made him some figure of curiosity out West, let me tell you.

I idled for a while, pitching my hat at a rhinoceros's horn and I would have lit up a seegar if I'd had one. Teddy didn't smoke, either, it aggravated his asthma and he would have been choking for three days unable to stir from his bed. We might have been spared much. So much can proceed from little things like not having a seegar. I long ago decided that if there is a God at all It's either blind drunk all the time, or dead; there's no one minding the store.

I waited maybe half an hour and then Teethadore come running in like his pants was on fire and the Mongols was right behind; he hooked a foot in the mouth of the grizzly rug and he went headfirst into a glass bell jar had a blowfish—dead and varnished—in it and TR's glasses shattered along with the bell jar and the blowfish—they are brittle things—and a big chunk of blowfish stuck in Teddy's left cheek—spiny little bastards, too. All this pain and blindness caused Teddy to holler manfully, and while he was clawing the blowfish off his face he barked his shins on a deal table and fell on it, sending about forty little model ships in bottles flying. He laid out flat and slid along to bounce hard off a mapcase and then sweep the legs out from under an aquarium full of the ugly little fish you see in whiskey dreams.

I looked at the happy sight. The Assistant Secretary of the Navy was laid out bleeding in a puddle full of flopping fish whimpering faintly for something or someone. It seemed one or three of them fish was being ground up by them monstrous Roosevelt choppers and interfering with the Roosevelt diction as it went to bits and fell down his windpipe. (Screw yer damn Frog painters, this was a *pretty* sight.)

Teddy finally choked his way upright and spat out fish parts here and there; he fumbled around his soggy waistcoat and found another pair of glasses—he broke six or so pairs a day—and he got them on and looked up to see Luther Kelly, Major, USA, looking down and laughing fit to bust. Laughing like a whore with a dead john who's already paid.

"Brap you, Kelp," said Teethadore, still mushmouthed with the fish parts in his works. He hacked and coughed and struggled up, shedding tinkling bits of glass and bleeding from about twenty small punctures in his cheek.

"Long get off all right?" I says, trying to bridge the awkward part of the conversation.

"Express to Lake George." said Teddy. "He'll be gone a whole *week!*"

"Why, you could have us fighting the Rooshians, the British, and the Bolivians by then. All of them at once," I says. "I think I'll go wire Secretary Long and say *please come back.* Urgent."

"This is not time for your blasted levities," pouted TR. "I could carve a better government out of a meringue." I took that to mean if the goddamned fools would have listened to Teethadore he'd right now be entering Madrid at the head of a conquering army.

"Come along," said TR. "You will find this interesting."

Some folks snap when their gods are ill-spoken of, or their mothers, but I go berserk when anyone in command says "interesting," and I do that for excellent reason. I have fifty-six visible scars in my hide I got in the course of going someplace that these bastards called "interesting."

Teddy was built solid, like a sand-filled barrel with feet, but I got a good clamp on his windpipe and I roared, "I DON'T LIKE THIS AT ALL WHATEVER IT IS YOU ARE GONNA DO YOU ARE GONNA DO IT WITHOUT ME THIS TIME YOU INSANE DUTCH PECKERWOOD . . ." and other endearments. Teddy nodded an eighth of an inch, grinning at me all the time.

I relaxed my grip.

"While you were choking me . . . . . . I thought of how hemp must feel . . ." he said, still smiling.

I follered him glumly down the corridor to a guarded elevator and we went down and down and down. The door opened and TR led the way past eight guards to the Code Room. TR motioned me on past a couple of Marine sergeants and came along behind me.

A shaky—malaria, I suppose—captain come up to TR and he saluted. Teddy nodded in a practiced, condescending sort of way—hell, he couldn't have *enlisted* in the Army with his eyesight—and he looked around the dark room at the bustle and scratch.

"I have a message for Admiral Dewey," said Teddy. "Who, I do believe, is in Singapore."

"Yes, sir," said the captain.

Teddy carefully wrote out his message to Dewey, in big block letters, and he grinned hugely while doing it.

He showed it to me.

COAL PROCEED MANILA WAR IMMINENT ROOSEVELT
ACT SEC NAVY

I was shocked into speechlessness. I knew we would mix it up with the Spaniards, but I thought it would take months or years of sashaying and flannelmouthing by diplomats who all the while would protest they was trying to avoid that horrid circumstance.

"Come along, Major Kelly," said Teethadore. "We have our duties." I follered along like a broke old dog.

Up in TR's office, I jangled the coins in my pockets while Teethadore wrote out his resignation from his high position. He tucked it into his coat.

"Major Kelly," he said, "I will even buy you a drink."

"Uncommon decent of you," I said. I had a few words I could have said on all this but they was of no moment, like me.

We walked on over to Ollie's.

I had about twelve fingers of sour mash in a posh saloon that was nearby, and then I had a seegar. Teddy sipped bottled Saratoga water.

"I am going to form a division of picked troops," says TR. "And I am going to call them the Rough Riders. Those fine specimens who breathe the free air of the Great Plains and the High Rockies will make splendid solidiers!"

"Yer drunk on gaddamned Saratoga water," I said. "You can't *tell* those sonsofbitches to do *anything.* They'll shoot you."

"Cowboys, hunters, scouts, trappers, wranglers, muleskinners, the hardy sons of our Great West."

"Christ," I says.

"Officered by the manly graduates of our finest schools," he went on.

"Meaning them fellers you went to Harvard with?"

"Oh, we'd take Yale men and some from the other lesser schools, and I will *require* your services, *Major* Kelly," said Teethadore, and all teeth at the moment. "Quit trying to cravenly steal away from this priceless test of your valor."

"How about I boldly steal away from this here priceless test?" I snarled, rising. "And I don't know if 'valor' is dyestuffs or bolt goods anyway."

"This simply won't do," said Teddy, looking sad.

"Send one of them Harvard brave boys you're always gassing about. I'm old, I have gout and bad dreams."

"I will need a stout recruiting officer to assemble and sign up the men for the Rough Riders," said Teethadore.

"West Point," I said. "Finest kind of officers. I pay taxes to train the ninnies."

"You are correct," said Teddy. "They wouldn't really *understand* one another. I need to send . . . . . . one of their own."

"Own what?" I says, goggle-eyed. "Me? Me? I might have shot their brother or third cousin twice removed or something and you want *me* to go sit behind a damn *table* all day? Where they will know where I'm *at*?"

"Surely they would not take such rude advantage?"

Theodore and I had had this conversation before. He thought war was chivalry and that the West's famous gunfights was fought fair. As a rule, you shot for the back and took ruthless advantage every little chance you got. Or you were dead. I did not waste my breath.

"Where do you want me to go?" I said wearily.

"West Texas, New Mexico, and Arizona."

These was all fine places to run if you had plumb wore out the patience of the forces of law and order. My friends and acquaintances of the last forty or so years were pure and simple the scum of the damn earth, and proud of it. I about wanted to go to West Texas like I wanted to go to Devil's Island.

I whined and begged and mewleypuked and sniveled and moaned and pleaded and wept and blubbered while Teddy sucked down soda water and said "tut-tut, couldn't I be more manly?"—which meant do as I was told.

Teddy bade me farewell, clapping a fat hand on my shoulder and bidding me buck up, smile, think on the flag and glory, keep my upper lip stiff, and catch a train the day after tomorrow when he would meet me at the station to assure I was *on* the train along with ten thousand recruiting forms and a few Regular Army noncoms to fill them out. Also twenty thousand recruiting posters, and a lot of gold—I perked up—to pay bounties with if the posters didn't bring the recruits in fast enough.

"Theodore," I said, to the empty space beside me, "if you offered two hundred in gold and a pardon, they'd come *here*."

I ordered another drink. In it again, goddamn it.

Gussie was waiting on me.

She was a wonderful actress I had known and liked for years, a fine girl from a little town in Ohio who had left there probably without shoes and who had finally married her millionaire who had shortly expired, of heart failure, in bed. Gussie planted the feller and then she scandalized all New York and all Washington (a mansion in each, you see) by tossing the accumulation of her dead millionaire's life out on the ashheap and redoing both castles in lovely things and not a lot of them. Then she went back to the stage, exploding half the hemorrhoids of the leering socialites intent on her delicious scandals.

The brighter ones among the swell set grasped that Gussie did not give a fig for their opinion. That was about four out of four thousand. The rest had the vapors regular-like, thinking on her.

All invitations to dinners and balls and swell parties ceased, which was fine with Gussie, who said that the rich ate very badly, smelled worse, and were so stupid that they needed metronomes to breathe. That was the gist of it, though what she *actually* said I wouldn't even write down, since Gussie's command of language common to harbor towns and cow camps far outstripped my meager talents. And my talents was sufficient to have once caused Shanghai Pierce to reach for a Bible to ward off lightning bolts from a blue sky. Shang being afraid of anything was news to me, and here I had forced the old boy to reveal himself.

We met at a restaurant and et oysters and drank champagne and went to her mansion bold as hell, with all the neighbors' eyes on us, and I didn't leave until late afternoon the next day, fucked to a standstill.

I had a couple belts in the hotel bar and went up to my room and I hadn't been in it five minutes when one of TR's jolly Harvardlings banged on the door and marched in, his teeth gleaming so bright in the gaslight it gave me a stabbing headache. He handed me a packet of sealed orders.

Then the Harvardling handed me a train ticket. He handed me a huge wicker hamper. I opened it and picked out a jar.

"Christ," I said. "Take a note."

"What? How?" said the Teeth.

"I'm gonna call off the labels on this mess of jars in this hamper, you asshole," I roared, "and you will write down what I say. And it's *Major* Kelly to you, you damned wet pup."

All Teddy's little pets carried notebooks and pencils in case they spotted the last survivor of some once multitudinous creature, so they could note critter, date, time, and place and give Teddy a leg up on shooting it. I suppose. (Perhaps I am being harsh. Maybe he just wanted to drag the critter home, cage it, and put it on a strenuous weight-lifting program.)

The Harvardling handed me the list, and I signed it. "Thanks ever so much I don't know what I would *do* without all of your help. God, am I sorry I shot that grizzly, the one in your office."

Teddy was in a hunting mood once and his guide got crippled by a mule, and I happened to be wandering near and was pressed into duty after a lot of whining on Teethadore's part and the laying of much gold in my large sweaty hand.

Teethadore hunting was a triumph of will over blindness and idiocy.

I wasn't keeping a close watch on him—how was I to know?—and Teddy spotted a mountain goat on a high cliff above him and he shot it dead and it fell on him. It knocked him off his perch and he slid and bounced down a hundred feet or so and caught a handy juniper bush. I laid down a rope. He indicated he would tie the rope to the tree he was on, slide down it, and let go the end and drop into the river, which would still be a good hundred feet below.

The river was sharp black rocks sticking up through white foam, so I talked him out of that idea. I damn myself every time I think on it.

I couldn't pull him back up right away, because the edge of the cliff was very sharp. With Teddy hollering about all the good hunting time we was wasting because I wasn't game, I made a crude windlass out of lodgepole and drug him up fast with the horse. It was a cheap grade of cliff and he only got scraped up a little.

"Invigorating! Bully!" he said.

I was beginning to grasp I was dealing with a mental defective and thought I might go back to the cabin and see if I could coax the mule into a repeat performance.

We found a grizzly in an hour or so. The bear was sleeping, but when he smelled us he went *woooooofff!* and hightailed it dead away.

The future President shot it in the ass. It is all you can *see* of a bear so headed.

The bear stopped cold, turned 180 degrees, and come running back right at us.

Teethadore stood manfully, Winchester to shoulder, and he shot a whole lot and the bear was still heading our way.

I stepped out in front of Teethadore with my four-gauge shotgun and forty-aught-size buckshot and hit that bear, stopped him like he'd hit a glass dam.

"Unsporting," said Teddy.

"Go to hell, you perfumed ninny," I said.

Now, at that time I could have quiet-like scrambled up a tree, but I didn't. I'd taken the man's money. I couldn't see the future. I could have been the man who saw Teethadore et before he got big enough to be dangerous. I have no excuses.

As so often in life all that I had to do was nothing at all and I would have spared myself and others grief, pain, and scars. (Well, the only time I was ever a main attraction at a wedding, I stood mute, causing the bride's kin to throw me through a stained-glass window, one dedicated to the fallen boys in Union Blue, which, that day, I sure was.)

2

Me and ten sergeants who could read and write (the entire supply the Army had, I suspected) arrived at Fort Sedgewick to recruit soldiers. War hadn't been declared yet, but Theodore's confidence and the big sack of bonus money—gold coin, collected from them of Teddy's friends as wanted to see him President, a thought which gave me the staggers and jags—guaranteed a turnout.

Fort Sedgewick was named after my favorite Civil War hero, one John B. Sedgwick, whose last words were, so help me, "Don't worry, boys, they can't hit an elephant at this dis . . ." That is the sort of optimistic exit a feller can only hope for. I will never be that lucky.

Of course, the military misspelled his name, but you can't have everything and fame, too, as Bill Cody was to never quite learn.

All along the railroad route there was militias drilling beside the tracks, and bandstands in every town square, and all the passengers was enthusiastic about the coming war which everybody seemed to think had already started. Or would have if them yellow-bellied Spanish had any sand. Enthusiasm for things that is military usually lasts till breakfast the second day and I have myself seen countless young boys go off to battle with heads high and chests puffed out. They don't come back that way, and all the ones left on the field are either too bad wounded to move, and crying for their mothers, or still.

Right then I did believe that if I went down the center of any town *all* the townfolk and most of the dogs would foller right along to whatever carnage I had to sell, long as I had a flute to tootle and a couple square yards of cheap cloth in the good old red-white-and-blue.

First night the recruiting sergeants went round the saloons and tossed about the rumor that Teethadore was looking for a few hundred good men and true, stalwart, brave, superb horsemen, crack shots, tough as oil-tanned leather, and like that and the drunken saloon telegraph carried this priceless piece of horse shit to the farthest and most desolate places of Texas, which is all of them.

(When Phil Sheridan said that if he owned both Hell and Texas he'd live in Hell and rent out Texas, he was standing in the most beautiful part. I don't know where it is.)

On the eleventh of April war was declared on the Spaniards and we was able to properly open the doors for business. Well, the fellers as wanted to fight the Spaniards with Teddy came to Fort Sedgewick in the thousands. Not a few hundred. Thousands. They fought each other for places in the lines, and several of them died of gunshots or knife wounds. There were so damn many the garrison could only watch.

The ten sergeants sat at trestle tables—the damn gold got shipped back entire, no need to bribe 'em—and took hard looks at the recruits, most of whom was a lot harder-looking than the sergeants.

I stood behind the sergeants, whittling.

A couple gents come up whistling and I looked up and almost took off a finger with my pocketknife.

The gents allowed as how killing Spaniards was a line of work they had long admired and felt that they would do right good at it.

The gent in front was a sandy-haired feller with a beard to match and merry blue eyes and he was dressed like a dude hairbrush drummer save for the custom riding boots with four-inch heels and a pair of silver-chased-ivory-handled Colts in well-worn tooled holsters. I warn't sure it was who I thought until I spotted the thumb he'd once caught between the saddle horn and rope, long ago when he was being a fair to middling cowboy at forty a month and found. This was long before he commenced into making life miserable for E. H. Harriman's railroads and for E. H. Harriman himself by robbing his trains. His sidekick was a tall feller with flat pale blue eyes that never changed with the light or seeing that they done. This customer had habits of rolling coins across his knuckles and pulling a gun and shooting so fast the eye could not follow. Like all good gunmen, he carried talcum powder for his holsters. I saw Harry shoot three men in the head in Silverton, Colorado, once, so fast they was all dead before I heard the *noise.*

Bob Parker and Harry Longabaugh, or Butch Cassidy and the Sundance Kid if you were some other places.

Butch looked up from the sergeant, saw me, and grinned and winked. I grinned back. He was a likable feller, sure enough; hell, he even liked the people he robbed. He drove E. H. Harriman near on to crazy sending him postcards and chatty notes from here and there, like twenty-four hours after he'd robbed E.H. of a pile of money.

I decided a julep or ten would taste nice, and I headed away from the crowds in front of the recruiting tables toward the little town and beat the rush to the saloon. I went on in the first one I come to still had glass in the windows and had the barkeep fix me a big one with plenty of ice and I went back out on the porch and found a nice place on the bench didn't have too many splinters in it. Butch and Sundance come along presently, chaffing each other like schoolboys. They had a sort of running vaudeville routine didn't seem to be rehearsed even.

"You boys got faces sorta familiar and names I can't recall," I says. "So what are them names I can't recall? You tell me them names and I'll practice them while I go and fetch you some drinks. Can't remember them drinks you used to drink neither."

Butch allowed as how they was stout Mormon lads named Nephi and Hoopoe.

"Mormons don't drink or smoke," I says.

"Jack Mormons drink and smoke," says Butch. "I'sa raised Mormon but it didn't take."

Me and Nephi and Hoopoe sat there for an hour or so talking about the coming war—I didn't wish to bring up anything in their past that I knew about which might embarrass them and they was equally tender toward my feelin's on similar subjects. Good manners makes the world a bearable place, I always say.

There was a lot of us out west in delicate circumstances and it accounts for our discreet ways. For instance, it is considered most impolite to ever ask anyone their *name.* You can get shot for your poor breeding and worse manners.

"I've never met Teddy," said Butch. "We robbed a train we was supposed to find him on, but he'd missed connections in Chicago. We only got four hundred dollars for the eighty of us . . . . . . well, it was a nice thought."

"Eighty seems a sort of large . . ." I glanced back of me. The window was closed and the glass whole.

"The point was to meet Teddy," said Butch. "Some of the boys was awful disappointed."

It seemed that the votes in the West was secure for Teethadore. I didn't count. I'd met him. I wouldn't vote for the goddamned fool if he had a gun to my head.

"Where's Cuba?" said Sundance, I mean Hoopoe. "I never heard of it till now."

"South of Florida," I said.

"I never heard of that neither." For a boy born in New Jersey, Sundance's scholarly upbringing had not been top-notch. Well, I was wrong there, too.

I drew a map, using the back of a recruitment poster and a pencil borrowed from the barkeep.

"Why does Theodore want *that?*" said Hoopoe, pointing at the island.

"Why are you named Hoopoe?" I says.

"Great Mormon prophet," says Sundance.

"Teethadore is a great general," I says.

We drank to that. I watched them go off looking for a game of cards.

The instructions was to recruit one thousand men at each of three stops. After the three thousand enlistment forms was done our work was finished. Since the sergeants did all the paperwork, my labors tended to be in the saloons. As military duty goes, I have had worse.

We saw the first thousand boys off on a special train to a camp in Florida where they would be taught how to ride and shoot. I figured only half of them was actually escaped from prison, and the other half ought to be in the jug on general principles, so it was as fine a bunch of soldiers as ever I seen.

No sooner was the train over the horizon than all hell broke loose at Fort Sedgewick, where it had been discovered that the payroll was gone, all the whiskey from the officers' mess had taken wing, and then there was a long list of miscellaneous lost items—all the musical instruments from the post band but the bull fiddle and bass drum, all the flags, all the officers' silverware, two mountain howitzers, a flagpole, and a shipment of six hundred Krag .30-40 rifles that was being held for another cavalry division to send an armed guard to pick up.

"The bastards stole every damn thing but the dust and the sunlight," said the Fort's colonel, shaking his head sadly.

The next two places was just the same, and we sent on a picked bunch of renegades, gunfighters, tinhorn gamblers, card sharks, dice-shavers, horse thieves, bushwhackers, and a couple hundred Injuns I'd shot at one time or another and vice versa.

"I ain't scalped anybody in so I long I can't hardly recall how," said one, Rains Black, his voice rising and falling. He'd got most of his English from books, but the song in the words was Sioux.

I waited as long as I decently could to go back to the camp in Florida, only a couple thousand miles away. I had good reason for this, as I suspected that these trains full of our recruits would pick any town they passed through clean as raked sand, and I did not want to arrive in them towns just as folks was getting their breath back. I did pass one pathetic sight, some old geezer wailing from the platform at some tank town in Mississippi.

"They even stole my teeth!" he wailed, sort of sloppily as his diction weren't too good.

The day that I arrived news had just come that Admiral Dewey had met the Spanish fleet at Manila Bay and the Spanish fleet was on the bottom of the Bay and Dewey hadn't lost a single man. I did not care much for the news, for though I always like to be on the winning side, long casualty lists do have a sobering effect on the country and all this victory did was whip up the blood lust to a frenzy. There was also a lot of hoorah about how the vicious Spaniards was shooting women and children and little puppy dogs, and trampling the petunias—and

Wee Willie Hearst and his godawful newspapers was out with a fresh batch of horror stories every morning. The Spanish was like every other colonial power on earth about then. They were *tired,* is what they was.

Teethadore had gone to his tailor and got a dozen uniforms made up, ones with epaulets that unzipped to reveal a couple pair of spectacles in each, plus padded pockets here and there in which a dozen more was hid, so that Teddy would never want for being able to see. Unfortunately, there was no lightweight uniforms for the men, who was issued heavy wool garrison uniforms. Though it was only April, Florida was a sweltering and damp place, and the uniforms were sheer torture.

Teethadore had been a rancher for about two years maybe fifteen years before, and in the time passed he seemed to have plumb forgot what cowboys is like. If you *tell* a cowboy to do something, he will tell *you* to do something involving your mother and a goat. Cowboys is gentlemen, they know it, and they expect to be asked polite. In town, cowboys practiced their in-town manners, which was beating each other witless.

The Regular Army sergeants was mostly in the hospital time I got there, with injuries mostly to lower jaws and noses. This threatened discipline something awful, especially when the Provost Guard would be told to arrest someone for telling a sergeant to go find his mother and a goat and the guard would sort of shuffle and spit and one of 'em would say, "Wal, damn it, I think ya want old Red thar arrested you ought to do it your own damn self, what I think." Chorus of yups and spits. (Chewing tobacco was a popular item. You could do a lot of things with it to an officer's shirtfronts and braid and blame the damn wind.)

Teethadore solved this problem with his typical flair and style. He made his scrawny little Harvardlings sergeants, and the recruits was so amused by these outlandish creatures that they would follow orders more or less so as not to upset the digestion of the little twerps. Also the little Harvardlings were accustomed to dealing with gentlemen, and so they prefaced their orders with "If you don't mind . . . . . . could we form right?"

Teethadore's Lambs didn't mind. So this was how the Rough

Riders was trained. An officer would give an order, some pale, weedy youth would take counsel with the privates in his care, they'd vote, and it would be done right quick if they'd a mind to.

Weapons was another problem. The recruits was armed like the bandits as they was, and they thought the Springfield rifles and black powder crude and beneath them.

Butch and Sundance ended up corporals in one company, and as Nephi and Hoopoe they had the troops in stitches all the time. Sundance was still wearing his gunbelt and Colts and a visiting officer commented disapprovingly upon them, whereupon Sundance whipped them both out and shot twelve times at a flock of pigeons racketing past overhead, and twelve birds exploded into puffs of feathers and blood. The officer nodded and went on, quite pale.

Some of the fellers had brought their buffalo rifles, antiques now, the buffalo having been gone for twenty years, and after it got through to the officers (me) how useful they would be for sniping at ranges up to a mile with plenty of force to kill when it got there, the buffalo riflemen was formed into a special company and allowed to wear their own clothes with an issue hat. Next day all the Rough Riders had to wear their own clothes because there was an accident in the night involving the garrison uniforms, lamp oil, and a match. The uniforms was all piled together, no one quite could figure how. The officer on duty ordered all them lounging bastards to put out the fire. One Stuff Simpson drawled as to how he and the boys here wouldn't piss on Major Kelly here if he was on fire, and with apologies that's the way things was. I nodded and said I understood the situation. Some kind soul gave me a bottle, and we jawed in the stinking wool-smoke and drank.

"Well, how does the work go, hey?" said Teethadore one evening as he looked out upon the serried rows of Rough Riders standing at attention if they wasn't scratching or pitching pennies or hunkered down playing poker.

"That is the most frightening collection of insubordinate sonsofbitches on the face of the planet. And you will be the very first dead hero of the war you don't think over very careful them orders you plan to give just when they collide with the Spanish."

"I don't understand," said TR. He seemed genuinely puzzled.

"When you holler 'Follow me' just be sure the boys here can see just why they ought to foller you. Any one of them bastards would charge hell with a washrag if they thought it a good idea. If they think your orders are a bad idea they will shoot you right quick as a menace to their health and dignity."

"I know," said Theodore, twinkling.

"This is a stupid war," I said. "The Spanish would like nothing better than to allow Cuba and the Philippines to be commonwealths, like England done with Canada."

"But I can't be President with that *Spineless Creature* in the White House preventing a good war. Why, he's done all he can to *avoid* war!"

"He was an officer in the Civil War," I said. "He's seen war."

"I simply cannot understand him."

"I can," I said. There was nothing else to say to Teddy, except perhaps go to hell.

3

Tampa, Florida, is an ugly, hot, sweaty, bug-ridden festering sumphole. It can be even more unattractive if you are stuck on a troopship out in the Bay, dead in the water, so the bugs can find you easy. There we sat, awaiting orders to go fight the Spanish.

There was only one place to bother fighting at for either of us, and that was down to Santiago, on the south coast. It was no secret to anybody but the Department of War, apparently.

We was in the books as cavalry, though cavalry in war (chasing Indians didn't count) was of no use at all except maybe as a messenger service. A horse and rider is a big target, and men fought from holes in the ground now. A horse will not go in a hole in the ground. You try it some time.

It was hard enough on us men, but the horses in the ship's hold died at a great rate. One by one the horses we was supposed to ride in some unstaged death-or-glory charge was pitched over the side for the sharks.

The Bay was full of bloated horse carcases and sharks and carrion birds. The flies was so thick that you actually got used to them crawling on you, and the bad food and bad sanitation began killing the soldiers and was to kill fifteen for everyone that got shot. Two thousand good men could have mopped up the Spanish, so America sent thirty thousand but not the supplies and food and medicine to keep them. I think that amounts to murder, just like I have always thought bad generalship amounts to murder.

The Spanish-American War was the easiest to avoid of any war we ever had. It was fought for other reasons, for promotions in the Army and Navy, for Theodore and Hearst, for the Sugar Trust, for money. As a war, it is damned hard to brag on it.

Any of 'em ain't much to brag on, you ask me.

A couple of TR's scrawny Harvardlings come by one afternoon and fetched me ashore to where Teethadore was holding court next to a polo field. The soldiers was out on the troopships and beginning to die off and TR was playing a fine, manly, masculine game of polo with his like chums, all of whom would end up in the goddamned government. They was that sort of folks.

After a few more fast chukkers TR cantered over to where I was leaned up against a live oak and drinking lemonade with ice in it. He swung down and a lackey took the horse's reins and led the animal off to be cared for a lot better than the troopers sweating in the stink out there in the transports.

"Luther, my good man, I have a job for you," said TR. I felt like breaking his teeth. My good man. Shit.

"You want me to go to Santiago and spy out the Spanish and let you know of their troop dispositions and numbers, artillery, supply, morale, fortifications, and such. When you arrive in the harbor you would like me to be bobbing around and easy to see so you can haul me aboard to hear me sing. Well, I did that three years ago (saving the bacon of that little shit Winston Churchill) and I can assure you that not one goddamned thing has changed because the Dons don't like to rush things. There's a report on file in my office."

"I would hardly think a three-year-old report could possibly still be accurate," said Teddy.

"The war is unnecessary, the report's unnecessary," I said, mad clean through, "and I assure you all is as it was three years ago."

"It's the only possible war," said Teethadore.

"The poor, pisswilly Dons do not want this war, they do not want what they have left of an empire, they are old and tired and they need a lot of rest. They'd give you everything but Spain itself if you'd just allow them to save a little pride. Oh, to hell with it, I don't know why I bother."

Teddy braided a hangman's noose in string and played cat's cradle with the rest.

Now, Theodore enjoys pissing me off, which he is quite good at and I don't do so bad myself on him. (He once called me "his conscience," which set me to shivering. I gave the world a week to live.) I roared and cussed and stomped and snorted and kicked things and I still caught the nine-ten southbound, which would put me in reach of a fast boat in the morning. I had a couple of friends who was in the gunrunning trade down to Key West, and I thought I might work something out with these pirates. I always have a moneybelt full for emergencies like this.

The train pulled out and I stuck out my tongue at the gigantic Roosevelt choppers beaming lighthouse-like on the platform.

Friends I got I ought to shoot myself.

I took a coaster down to Key West, a five-day proposition, and when I got there and hopped out upon the dock, still in a red rage over this nonsense, it was about a hundred and ten in the shade and the air so humid if you breathed deep you'd drown. The cockroaches on Key West is six inches long and they have been known to carry off the impolite. Me, I don't throw things at them or raise my voice much.

I stumped on up into the town—twelve shacks, two saloons, and a warehouse. There had been several attempts to start a church here but all of 'em had starved out or burned down; on the point there was a customs station and a lighthouse.

The local residents was all fugitives from justice somewhere—this was as far south as you could go in America and still not be swimming. It was my kind of place.

I went off to look up the import-export firm of McGarrigle and Deleage, and I suppposed them two worthies was in the saloon if they wasn't hanging from a Spanish gibbet somewheres. I went in to the cool dark and it was about half an hour 'fore my eyes widened out enough to see the damned floor, the glare on the sea and sand was so bad outside.

There I am, blind as TR without his specs.

"Looky there, it's familiar, I think I knew it once; yes, memory speaks. It is that coyote and buffalo and grizzly-bear molesting hero of our great West as told us by Ned Buntline. Who speaks the truth.

Perhaps we should hose the sea gull shit offen it and see if it's thirsty," says this voice, the Irish one.

"I perspect it's down here wanting to make money on the misfortunes of others. It's the best time, because they are distracted, but here it is anyway. I wonder does it drink only whiskey, or if it would stoop to drinkin' rum as we ain't stole no boatloads of whiskey lately," says the Froggy one. They didn't have much in the way of accents left, but they were there.

"I don't get a goddamned drink soon I swear when my eyes work I am going to have a terrible attack of the hydrophobia," I says. "And I'll make sure you both get it, too."

"Just walks in here and starts to threatening," says the Mick. "His damn manners never improves as he gets uglier. I could give up hope."

Someone screwed a tall cold glass of something into my hand. I could about see them setting at a table and I slurped and staggered over and flopped down in a chair.

"You ask it to sit here?" said the Frog to McGarrigle.

"I'se terrified to ask it to leave, though," said the Mick.

"Why don't the pair of you fuck some clams—they're right out that door and turn right," I says.

"Yup," says the Frog, "I think it must be exactly who we thought it was. Been a bad day all day, I think it must be him."

"Oh, it's him all right. No other man would walk in here feigning blindness to make us pity him and give him a drink."

"Right, no morals; it's him."

"Couldn't be nobody else."

"The genuine article."

"Luther the Kelly," they chorused happily.

"Gaddamned good to see you boys," I says.

"We expected you," says Deleage.

I was stumped.

"Who else would Teddy send? An admiral?"

I didn't know how much more of this good luck I could stand.

I could see now. There was an oilskin packet on the table. I reached for it.

"It's the truth as of a week ago. 'Course, another hundred poor Dons is dead since of that slop they feed 'em."

I looked at my friends. McGarrigle weighed about two-eighty and Deleage about ninety-four. Spending so much tense time together smuggling made them chirp like caged birds.

"We was worried about you," said McGarrigle.

"Looked like the war would be over and you wouldn't even stop in to say hello and borrow money."

"Day after day we have worried ourselves flat drunk here over you, that there had been an accident or a husband who was a good shot."

"That four-eyed little shit has his war, all right," I said, thinking on that dignified scene with us in the hedge and Long getting into the carriage. All them thugs, thieves, and bunco artists I had bagged for Teddy. Christ on a bicycle.

"God, how we worried. We thought maybe Teddy was fighting someone else we hadn't heard about. Good wars are so hard to find. In our line of work we hope to hear of every one of them," said McGarrigle. "But we thought that four-eyed little bastard would want some information so he can wring the last possible bunch of votes out of this war by him being a hero and all."

"We even worried that you and Teddy had had a falling out and he wouldn't let you come to his war."

"Nothing's changed since I was here three years ago?" I says.

"Just like it was, only more so," said McGarrigle.

We got good and drunk that night and then we went fishing for a few days, landing marlin—it tastes like veal, not fish.

I did not go tramping around in the sweltering jungle making notes and drawing maps. For one thing, that sort of scouting is called spying by most folks, who take ill to it. In the case of the Spanish, they got so vexed that they removed your fingernails and other whatnots and slow-skinned you, all the while trying to save your soul. A priest was always at hand to administer baptism and the last rites.

McGarrigle and Deleage had a small and efficient corps of spies and we would get ample warning of the American troopships sailing and we could take our steps then. We hung around the saloon and played dominoes and backgammon and liar's poker.

From little snippets of information dropped careless out of the lips of one or the other of them I learnt that they owned the saloon where we ate, drank, and cheated each other. They owned the warehouse which was a legitimate bonded warehouse; they owned all of the other buildings and most of the fishing boats; and they were going to put up a hotel as soon as the war was over.

"I don't think the Dons own a ship can sail this far," said McGarrigle, "but we are cautious businessmen."

"Is the Spanish fleet really that bad off?" I said.

" 'Tis, 'tis," said Deleage, "and if they bombard any American port it will be this one—it's closest to 'em and they can run in all four directions if need be."

"I take it that you boys is going to make a stab at being honest businessmen?" I says.

"I know it makes you disappointed in us," said McGarrigle, "but we're along in years and running guns isn't any fun anymore."

"When I was younger I thought nothing of being hung or shot or drowned," said Deleage, "but now I think about it all the time and it scares me peeless."

" 'Struth," said McGarrigle, "we're old and lost our nerve."

"For old-times sakes you will of course drop me in the right place, near on to Teethadore's ship?" I says, waiting on the answer, for if they wouldn't I was going to get lost.

"For our friendship with Luther Kelly, the Legend His Own Sorry Self, yes!" they chorused.

One moonlit night we went out to a beach on a tiny cay no more than ten miles from Key West, and we watched sea turtles come up on the sand to lay their eggs. The turtles was clumsy on land, and huge tears dripped from the corners of their eyes while they waddled away from the surf. We killed one and dressed it out there on the beach, and took the meat back to Key West and ate turtle steaks for the next few days, and delicious it was.

Word come that Teethadore's flotilla had upped anchor and gone to sea, sort of. Well, they was having more trouble than the observers deemed possible. It took *five days* to get all the ships out of Tampa Bay, what with running into each other and finding out that they had plumb forgot to fill the coal bunkers or something.

So McGarrigle and Deleage and a few ladies from their whorehouse on Key West took Mrs. Kelly's young son Luther south and we enjoyed each other's company and scrawled together some maps and shook our heads over the fact that the Dons had been ordering shells *for four years* and they still didn't have any for the guns of the forts.

I guess they was supposed to throw rocks.

I tucked all the maps and evaluations and additions and such in the oilskin pouch and Deleage dragged my clothes in—they'd been dragging behind the boat for days with a chain tied up the rope so it whacked them and they was nice and tattered like they would have been if I had been hotfooting it through the jungle for weeks like I was supposed to. We waited for nightfall and run close to the entrance to Santiago harbor and waited for TR. The running lights of the fleet appeared and we tacked back and forth and when they got close on in I tossed an India-rubber raft over the side and scrambled in it with a flare gun and some flares and my oilskin packet of reasonably accurate lies.

The last thing I did was eat a small piece of guncotton. It makes you look sick and hungry and tired and wears off in a day or so.

The guncotton tasted terrible, and it was tough, and I was chawing away on it when something bumped the bottom of the boat. It lifted me a good foot in the air.

I knew it wasn't a rock, because whatever I felt had *pushed.*

I was puzzled as to what it might be. I had the flare pistol loaded and I was just waiting on the flotilla to get a little closer.

The whatever bumped me again. This time it lifted me about two feet and slopped water in the raft.

The leading patrol boat was coming on. A few drops of water hit me from behind and I turned and there was the biggest damned shark's head I have ever seen. Up close. It swiveled some so it could look at me with the other eye. Then it went under. I thought I'd be very, very quiet.

The shark's head shot up right in front and the jaws was open from here to there and I shot the flare down the bastard's gullet and I saw it hang fire a moment before it burst into flame. The green flames licked at its gill rakers and it seemed a damned long time before the shark shut its four-foot-wide mouth and dove.

I quickly shot off another flare and commenced hollering for help. The patrol boat saw my flare and turned on a searchlight. The destroyer behind the patrol boat started firing its four- and five-inch guns at me. Out there in the ocean in my rubber duck. I couldn't remember when I had been so happy. Great gouts of water shot up on every side of me. The shells was armor-piercing high explosive and when they burst underwater I got spanked but good.

So there I am trying to outshout a naval barrage and all the time wondering when that damned shark was going to come back and eat what had give him such indigestion.

Busy remarking on Theodore's ancestry it took me a moment to see the shark was coming toward the stern of my boat, mouth open and belching green sparks. So I give him another helping and the mouth shut and it disappeared. The brief light helped the gunners to correct their aim and their shots was damned close and the waterspouts was filling the raft rapidly. I grabbed the oilskin packet and the flare pistol and waited for the shark. It rose up a couple hundred feet away, in a searchlight's beam, mouth open as far as it would go and one of the gunners put a shell right down the monster. Pieces of my most recent acquaintance rained down for several minutes and one of them, a portion of jaw with several razor-sharp teeth in it, thumped into my raft and tore the tubes open.

I couldn't remember when I had been so deliriously happy.

I was cussing a blue streak a yard wide and a mile long as I sank ungallantly beneath them black, greasy Caribbean waters, and I come up and I dogpaddled and treaded water cursing that goddamned four-eyes Dutch dwarf and accusing him of perverted lusts and the many horrible things I knew he did to small barnyard animals.

My invective was rewarded by a searchlight beam that blinded me and a faint order "Away boats!" come to my ears and soon I was being hauled over the side of a longboat.

I was near on to running out of things to call Teethadore anyway. Someone flipped open a dark lantern and shone it on my face. The lantern moved. TR's monstrous choppers gleamed white in the light.

"Kelly," says my good friend, "I knew I could count on you."

I was shivering with anger and fear. I must move to Nepal and change my habits. I wasn't sure where Nepal *was,* which was encouraging, come to think on it.

I managed to grab the ladder and hoist myself up, the packet in my teeth, and I tumbled to the deck of the destroyer. Good old Teethadore was right behind me. He had them signal with an Aldiss lamp to a big ship a couple miles away, and the destroyer raced toward it.

The seas was heavier out there, and they had to rig a bosun's chair to get us over from the destroyer to the battleship—the *Texas*—and after woozlebumbling about the decks a while I got my balance back. Blasphemy does that to me when I practice it as religiously as I just had been.

Col. Theodore Roosevelt and his aide, General Wood, pored over my bogus maps and notes and seemed well satisfied.

"Fifteen thousand troops in Santiago but you say no more than three thousand can be mustered against us?" said the general.

"Probably less than two thousand. Ten thousand troops are needed just to hold Santiago from the Cubans, who kill a few Spaniards every night. There are two to three thousand troops too sick to rise from the floors of their filthy hospitals. Many of the ones who can still stand have malaria, yellow fever, and typhoid—all them jungle camp diseases. Them as can move can and will fight bravely, but they are drawn from all over and don't know their officers. They'll fight defensively. Anything you take, you keep. They won't counterattack. Your biggest worry is the snipers. They have the new twenty-five-caliber Mauser needle gun. Good to fifteen hundred yards. The Mausers aren't sent by Madrid. A local Don paid gold for three hundred of them, and ammunition."

"Gold to who?" said TR.

"Gunrunners," I said, and no more.

General Wood snorted.

Like I had told Theodore, Spain wouldn't do anything more or less or different in the three years since I had last been to Santiago. (That was a fairly exasperating trip. I was trying to keep a bumptious little scamp named Winston Churchill alive long enough to see his dear mother once again. I was fond of his mother my own self. Jennie was unlike any other woman I ever knew. I can't tell you why, but she sure was.)

I yelled and threatened and sniveled and whined at Teddy to let me return to the States. I would, I said, forgo all the medals he was planning to give me. I even said I'd vote for him, goddamn me.

He waved aside my pleas like he was brushing away gnats and I stormed off and sat down on something I thought was a locker. It was a vent to belowdecks and I got stuck in it. Just in far enough so that if I got my muscles bunched to pull myself out I was stuck.

The watch pulled me out.

I have had worse days, I thought, but not lately.

4

I shall spare you the revolting details of the off-loading of troops. For one thing, once again they had been issued winter garrison uniforms, heavy wool serge, in which they were expected to work and fight in damp tropical heat. Men keeled over and died of heart failure or convulsions from heatstroke. When the bully beef was opened it stank of formaldehyde and was a livid fishbelly white. The sailors had good food and it did not endear the Navy to the Army.

The Army always gets the shit end of the stick anyway.

Five days later our troops were ready to advance on the entrenchments of the enemy. Some of our troops, that is. We landed fifteen thousand. Six thousand was down with any mad number of ailments and half of them was to die. The Spanish shot a few, the profiteers who had supplied to the Army the poisonous beef and the peas colored with copper sulfate and the hardtack full of mold killed fifteen for every one met a Spanish bullet.

In the wee and small hours of the sixth day, Theodore, mounted on the least sickly horse left, led in a charge up a hill such of his Rough Riders as could stand. They had to march about five miles through a jungly forest to get to the grassy hill, and green-uniformed Spanish snipers potted over a hundred—the Mausers was good to more than half a mile.

Theodore had sent me skulking off to find out if the Spaniards had moved forty thousand troops or a lot of machine guns in overnight. I shinnied up a very tall tree and slapped mosquitoes and biting flies for a few hours and then slithered back down and said no, they hadn't.

The Rough Riders' charge was not awful military-looking, what with the insubordinate cutthroats that was private soldiers, the Harvardlings that was junior officers and convinced this was some sort of strange lacrosse game, and Teethadore, who sweated like a hot hog so bad his glasses was dripping and he was blind, and he zigged and zagged until the Sundance Kid, of all people, grabbed the reins and led Teddy's horse up the hill.

"Follow me, men," said Teddy, furiously rubbing his glasses with his sopping kerchief.

"SAY PRETTY PLEASE" bellered a couple hundred assorted bank robbers, train robbers, cattle rustlers, horse thieves, regulators, bushwhackers, claim jumpers, tinhorn gamblers, pimps, and other such solid citizens as the West has been so justly famous for.

The boys had got the hang of the Spaniards' green uniforms, which was just a little bit off—no cowboy or gunfighter ever wore glasses, they all had eyes like hawks—and soon as one would spot a sniper half a mile off and point it out a passel of .45–90s and .45–120s would let fly and the Spaniard would have many holes in his dead ass.

Theodore was beside himself with rage. He'd just about get his glasses clear and slap them back on and another cascade of sweat would slosh down off his forehead and he'd start again. Finally, Theodore made a sweatband of a spare kerchief he found somewhere, clapped his glasses on, and saw maybe five hundred of his Rough Riders standing here and there about him, keeping close guard on a huge kettle of peas and ham hocks the Spaniards had abandoned. There was a little gunfire now and again as one or another of these bandits come upon a Spaniard.

We was in sole possession of the field, the ham hocks, and the peas.

Just then a Mauser cracked and Theodore's hat had a fresh hole in the brim—and the Sundance Kid had drawed and fired damn near straight up, a sniper had stayed quiet in the tree directly overhead. The sniper fell sort of slowly and landed on his back in front of Teddy. His horse shied and Sundance grabbed the reins again. I went over to the body. The slug from the Kid's Colt had gone right up through the lower jaw and tongue and out the top of the man's head. The Kid didn't aim, he was so fast his hand was empty, then one fraction of a second later the sniper was dead. He was no one to fight with, for sure.

"Follow me!" Teddy yelled, urging his horse forward. There was some scattered shots off to our left.

"THE HELL WE WILL," bellered his loyal soldiers.

I went on over to him. "It's over," I said. "There's nothing for the Spanish to do but surrender. We're on both their flanks and we have the high ground."

Teddy sagged visibly. He wanted to be known as a brave man. Well, sheer lunacy is as good a substitute as any that I know, and Teddy sure had that in quantity.

His Rough Riders had to a man thrown away the serge blouses, and they was either barechested or wearing light cotton shirtings. Someone brought out a deck of cards and they cut the cards six times and the thirty men who lost out the worst went off without a word to picket duty while the others sampled the peas and ham hocks that was the first real food they'd had since they joined the damn Army.

"I thank that yu'd best get us off this here pesthole 'fore we're all dead of the rot," drawled Badger Dick Boskill. He was a six-foot-eight half-Kiowa who did card tricks of the variety you can get shot for. Badger Dick was so damn big no one had tried yet.

"Uh, um," said Teddy.

"Othersome," Badger Dick went on, "we might have to all sign this here affidavit about how—what is your name these days, Sundance?"

"Jones."

"No you ain't," said Butch Cassidy, "you are Smith. *I* am Jones."

"Smith," says Sundance.

"How Private Smith here had to lead your horse up the hill on account of you is as blind as a damn mole and woulda rode out to sea and drownded Private Smith here hadn't come to your aid."

"Ah, ah, ah, ah," said Teethadore. He was now getting ready to impress us all with his very best empurpling asthma attack.

I shoved a pint bottle of tequila I'd taken off a sniper's corpse at Teethadore and roared, "Pour that down yer gullet or you'll smother." Teddy drained off about half of it and his eyes sort of lolled around for a moment and he shuddered top to the soles of his feet and back up. "Hoomph," he said, swaying in the saddle.

"Oh ma God," he said, whisper-like.

"Oh fer Chrissakes," says Butch, "we don't want to go back on them damn transports. Let's us just go kick the rest of them greasers out of Santiago and see what they got in the way of grub and liquor and when the goddamned U S of A wants Santiago all they got to do is ask polite and have us a way home and we will give it to them right away."

The Rough Riders allowed as how that seemed a good solution.

The Harvardlings having observed the fulsome awe with which the soldiers regarded good old Teethadore chose to keep a discreet silence as the Rough Riders fell in and marched on Santiago. They slouched along any old way, blowing snipers out of the treetops at a half-mile and appropriating a couple of fieldpieces had ammunition by the way and about four hours later this slovenly army approached the ancient fortifications of Santiago.

About ten heads showed, barely, over the stone breastworks.

The Sundance Kid and Snakefoot du Plessis flipped for which side and went out front. When Butch fired a shot in the air them two drawed and it sounded like cloth ripping the shots come so fast. The heads went down like some sort of carny game.

In five minutes a white flag waved from the parapet. The gates was flung open and a podgy little Spanish general stalked out and handed his sword to Sundance, who hefted it and walked back and gave it to Theodore.

"You want his balls, too?" said the Kid.

"Who speaks Spanish here?" yelled Teddy.

"It's not necessary," said the Spanish general. "I went to Harvard."

So him and Teethadore had a fine old reunion and compared notes on football games and racing shells while hundreds of men in both armies died of neglect.

The Spanish just put down their arms and went to the business of trying to stay alive in a tropical city which had tainted water and every disease known to man but chilblains, and the Rough Riders joined them.

About a week later the Spanish admiral took his ships out through the harbor's roads to give battle to the Americans and in fifteen minutes all the Spanish ships was burning or sinking. The U.S. Navy didn't lose a single man.

As our wars go it was damned hard to brag on it, like I said.

Theodore went off and telegraphed his mother or something because it wasn't but about two weeks before there were transports for us down at the docks and them full of food and nurses for our sick and wounded that hadn't died yet, and it was very few of them hadn't, and we was marched on board, the Harvardlings having mysteriously got their voices back, and off we went, save for a hundred or so of the Rough Riders who felt the outpourings of thanks for their heroism might result in their identification and eventual trial and hanging.

Butch and Sundance was of this number.

I wished them tall grass, deep watering holes, and pretty ladies, and they said that they might try Argentina or Australia. The Pinkertons was hard after them along with Harry Lefors and Charley Siringo and some other hardcases that happened to be law abiding.

"Siringo is as fast as the Kid, here," said Butch.

"No he ain't," said the Kid.

"Like I said, Argentina or Australia or something," said Butch.

I told Teethadore I was damned if I'd waller all the way to Long Island, where he planned to muster out the Rough Riders, in one of the rusty tubs the Navy had commandeered to haul us home.

I was yelling at the top of my lungs at Theodore when McGarrigle and Deleage come in and told me to quit waking the damned dead we'd leave that very hour for "the south coast."

"You seem to be well taken care of, Major Kelly," said Theodore.

I just walked away. I wondered how that man slept at night or shaved himself.

McGarrigle and Deleage had some business to attend to in New Orleans, so we sailed there. Actually, we sailed to Bayou Teche, since the business was with a few dozen of Deleage's Cajun relatives.

Neither the Mick nor the Frog bothered to mention just what this business was, and being the soul of courtesy I did not ask.

My polite discretion was taken for eagerness to help them in liquidating their import-export firm. While I had been helping Theodore beat hell out of the Dons the Mick and the Frog had held a fire sale, and the last of their munitions had been bought by one or another revolutionary band at or in one or another of them tinpot countries that line the Caribbean like cheap hotels in a gaming town.

Cajuns is clannish folk, and a relative of Deleage's named Cousin Moutard led a long line of pirogues back through the swamps till we come to an abandoned plantation. There was a huge old ruin of a house had the roof caving in and the wallpaper hanging down in long sheets from the ceilings. Snakes slithered away when you walked on the floors, which was a hard yellow pine all tongued and grooved.

The house was full of cases of rifles and ammunition and a few mountain howitzers taken to pieces. We loaded everything and Deleage set fire to the old building.

When he come to the dock where we was waiting I asked him if perhaps the plantation had been his family's. He nodded and shrugged and we poled away into the dark swamp.

The next morning I firmly refused to go on any delivery mission down in the Caribbean. Cousin Moutard offered to take me to New Orleans to catch whatever train suited me.

They was still loading their ship with the cases of guns and bullets when me and Cousin Moutard headed away from the landing.

As the pirogue moved on the flat water, I reflected that I had come out of many adventures much worse chewed up than I was at the moment, probably because I was nearly fifty and I didn't debate overlong with myself as to whether or not it was time to run yet.

This was an extremely dangerous time for me. America had come in to lots of new possessions and I knew who several officers was that would like nothing better than to tell me go look at 'em and look at 'em carefully.

It was a good time for me to take a quiet sneak off in some direction no one would credit, and using a name and passport no one knew at all. A very good time. Never been a better time. I thought on where and couldn't come up with nothing.

That night Cousin Moutard and me stayed at a hotel at a steamboat landing—water was the roads here—and about midday next we come to the Mississippi.

"You can catch a ferry this evening," said my Cajun cabman. "Good luck to you. Those two scoundrels will be in Key West in two months, if you wanted to write."

We shook hands.

I spent the next week in New Orleans, going to the races and eating good food. I caught the train west, for San Francisco. I figured when I got there I'd look on some maps and find a safe place to go on to.

The Spanish-American War was over. One good thing about it, it was short.

I should have booked myself on an extremely slow world tour under the name of Parker but I had forgot that the way to stay alive in this world is never be regular in yer habits.

It was how I had kept myself alive when scouting and I should have knowed that it would apply to the rest of my life.

Gussie had wearied of the cosseted life of a millionaire's widow and was playing in a perfectly godawful play which opened the day that I got there.

I was about trained out. Dirty, hungover, and reeking of seegars from the smoking coach. I got a room at the Palace and sent a bellhop to a tailor I knew over on Powell Street with a note ordering me fresh duds in the morning or even later that night. I soaked in a scalding tub for a couple of hours and ate a room service dinner of seafood and champagne.

I slept for a few hours and the tailor woke me up. He'd altered a ready-made dark blue suit and had brought all the accessories such as shirts and cravats and studs and a creamy new Monarch of the Plains Stetson and boots and linen handkerchief and small clothes. I paid him and offered him a drink, and he grinned and had one quick one neat and went out, his pigtail bobbing. Wang Chu understood English all right but he didn't like to speak it much.

The clothes fit perfectly. For years the good white citizens of San Francisco had been passing laws making it more or less illegal for Orientals to do any sort of work but laundry or cooking, and Wang

Chu had his tailor shop behind a laundry and more than one of the city's swells gave his custom to the little Chinese tailor.

I waited at the door with the rest of the stage-door Johnnies, sort of slanchwise across the alley, tipped against the brick of another building. An earthquake struck, a mild one, and I felt the brick ripple through the cloth of my coat.

Gussie weren't an ingenue anymore, and I was no young swain. But she spotted me before she had got all the way outside and she blew me a gay kiss.

"Oh, Luther," she said, "is this really the wickedest city in all America?"

"No," I said.

"What's the wickedest?"

"Washington. Very few people die of San Francisco. Tens of thousands die of Washington every year."

"Hmm," said Gussie, "are you developing a conscience?"

"Hardly," I says. "I just like to keep an eye out is all."

"Let's walk and walk and walk," she trilled. Gussie had the loveliest speaking voice I ever heard, cream and sand.

So we walked up hills and down hills and we went down to the wharves and walked up to the top of Russian Hill and watched the sun come up. We went over to the Italian neighborhood and ate breakfast in a tiny place had room for only two tables out in front.

I took Gussie back to my room and we had a grand old time for aged folks like us and she went to sleep with her head on my chest and after a few minutes I slept, too.

For a few days that was our regular routine. The play was so awful I couldn't even find the patience to sit through it once and I have mercifully forgot what the damned thing was called. Gussie was a fine actress but not up to lifting this dead hog off the floor. She laughed it off, saying when you'd been away from acting as long as she had you took what you could get and this was what she'd gotten.

We was walking in that light, misty San Francisco rain once and Gussie stopped real sudden and put a hand on my cheek.

"Luther," she said, "why don't we get married?"

"Who to?" I said. I warn't surprised, I had been expecting this.

Gussie looked at me, smiling and sad at the same time.

"You're right, Luther. It's just I missed you when you left the last time."

"Gussie," I says, "I'm going to take you to your hotel now."

She cracked me a good one with her handbag, the jeweled clasp cutting my cheek.

I watched her stalk off, and, no, I didn't go after her. She needed to be alone and maybe she needed to never see me again. I would find out in time. You get into your forties having not stayed more'n a few months in one place since you were fourteen you find you don't want the road home all that familiar. I had got used to loss. I was comfortable with it.

Times like this a feller wants a drink or eight, because Gussie was a great friend and I had had to fail her, easier to do it and get it over with than go along knowing that one day I'd have to sneak off leaving no more than a note on a pillow and my best wishes.

San Francisco was a great place for saloons and most of them open twenty-four hours a day. I found one with a few gents in it who were more or less in the same funk I was and did not wish to talk. We had ourselves a good community mope till the sun come up and we all rose at the same moment and went our separate ways.

When I picked up my key at the hotel's desk the attendant handed me a red parchment envelope which had been sealed with black sealing wax. My full name was on the front—Luther Sage Kelly—and the letters looked rather curious, none of them was exactly curved—they was assemblies of lines.

I was as tired as Noah's dog and I slipped the envelope in my coat pocket and went on up to my room, slipped off my coat, and flopped on the bed in my boots. I slept for a couple hours, that unhappy, drunken sleep that don't rest you, just stretches you out thinner than you was before.

All them years of being out in bad country alone and that country full of folks who would kill me if they could has made me uncommon good at sorting out noises, and the softer the noises the quicker the sort. Half asleep, I heard the faint brushing noise of feet with no shoes on them and I opened my eye a slit and when a shadow from deeper in the room got close enough I come up off the bed with a pillow in one hand, to distract who it was as my right foot headed for a kneecap.

Wang Chu's eyes was about as big as black overcoat buttons. I pulled my foot back and come up to my feet.

"Gaddamn it, Chu," I says in a low voice, "I could have hurt you. You're welcome here anytime, just knock on the damn door. If I'd have been a little more nervous I'd have had a gun to hand and you might be dead." I *was* concerned as hell, even half asleep I grasped that Wang Chu must be in some trouble. Well, I liked him and I liked his clothes so I'd listen, I thought. (I ought to have known by now that noble impulses are only slightly less dangerous than scorned women.)

Wang Chu bowed and delivered a speech in better English than I got about how gracious and fine a person I was.

I told him to cut the crap and tell me what he wanted.

Chu allowed as how he appreciated my urging him to cut the crap and the problem reduced to the sorry fact that someone was trying to kill him.

"Someone is trying to kill my tailor," I said, eyebrows raised. "Why, the nerve of the son of a bitch. We cannot have this."

So I then asked *why* someone was trying to kill the good citizen Wang Chu.

Wang Chu expressed surprise that anyone would wish to kill a humble laundry owner, but having thought of not much else for days he supposed that it had possibly to do with smuggling . . . . . . since times . . . . . . were . . . . . . hard . . . . . . and . . .

"And it's every pigtailed Chink fer himself," I says. "I think I do divine the picture. Now the real question is what are you smuggling? Opium? Girls? Coolies?"

Wang Chu shook his head vigorously. "Jade," he said.

"That's ridiculous," I said, "I know where there's tons of gaddamn jade. I know where there is a whole *mountain* of jade. Pink, white, green, red, yellow, any color you want."

Wang Chu sucked his teeth for a while. "Entire mountain?"

"Yup. Big mountain, too. But why are you smuggling jade into . . . . . . you are smuggling jade *into China.*"

Chu allowed as how the honorable and gracious Kelly was tits-on right on that score.

"Where is the mountain?" he asked, innocently.

"Alaska," I says.

Chu allowed as how he had heard of Alaska and heard it was a big place. Also a long ride away.

"Any jade closer?" he asked.

I allowed as how there was lots of jade much closer.

"Where?"

"Wyoming," I said.

"How big?"

"Oh, a ton, maybe."

"Ah, what color?" said Wang Chu.

I picked up a green sour apple from the fruit basket on the night stand. "This color," I said.

Wang Chu's impassiveness went missing for a moment.

"Pay two hundred thousand in gold."

"Fine," I says, "I'll go fetch it. Half down, half when I bring it."

"All on delivery."

"Goodbye, Wang," I says, pulling on my pants.

"Half down, I go with you to get jade boulder. Don't worry about other problem."

In two hours, after having swelled the bank balance of Kelly so fat the manager soiled himself at the mere sight of me, Wang Chu and Mrs. Kelly's son Luther was going across the Bay to the train station in Oakland. We carried no baggage to speak of, and I had wired ahead to some friends telling them I required a freight wagon, stock, and a reason for driving the wagon north from Cheyenne and thank you very much. As I could have easy turned these boys in for a fat reward long ago they would not ask me any prying questions neither.

"Whole ton," said Wang Chu.

"Yup," I said. "And if you are smart you'll sell it slow. Don't want to flood your market."

When the train pulled out we was installed in a suite with all the comforts—had half a car, study, parlor, and bedrooms—and I got into a for-blood poker game with Wang Chu. He beat me out of five grand before I gave up and rang for dinner.

We et canvasback duck, oysters, potted shrimps, and such. I had had a long night and day. As the train climbed the Sierra I went to sleep, and when I woke up late the next afternoon we was pulling into

Salt Lake City. I pulled the blinds. I don't even like looking at the goddamned place.

I went to the bar in the smoking car and got a nice big drink, and looked balefully out on the City of the Saints. I did not allow them much hope of improvement.

Chu found me, and he sipped at a glass of wine while I guzzled a tumbler of bourbon.

"How you find this jade?" he said.

I knew about the jade in the Owl Creek Mountains because I had guided one of the early geological surveys—it was hardly any problem, as the Cheyennes swooped down on the wagon hauling the specimens, run off the driver and guards, dumped out some of the sacks of specimens, and scratched their heads a moment before agreeing unanimously that anyone who filled sacks with these worthless rocks was insane and therefore sacred to the Great Spirit, and so we was left alone and never bothered—at a time when half the track crews laying the Union Pacific was in trenches fighting off raids.

I had happened on the jade solely by accident. I had tossed a fair-sized rock down in a dry wash to see if I could flush a deer or an antelope for camp meat. The rock hit a good-sized boulder and busted off a flake of it. I happened to be down in the wash the next day and I picked up the flake—a sour apple green—and took it to Professor Herndon who said it was jade, the most valuable color, and he would not mention it in his report because we must at all costs discourage Oriental immigration.

I shrugged. I hadn't met many Chinese and didn't care one way or another, there was always some idiot with a dislike for one or another color. People are generally fairly vile, you ask me, tint no matter. So I pitched the jade off into the brush and thought no more about it—until now.

As the train began to labor off toward the pleasures of Denver I rang for breakfast and ate a lot of pancakes and bacon and eggs and I was addressing a seegar and some stout coffee when Wang Chu come in and bowed.

"Now what?" I says.

"Just being polite," says Wang.

"It's wasted on me," I says.

"You Americans have abominable manners."

" 'Struth."

Wang ordered a simple breakfast of melon and coffee.

"By the way," I said, "did you not make mention of someone trying to kill you, implying that you would like to have me kill *them* or something?"

"Hired other man."

"Which other man."

"He say he know you. Thomas Horn."

Last I had heard of Tom he was "regulating" up in northern Wyoming. A regulator shot down rustlers like coyotes, sparing the ranchers the trouble and expense of due process of law. When I'd last seen him he still looked boyish enough, which I have noticed the worst killers always does, I don't know why, maybe it's that sorrow and pity is not known to them.

Horn always left a pebble in the cheek of a victim. I had it on good authority that he had killed over four hundred men, maybe more.

"Well," I says, "I would have flat refused that kind of work anyway."

Chu nodded. "Horn said you would. I am glad that I did not embarrass you."

We got to Cheyenne in the forenoon of the next day, and I stepped off into that damnable Big Horn wind that can pick you up and have you in Kansas in minutes. I swear I once saw a whole flock of sheep passing over a mile up.

My chums was there with the freight wagon and saddle horses and such, somewhat older than I remembered them and then I realized it was better than ten years since I'd seen them or they had seen me.

"You require that we go with you or anythang?" says Poke.

"Nope."

"Well then, we'll go back to the ranchin' trade." And off they went without another word.

"We don't pay them?" says Wang Chu.

"We pay when we get back." I was tired of explaining.

We tossed our traps in the wagon, and I checked to see what in the way of grub we might need. It was all there and the water barrel was freshly filled.

We took off to the north—had some hundred and fifty miles to do, and there wasn't no railroad spur to that lonely country. By the second day we had long outrun the last of the little spreads—here you had to have the water, the land was worthless without it. So a feller who proved up on a homestead that contained a spring could have tens of thousands of acres to call his own. It made the ranch holdings circular.

Wang Chu was awful put out at dinner because all there was to eat was bacon and beans and corn dodgers.

"You live on this?" said Wang. "No damn wonder you are all so pale."

It took us two weeks to get to the country I remembered and it was such a bleak place that there wasn't even a trace that pointed to men ever having been there. The water in the springs was poisonous—arsenic and what have you.

I poked around and found the boulder, still gleaming apple-green where the rock I had tossed on it twenty-five years before had hit.

Wang went on his knees before it and stretched a trembling hand out to it.

"There's an even bigger boulder up there," I said, pointing up the dry wash to a six-by-six rock face half eroded out of the yellow earth.

Wang Chu give off with croaks.

"I don't expect to winter here," I says, "so if you'll oblige we need to get this here boulder onto the freight wagon and back to the railroad and back to San Francisco where another hundred thousand is due me."

My lack of sentiment hurt Wang's feelings. "Such jade is seen only once in ten thousand years."

"Balls," I says, "I can see twenty of them boulders in a five-minute walk."

Wang's mind came a bit unhinged at that and he scampered off in them funny Chink slippers they wear, and I could hear him drooling and babbling around the curve of the wash.

"Jaysus Kayrist, Kelly," I says. "Think of all the pain and suffering you could have avoided if you had known . . ." Such thoughts is discouraging so I quit having them.

While Wang, my esteemed tailor and partner, was having the vapors I went up to the wagon and got a six-foot spud bar and came back down and shoved the chisel end under the boulder and slammed a piece of rock under the bar and levered for all I was worth. The boulder shook in the earth. A ton or so. Well, it could be rolled down the wash to a flatter place and I could build some sort of skid to get it up the bank and into the wagon.

After a bit of grubbing the earth away I was able to get the boulder to move, and by crowing it up and sticking rocks under it I got it out of its hole and onto the big gravel of the dry wash, most of which was jade, too.

Entertained enormously by the sounds of my Chinese chum becoming completely unhinged I occupied myself rolling the boulder along. It was shaped like a giant prune.

After much reflection I was able to wrap this here giant prune with chains and I hitched up the draft horses and dragged the boulder up a shallow incline, to a sort of high bump cut straight off on one side damn near the height of the sides of the freight wagon.

As the sun sank I crowed the boulder the last fraction of an inch and it crashed down onto the bed of the freight wagon, crushing the bits of driftwood I had piled there to slow the fall. The wagon went flat on the springs and then they bounced back up and the wagon rocked a little. It was about as much load as the wagon could take. I wedged things in around the boulder, made sure it was about centered between the axles, and went in search of my Chink chum.

Wang Chu was sitting on a jade boulder twitching now and again.

"Wang," I says. He snapped some out of his daze.

"All the jade here is priceless," he said.

"Well, we got a boulder in the wagon and that's all the weight that we can afford. So in the morning you come on down because I am leaving for the railroad."

I was getting a mite tired of beans and bacon so I allowed as how I would shoot an antelope tomorrow and so I et the beans and bacon anyway and then had a seegar and some coffee and went to sleep whilst Wang sat in a daze of overpowering greed most of the night. I heard him walk in about three in the morning. I heard him climb up in the wagon, and when I got up at four-thirty he was asleep next to the jade boulder.

I hitched up the horses and looked round and figured we was packed.

I clucked to the horses and off we went. It took near on to three weeks to make it back with the heavy-loaded wagon, the narrow wheels would sink in the sand and once we got caught in a sudden cloudburst crossing a white clay plain. The clay turned to something like axle grease and the horses both went down. I jumped off to untangle them and I landed on my butt and skidded fifteen feet before a handy tarbush stopped me.

The sun come back out and in half an hour everything was dry again. That is some strange country.

Wang was recovering and after the first week when he spent all his time petting the boulder and crooning to it his true self come forward and he was once again the greedy, avaricious little Chink bastard I liked as I could expect him to act reasonable, or anyway predictably.

We got to Cheyenne, saw the boulder crated and onto a car, insured for ten thousand dollars. It was worth a lot more than that but the insurance was large enough so it would be checked on regular. I told the train folks it was a meteorite.

San Francisco looked very good to us and Wang punctually paid me the second hundred thousand dollars. I thought this business was over and done with but of course it weren't.

6

I had any number of irate letters and telegrams from Teethadore, who had suddenly discovered where the Philippines was and wanted me to go and see if they were really still there. I read the letters and telegrams in sequence, hoping against hope that the next one would say "I am finishing this letter for the late Theodore Roosevelt who died of the apoplexy this morning." No such good and glad tidings.

I had been living by the month in the Palace, paid up six months ahead, and I was therefore a valued customer. So I saunters up to the clerk and says, "Any strange folks been around asking for Kelly?"

"Just the police," said the clerk.

I couldn't remember when I had last been so happy.

"The *what?*"

"Mr. Kelly," said the clerk, "you left no note and somehow a rumor got started that you had been murdered and dropped in the Bay, chained to a cast-iron lamppost. So the police heard it and came around. That's all. This Roosevelt fellow is certainly rude, isn't he, Mr. Kelly?"

"You could easy say that."

A couple of Army captains come in the front door and Army captains don't get paid enough to come in the front door of the Palace Hotel in San Francisco on their own affairs. I did a quick slither behind a potted aspidistra and hung both ears on one side of my head.

"He show yet?" says one of them.

"No, sir," said the clerk.

They left. I went over to the clerk and inquired if it was me that they was after. It was. I dropped a double eagle on the counter and said how much I liked him not having seen me yet.

He allowed as how he would not see me for a considerable time. Years, perhaps.

I had this gut-sure feeling that I ought to get low and stay there someplace far away. No doubt booking passage wouldn't do any good, the customs officers would be on the lookout for me. I would have to go slithering away and devil take the stamps and passport.

There was one likely way, and I snuck round to Wang Chu's shop and went through the laundry to where he tailored. A young man said Wang Chu was not in. I said that was fine, I'd wait. The young man said he didn't think that Wang Chu would be back anytime soon. I said to tell Wang Chu that the Jade Soldier would wait until Wang Chu could speak to him.

"Why in hell didn't you just say Kelly?" said Wang Chu a few minutes later. "All you pasty Europeans look alike as so many frog's bellies."

"Kelly is something of a valued acquaintance to many who Kelly does not wish to see right now."

"Roosevelt?"

I nodded.

"You have been to China?"

"Once. But just a couple of the Treaty Ports."

"I gather you are something of a cocksman," said Wang Chu. "I think the girls of Soochow would like you."

"I can get my bellrope hauled on right here," I says, a little testy. "I would like not to find myself sketching fortifications in wherever Teethadore wants to invade next."

"The Jade Soldier, eh?" says Wang Chu. "That would solve a couple of difficulties for me. The Jade Soldier can guard the priceless boulder of jade. It is a gift to the Emperor."

"Now just a gaddamn minute," says I. "I am damned if I am going to Peiping. Canton will be fine."

"You wish to miss the City of Northern Peace?"

"I wish to miss that deranged bitch who rules China. I know about that one."

Wang Chu laughed so hard tears flew from his eyes. "She might hang you up by the plums," he said. "She would enjoy such a sight."

"Not to blunt the edge of yer merriment, ya little shit, but I am not finding any of this funny."

"Hoo hoo hoo," said Wang Chu.

I pondered a moment that my misspent life now had me asking an obviously deranged Chink to help me avoid the attentions of an obviously deranged Dutch dwarf. Christ, I said to myself, I hate these little short bastards.

"Ah," said Wang Chu finally, "enough laughter. We shall get you out of the city and send you to China." He clapped his hands once. A gigantic Chinese stepped out from behind a curtained doorway. The son of a bitch must have weighed three hundred pounds. He looked as big as Liver-Eatin' Jack, which I had never thought I'd see.

It was going on dark and the fog was rolling in. I took a cloak and wrapped up good, and me and the huge Chink stalked through the fog, coming down the wharves. There was a longboat waiting with eight stout oarsmen in it, all Chinese. The moment that we had hopped in the stern the oarsmen pulled away. They'd a steady stroke, and in an hour we pulled up to a small steamer, a lacquered one, red and black. I stepped up on board and so did my escort—he caused the whole boat to quiver over to one side—and the steamer's engines began to thrum and we moved up against the gentle current of the Sacramento in the delta and braided channels at the head of the Bay.

There are over two thousand miles of channels in that delta, and to this day I have no idea how the pilot found the right ones on that night.

We kept winding up through cattails and water weeds, the moon lit the fog from above, and ghostly ducks would rise from the water, once a flock of geese rose up, honking shrilly.

The fog was even thicker in first light of morning. The luminous mist seemed weightless, we could have been chugging along two thousand feet in the air.

A dock appeared. The little steamer slowed her engines, Chinese roustabouts came out of the mist and tied her to. I stepped up on the dock. I walked along it and smelled the marsh gas. I followed a path which led soon to a little Chinese village—right there in California.

There were perhaps thirty houses, some sheds, racks for fishing nets to dry on. Young Chinese mothers and their exquisite and spotless children walked past me. The recent immigrants call whites "ghosts."

I found a little inn, went in, the owner brought me rice wine and cakes. I could well have been in China.

I stayed there in the little village for a week. No one spoke to me, or indeed even looked at me. Except for the giant, Wu, and the innkeeper. I tried to pay only once, and the innkeeper set up a fearful great caterwauling.

"You no pay," said Wu. "Wang Chu pay. You dishonor him not again."

Wang Chu also sent lovely girls to me every night. They would dance on my spine before we screwed. I liked this ever so much better than stomping around some malarial swamp counting Igorotes for Teethadore.

The Chinese who were in the village did almost all eventually speak to me, the Jade Soldier, and the girls who came at night laughed prettily with their hands over their mouths. I smelled like raw beef to them, because of my usual diet with half of it meat.

The fog went on and on. Sometimes it would lift and I could see a mile or two out across the waving tules, but it never pulled far enough up and away for me to get a fix on a mountain or any landmark.

One fine early morning Wu fetched me. We went down to the dock and got on the little steamer and chugged off through the mist. At nightfall we reached the Bay and a light skiff come out of the fog. I got in and sat in the stern. The oarsman got out, and Wu took his place. There wasn't but a few inches of freeboard what with Wu in the middle and me in the stern. I weigh near on two hundred myself.

Wu danced that skiff along the Bay right speedy, never slackening his pace until we saw a green lamp blinking off to starboard. Wu looked at it, turned the boat, and we come to a tramp steamer, a rusty tub that had likely seen a thousand ports. It was so common I took to it right away. It would not attract the eye.

We cleared the Golden Gate before dawn, threading our way through the foghorns and answering with our own.

When we stood well out to sea Wu come up on deck. He had changed out of his Chinese duds into seaman's truck—wool shirt and pants and seaboots.

"Where is our next stop?" I asked him.

"Macao."

Hoo boy, I thought, maybe the most dangerous city in the world. Well, I supposed I could jump overboard and go back to Teethadore's tender mercies. I elected to go where the violence and depravity was of a general nature, rather than directed at me alone.

The voyage, such of it as there was, was the usual nauseating bore for me, as I get seasick easily and stay that way. For some reason I am all right in very small boats and very large boats but the ones in between near on the fatal for me. Wu, in whose charge I was, plied me with all manner of foul soups and noxious potions. I wasted away and practiced looking pitiful, which weren't hard.

The Pacific is a very broad ocean indeed, also it has waves and swells, all of which settled in the stomach of Kelly, though nothing else did for long.

The ship itself was registered in Hong Kong to a Chinese company, but the company was registered in London so the flag was British even though none of the officers or crew were. Matter of fact, I was the only European on the ship. Some wag who had been asked to translate the Chinese to English had got the ship named *Glanders.* It amused me even in my sorry state.

Then one fine morning all seasickness went away and I felt weak but otherwise all right. I gorged myself on rich foods for a week and got back most of the weight I had lost—I didn't need *all* of it back—and as the little steamer plodded slowly across the Pacific I paced around and around the decks.

The jade boulder had been carefully crated and sealed, even to a bolted double band of iron with one big eyebolt welded on top, so the steam winch could hook it easy.

Everything was tickety-boo save for the time of year, which was the one in which typhoons live. A Pacific typhoon is sort of like an Atlantic hurricane. You know, lethal and unexpected.

One afternoon after a bloody red dawn the sea itself took on a coppery sheen and the swells were disturbed by crosscurrents; the air itself was thick and wet and choked you when you breathed.

The crew looked scared when I passed them. The captain would step out of the flying bridge and look off toward the southern horizon and scream more orders at the sailors, who were lashing everything down in the holds and on deck.

I hadn't been in the chartroom and other than a vague sense that we were headed east by south I couldn't have told you where in the hell we were, except in the Pacific someplace. For all I knew, we could have been plodding in a large circle just over the horizon from California. I didn't even know how many days we had been at sea.

The typhoon hit us in the middle of the night. The wind picked up and went from a low moan to a scream through the thrumming rigging. The ship nearly broached to, and it gave three sickening lurches before going back to its customary wallowing.

For three days and nights the little ship battled to stay afloat. Wu, my guardian, was killed on the second day. A sea anchor had been tossed out in a desperate attempt to help the rusty tub hold into the wind. A sudden burst of wind and a crossing sea snapped the cable; the broken end lashed back and took poor Wu's head off as neat as a muleskinner flicks horseflies off a mule's rump. Wu was maybe twenty feet from me. His headless body crouched and the arms and legs quivered and then the boat rolled and he was tossed into the sea.

The third day the ship began to come apart. All of the crates and cargo on deck had long since burst their stays and gone overboard. The lifeboats were still usable, but the seas were so big they would have swamped, most likely.

The constant twisting and pummeling was working the plates loose. The pumps were running at full capacity and falling a little farther behind every hour. The ship was becoming crank with the extra water in the holds.

Then suddenly the winds died and we drifted to a flat glassy calm. The eye of the storm. Hundreds of thousands of seabirds floated on the smooth black water.

Even with the bilges pumped dry and the decks cleared and the hatches sealed it was damn clear to Mrs. Kelly's son Luther that another three days of pummeling would tear the ship apart, and that when it went it would go all at once—and likely with little warning.

There was a very small lifeboat abaft of the after smokestack, and I simply appropriated it. It had a canvas cover in good condition and oars shipped to it and a full water keg. I tossed the boat over the side—well, slid it, actually, and let it drag behind on a rope. The ship was hardly moving and the crew was all below trying to make the ship seaworthy and the lookout couldn't see behind him, so I was able to lower a bag of food—canned stuff and ship's biscuit—down and I took a medical kit from another boat. Then I shinnied down the rope to the little boat and cut myself free. I shipped the oars and drifted, and before too long I was alone on the flat, black, glassy sea, except for the seabirds. Some of them was ducks and I was able to use a fishing rod I found in the boat and a loop of catgut to catch them round the neck. They seemed dazed and wouldn't swim away even if another duck was frantically strangling two feet from them.

I had many hours to wait. When I could see the wall of the typhoon coming on I threw out the sea anchor and buttoned up the canvas top over me and I lay there waiting to die. I didn't figure my chances were any good a-tall. Not even a little bit, but better than going down in the bigger ship after it disintegrated.

The Irish fisherman has a saying: the sea has some mercy but the rocks have none. I wondered how far I was from islands or shoal water.

When death comes to sit on your shoulder it can be a very peaceful feeling. Things are over soon and it has all been decided. I lay back in the tarry-smelling darkness and offered up a prayer to a God I don't think exists but my mother does and it don't hurt to be polite.

The boat began to toss. I started whistling, though I couldn't tell if I was on key or not.

I will never know how long I was there in that little boat. It was just small enough to not attract too much attention from the storm. The canvas cover was tight and it shipped almost no water. I was bruised from being tossed around to the ribs and planking, and slammed into a seat hard enough to knock me out, and I don't know how long for. Could have been fifteen minutes or two days. When the storm's bellers died I cautiously unbuttoned one corner of the canvas and stuck my head out. I could smell land nearby, the smell of green things and earth. Other than the landsmell, I hadn't the foggiest damn idea what time it was other than it was pitch black night, or where I was give or take ten thousand miles.

When dawn come up I could see land over to the west of me. A fairly substantial island, with mountains cut off by a fleece of clouds. The boat was drifting toward the island at a slow pace, so I unbuttoned the top all round and folded the tarpaulin and put the oars in the locks. I drank some water and ate a can of beans and a ship's biscuit and ran my fingers over a bone-deep gash that ran from my forehead to the crown of my skull. The kit in the boat had a mirror for signaling passing ships, and I bathed the cut with seawater and found it warn't as bad as it felt. I sewed the cut up with a straightened fishhook and some light cotton fishing line. Then I rigged a drip for it and let it run saltwater on the cut. Infection could still kill me in a matter of a couple of days. I had lost good friends to the blood poisoning, and one of them had no more of a wound than a single thorn scratch by the corner of his mouth. (It was Bill Pentz, the rancher, and in two days he was one huge running sore and a fever of 109.)

The island come closer and closer and I kept an anxious eye peeled for the surf. I could use a nice sandy beach right now. I thought it would be a real shame after having survived that damned typhoon to die pounded to a pulp on the rocks.

By and by I could see the surf breaking on a black sand beach.

I kept the prow of the boat pointed toward the island and began to row. The swells gained as I got close. When I felt the keel begin to ground I jumped out with a line in my hand and got plastered down into the sand by a wave, jumped up, and sloshed up past the surf line and began hauling my boat up. I could barely drag it, but I got it above the surf line, though I would have to bring it farther by high tide.

A freak wave hit just then—I could see the seas drawing out quite a bit farther than they had. So when it come in I was ready, and I hauled hard on the line and the boat come up well beyond the tideline.

I had no sooner sat down to rest a bit than I heard a ship's horn, and one of Her Majesty's frigates hove into view from behind the headland. I peeled off my shirt and waved, and they put a longboat down with dispatch and the tars rowed in for me. I dived through the breaking surf and swam hard as I could, so they wouldn't have to beach their boat.

A couple of brawny sailors pulled me over the gunwales and the longboat turned to right smart.

When I got to the top of the rope ladder I felt suddenly weak and sick—I hadn't eaten in a long time. I fainted on the deck and was carried off to the infirmary. I slept for twenty hours or so, and when I woke it was just coming on dawn. I got up and went forward to where the lookout stood and asked a couple questions. The swabbie was full of news, though he didn't take his eyes off the sea ahead for even a second.

Having been more or less away from the papers for the last four months I was gratified that things had gone on as senselessly and bloodily as usual so the world still swung in its miserable and lethal orbit. Perhaps the harrowing events of the last few days had soured me. There was a rising rebellion in China, the Heavenly Fists (Boxers) who were hoping to drive all the foreign devils out. To this end a number of missionaries had been killed and various gunboats belonging to one batch of foreign devils or another was steaming up and down the Yangtze or the Yellow River loosing off an occasional round.

The British had for more than a century pursued the opium trade in China, often carried by ships owned by old American names. Britain did not want a strong China—she had quite enough difficulties with Russia—and so the poppies of Burma and India became smoke to cripple the Chinese dragon.

The Sirdar, Kitchener, had taken Khartoum and killed tens of thousands of the followers of the Mahdi. The Boers were about to go to war with the British. I had some experience of the Boers. I wished the British luck. The guerrillas in the Philippines who had been fighting the Spanish for forty years had took two deep breaths when the Americans replaced the Spanish and then had started in on the Americans. Since there was seven thousand islands in the Philippines, I figured that could go on as long as anyone had a bullet left.

I thought I might go back to the United States and quiet-like sneak up to the Thousand Islands country and set on a porch and smoke the odd seegar and stay good and hid. Take up building little ships inside bottles or tying salmon flies or maybe needlepoint or something. I had an adventurous life. Adventures clustered around me like stink on shit and I was damned tired of it.

After a few days we come nigh on to Ceylon and the ship went into Colombo's harbor. I was able to cable my bankers from there. Since the good ship *Arthose* paused for over a week I was able to get some actual gold money, which I hate leaving home without.

I stopped in at the U.S. consul's and had him cable Washington and New York that I was alive and well. This was a very bad mistake. Should have just let my friends wonder.

For the next morning the consul was at my hotel with a cable from I suppose I do not have to tell you, Teethadore, delighted that I had surfaced, all the best, and the ordering me to proceed to Southern Africa there to observe the budding war between the Boers and the Brits.

I tried to bribe the consul but the son of a bitch was one of those rich bastards can't be bought, so there I was, a valued associate of that damned Dutch dwarf again.

Jaysus Kayrist, Kelly, I says, long life and no friends to your wake.

I cabled Teethadore saying I'd see what I could do.

He cabled back a message to the effect that the statute of limitations did not apply to everything.

Well, I kept my temper. I bade a fond farewell to my shipmates—and waited a decent interval before taking ship on an American tramp steamer that would make Cape Town but not in any great hurry. I knew Cape Town would be safe—anyplace in reach of England's naval guns was automatically very peaceful—and perhaps I could weasel my way into a billet with a crack cavalry regiment, since they presented a fast and moving target, and they had chefs instead of cooks.

In about a week the tramp freighter was loaded down and outward bound and I stood at the bows and looked off across the Indian Ocean toward the east coast of Africa. In the twenty years I'd been away I wondered what had become of the Zulus I had known, and of Marieke, the hell-for-leather Boer girl who loved me. Ever since my young wife died at the foot of the Wind River Mountains I never stayed long with one woman or by any choice of mine more than a couple months in one place.

I could tell a few days later that we weren't far from the east coast of Africa because of the numbers of huge great white sharks that sailed in our wake. One of them et the ship's log, trailing as it was on a cable. The bright brass caught the shark's eye.

When the wind was from the west I could smell the smell of Africa, sandalwood and decay, some greenstuff smell, but mostly a smell of death this time, faint and far, but none the less a stench of honey on rotten fish.

We passed the bloated bodies of two whales, covered in gulls with sharks thick as flies in the water. I saw sharks so frenzied that they were biting each other, and I didn't know that there were other animals besides humans would stoop to such behavior. It saddened me. I had such hopes.

The little steamer first put in to the Portuguese harbor town of Delagoa Bay. I had never been there and it wasn't much to look at—the Shanganes had burnt it flat at regular intervals damn near since the first Portagees landed there. It was originally a watering and vegetable depot for Portuguese traders heading for the Spice Islands or coming back with loads of spices that made the bland European diet at least bearable. For a time, there had been a lot of slaving out of Delagoa Bay, but not for a couple of centuries. The air still reeked of human misery.

It would be a couple of days before the steamer went on to Durban and Cape Town, so I stomped down the gangway and damn near fell over—I had my sea legs and the land didn't move sufficiently. Shortly I would have my land legs back, which meant a sentence of seasickness. I hate the ocean.

There was some sort of parade going on up the ways there, a lot of cheering and such, and I was bored enough to go on up and find out what in the hell was the cause of all the fuss.

There was someone speaking in a hesitant and stammering voice, but the sun was behind him and I couldn't quite make the features out. The speech was a fairly fat, self-aggrandizing muddle of words, and then a heartrending appeal for help against the vicious and evil Boers.

The speaker had a lisp. It stuck in my mind. I had heard that lisp before some time back but I couldn't quite place it.

"Who *is* that?" I says to a monocled Brit standing near me.

I was informed that it was young Winston Churchill, having escaped gallantly from the odious Boers, he now felt compelled to tell us about it.

"Buzzard shit!" I said to the monocle, and I ambled away from the scene, but not fast enough.

"Luther! I say! Luther Kelly! What good fortune! Kelly! Kelly!" yelled young Churchill to my rapidly retreating back. I was picking up my boots and reaching out with them right smart.

"Luther!" that last seemed to be gaining on me so I broke into a flat out run. That little bastard was pure and unadulterated trouble; he hadn't enough wit to fear anything, and I knew sure as hell that if I didn't shake him in forty-eight hours there would be a telegram hand-delivered to me from Teethadore bidding me stand as close as possible to young Winston and watch him, by the by reminding me that there were some crimes not subject to the statute of limitations, etc., etc., etc.

Luther Kelly, a Legend in His Own Time, was running in abject fear from a fat little lisping limey bastard whose sole redeeming feature was his beautiful and ferociously intelligent mother.

Churchill always wanted to be a Great Man. I have had smaller ambitions, like being an Old Man, and them as wishes to give me medals are wasting their time. I have never done one damn thing out of bravery. If I fought like hell it was only because there warn't nowhere to run.

I finally stepped in a large deposit of elephant dung left by a tame elephant worked in a lumber yard. My feet shot out from under me, I cracked my head on the cobbles, and Winston overtook me, summoned help, and bore me to the British consulate, where a sawbones stitched up my head and gave me morphine.

I opened my eyes late the next afternoon and of course young Winston was waving the telegram from Teethadore, the usual "die nobly." I should have turned Mormon and gone into the prophecy business.

I called Winston a lot of names of the sort bullwhackers use when an axle breaks or an ox stands on their foot or they look down in the trace chains and one of their fingers is in there.

Churchill just nodded happily and complimented me on the variations and music of my words.

I couldn't remember when I had been so damn happy.

7

Young Winston proceeded to make my life miserable as quickly as he could find an unsettling routine and stick to it. For one thing, he wasn't there in the British Army, he was there as a correspondent. This meant that we could not rely, as I so often have, on sheer military incompetence to keep us far from maims and horrible wounds. Winston knew beyond any doubt that he was destined for great things, which had not yet happened, and he was therefore in no danger from anything at all.

I wake up shivering in the night sometimes at the mere thought of an artillery barrage or a sniper out there somewhere who is as good with a rifle as I am.

The British, among their other peculiar habits, dislike change of any sort. They were the last European power to surrender their muzzle-loading bronze cannon. The British leapt to meet the Boer threat of 1899 with an Army outfitted and trained for fighting the Russians in the Crimean War of 1853. Other inventions which had come upon the art of war were repeating rifles, machine guns, improved long-range artillery shells, and barbed wire. The day of the horse cavalry was gone—about all I could think for them to do was dress out their horses and fry up the meat for the infantry.

These were some of the sour remarks I made to young Winston. He beamed and said he could not agree more. He waved another telegram at me. It was from his mother. She had outfitted, largely with

American funds, a hospital ship. She awaited Winston in Cape Town. Do come.

On the twenty-first of December many stout Britons armed to their horsey teeth marched us down to the Royal Mail ship *Induna,* and they gave us three cheers whilst I, at least, amused myself by making obscene gestures with my hands high in the air. No one noticed.

The news of the war was everywhere bad—if you cared who won. Me, I did not much care, as long as I was not called upon to give my life's blood or a single drop of the damned stuff for perfidious Albion. I have never wanted *any* glory. Just the money, thank you.

Ladysmith was surrounded, so was Kimberley, so was Mafeking. Winston's aunt, Lady Sarah Wilson, was in Mafeking holding afternoon teas and bezique games in a whitewashed bunker over which floated an enormous Union Jack. It looked to be such a jolly little war. They all look jolly at the beginning. Them boys of sixteen and seventeen and so forth march off to battle whistling. They don't come back whistling. When they come back, if they do, they are looking out of old eyes. It can happen in a single morning, or afternoon. The look is something you never forget. They are young when they come back, still, but after that morning, they believe in death.

The Boers wasn't professional soldiers but they were a warrior people. They had to fight the natives, and when the fighting was done they went back home and took to farming again. They elected their officers from the best fighters.

A couple of them actually read books, which is frowned upon by the British as the ruination of good soldierly qualities and leads to quarrels with yer superiors. (I *always* quarrel with my superiors.)

By the time I landed in Delagoa Bay, near on to Christmas of 1899, the Brits had been routed, defeated, surrounded, outfoxed (no special effort or intelligence was required for that), and made to look generally like damned fools.

"Who is commanding this sorry effort," I says to Winston.

"Redvers Buller."

"OH, NO," I yelled, clapping a hand to a clammy forehead.

I knew the good Sir Redvers Buller. He was as brave as a lion and just about as smart. He was a splendid leader of men if the men were in range of his voice. In any Army *I* ran he would be my first choice for captain and the dead last for general. He was, uh, hem, haw, cough, wheeze . . . . . . stupid.

The *Induna* clanked out her anchor chain in Cape Town's harbor, and all manner of pleasure craft gathered round to hurrah Winston. Nothing like having a young patrician hero to lionize at a time when the soldiers of the Queen was getting their blocky little heads knocked off every chance the Boers got to do it. (If you read much history and notice things you'll find that if the weapons and numbers on each side are equal, that a citizen's army will beat a professional army all hollow.)

We didn't even get ashore right away. Winston's mother, the lovely and ferocious Jennie, sent a boat for us and hauled us to the hospital ship *Maine,* named after the battleship lost in Havana harbor. You will notice that while many mothers worried about their offspring getting hurt in this war, Jennie was the only one who just commissioned a ship and went to the war, and had a floating hospital just waiting should either of her boys have bad luck. And all paid for by her many, uh, friends.

The boat tied up to a long folding staircase hung down from the *Maine,* and Winston and I clambered up and there at the top of the stairs was the lovely Jennie. She was one of those grand beauties who stop folks in the street—when young because they are so lovely and as they age because their strength shows through; they are *still* lovely.

Jennie was also the pure quill. She was nursing wounded soldiers, emptying bedpans, changing dressings, assisting at amputations, bathing those wounded men who were delirious with fever—and she did that seventy hours a week.

She kissed Winston lightly on the cheek.

"Winston," she said, in that throaty purr I'll never forget, "is this the famous Kelly?" I thought of asking smartly if she'd forgot bedding me at Blenheim Palace—three times.

Winston made introductions. I bowed. Actually, Jennie and me was as close as friends can get, but I thought perhaps I would not bring that up at just this particular moment, since she didn't seem to wish to.

She took us back to her stateroom and ordered champagne and

oysters and caviar. Work she might, but she wouldn't stint on the necessaries.

Speaking of which, she had a new husband name of George Cornwallis-West, who was three years younger than Winston.

"Father!" said Winston, opening his arms.

George retired from the scene, muttering.

Jennie laughed. She cared for no one's opinion but her own, and I liked her for that.

Jennie fastened her dark eyes on Winston while he lisped out the tale of his harrowing and dangerous escape from the cruel clutches of the Boers. He didn't mention that if he'd waited one more day the Boers were going to toss him back to the British as more trouble than he was worth.

We had dinner with Jennie that night, pheasant, two soups, and sorbets, claret, hock, and brandy and seegars. A few times we heard some screaming from the hospital wards below, but, considering all, it was a pleasant meal.

Jennie saw us down the stairs to a longboat, and the tars pulled sharp at the oars and soon we were up to the docks. An escort of soldiers in the new khaki uniforms gathered around us to protect us from Boer revenge or some damn thing—silly, you ask me, Winston could be counted upon to offer himself at every opportunity as a target. If I had the opportunity to shoot him I would be sore tempted, as he was likely to affect my health, happiness, and well-being. (If I had the slightest inkling of just how much he was to do that, I'd have shot the bastard in front of his mother and taken the chance on pleading with the jury.)

Winston was about as popular as a plague of boils at Staff Headquarters. Subalterns are forever at odds with their superiors but damn few of them write for the *Times* of London. Winston being Winston, he went direct to poor overmatched Buller, asking for a soldier's billet. Buller harrumphed and said that Army regulations forbade serving officers from writing for newspapers.

That rule had been hastily added two years before solely because of Winston's accounts of the Sirdar's Nile expedition. And now this arrogant pup was demanding that the rule be *suspended* for him.

Buller was drinking a lot these days, and he stared off in befuddlement, focused his eyes on me, gave a start, said, "Kelly, you blackguard, is that *you?*" to which I nodded.

"I'll hang the pair of you on Bungo," said Buller.

"Is Bungo for us or against us?" I snarled. "Or a black king or something."

Turned out it was Gen. Julian Byng, Commander of the South African Light Horse.

Having this moment placed us elsewhere, Buller nodded off to sleep and an adjutant led us out.

"And where is the South African Light Horse?" Winston asked.

The adjutant said we'd have to find them he supposed.

Outside, I stopped and looked to the northeast, where I'd fought and run from the Zulus, where the Prince Imperial of France had been killed, more or less dying of flattery, and where I had lain with a lovely young Boer girl who had more guts than me and was a better hand with a horse, too.

And here I was once again, stuck fighting a war that did not concern me.

We went to look up our comrades, and they us.

As is its habit, the British Army came back to Africa fully prepared to fight the Zulus. The time they'd been ready to fight the Zulus before, the British managed to lose twelve hundred soldiers of a morning—to a foe armed with shields and spears.

I asked around and found that the Boers were armed with Mauser rifles, Krupp cannon, barbed wire, Skoda mortars, and other modern horrors.

I occupied myself whistling "Heads of Oak" and wondering if I could somehow make it back to my California spread and start over with whatever managed to survive without me.

Sir Julian Byng eyed us with extreme distaste. He hated Americans much more than he hated Boers, and he hated newspapermen worse than the Devil or Americans. He made this quite plain to us.

"I do not need some sucked-up snip of a scribbler," snarled Sir Julian, "or his colonial lout either. But I have to make the best of it. Either of you ever heard a gun fired in anger? Can you ride?"

"I'm a Sandhurst man," spluttered Winston.

"Oh, God," said Sir Julian, "that *too*?"

I liked the man. He was intelligent and a swift and sure judge of character and the secret hearts of men. He spoke without malice or forethought—hindthought, neither.

"Wul," I says in my best Rocky Mountain argle-bargle, "Tain't fer certain I don't think ya lime-sucking pansies could whip a passel of crippled wog nursemaids. Maybe you'd best hire some Amurrican boys that knows what fighting's about. Ya ain't whupped nobody since Napoleon and I hears his piles was actin' up bad that day. Mebbe yuh should just crawl back on the ships and go home. The brussels sprouts is in season."

Sir Julian looked at me down the length of his considerable nose and he rang for an orderly.

"Fetch two chota pegs of scotch," said Sir Julian, "and take this goddamned . . . . . . correspondent with you." The orderly grabbed Winston and dragged him out of the office. A short while later he was back with the whiskeys, and then he withdrew.

"An amazing performance," said Sir Julian. "All but trying to convince me you were chewing tobacco. You lack the visible signs of that filthy habit. The yellow drool down your clothes. I didn't get your name."

"Major Luther Kelly, United States Army," I says.

"Your Army dress like this?"

He had a point. I was wearing chamois-skin pants, high boots all tooled with gila monsters and gold, a gunbelt and twin Colts, a lace-edged shirt, a watered silk waistcoat, a silver and turquoise choker, and a tall cream-colored Stetson. Why? Well, there was this package waiting for me in Cape Town, from Theodore, who wished me well dressed for this occasion. There was no commission in the package. I also had a Presentation grade .405 Winchester rifle all chased with silver and gold, depicting Theodore killing things.

"No," I admitted modestly.

"Does entering battle dressed like a procurer give you advantages I cannot at this moment see?" Sir Julian asked.

"You ever met Theodore Roosevelt?" I asked.

Sir Julian nodded.

"Frightening, ain't it?" I said.

"Horrifying," he agreed.

"These duds are his little idea of a joke—he gets to tweak me and the British Empire."

"Could I, er, ah," said Sir Julian, "um, assist you in any way?"

An hour later my finery was boxed up and shipped off and I flexed some of the starch out of the khakis that Bungo had been so good as to find me. I still had the Colts, for protection against snakes and other mean animals. But now I wore good plain heavy high riding boots decorated only with stitching, and not much of that, and I by God had an observer's warrant tucked inside my coat. I'd watch this war and let Winston fight it. Buller's subtlest tactic was to gather as many men as he could and charge, which worked good against natives armed with spears but I didn't think it would be as effective and fun against entrenched troops with repeating rifles, machine guns, and artillery.

My God that Winston was a royal pain in the butt. He was a hell of a good horseman, and he lacked physical fear, but he was always posing at the goddamnedest times, with bullets cutting all around him, and quoted Macaulay or Shakespeare or himself at the top of his lungs when a wise feller would have been curled up behind a nice thick rock being quiet and as unobtrusive as possible.

I was just going to observe this little war, which looked like it might not be so little, and as a war it decided nothing at all.

Often I found myself with Sir Julian, and in the warm evenings we'd drink whiskey. Byng was a good solider, and he was an intelligent man.

"Other than the odd tribal war—Isandhlwana was the largest loss of troops since Waterloo—we haven't fought a real enemy since Waterloo," said Sir Julian, "and we are splendidly ready to fight Waterloo tomorrow."

I nodded. I had seen this before, many a time.

"The Boer is a cunning and resourceful foe," Byng went on. "He cuts and slashes and runs and when he stands he entrenches and arranges his artillery, firing from ten miles behind his lines so it can't be got at readily. Buller is a brave man, but overmatched here . . ."

That was true, for sure. Buller may have been the best major ever commissioned, but anything up from that he'd be as lost as a fish in a tree.

All hell broke loose down at the far end of the camp, a lot of hallooing and such, and eventually a subaltern came running to Sir Julian. The boy was breathless and spattered with mud. Winston came on soon behind him.

"The Boers have struck at the Cape Telegraph," said the boy, "not twenty miles from Cape Town."

"We must pursue!" Winston said, hotly.

I suppose it was four o'clock in the afternoon.

Byng nodded.

"Kelly," he said. "Whist?"

"No," I said, "but I'll play bezique."

We went back to the card table in front of Sir Julian's tent and fell to a hard-fought game of cards while Winston swelled up like a poisoned pup.

"I give him ten minutes," I says, watching the man of the hour darken with choler.

"Five," said Byng.

"We have had our honor insulted and you sit at cards?!" said Winston, glaring wrathfully at us.

"You've a better suggestion?" said Byng, solicitude dripping from every pore.

"Pursue them!" said Winston, jutting out his jaw.

"Winston," said Byng, "this fellow across from me is not a subject of the Queen. He is a citizen of an independent nation because we had generals like you there, in the 1770s. Now Kelly will explain what I mean."

"They are a day, day and a half ahead of us. If we chase them they will eventually let us catch them. Now, I don't know exactly where that would be, but I do know that ten miles behind them there would be several Krupp Long Toms. All sighted and set. They'd make forcemeat out of us. Then they'd come down and cut Cape Telegraph again, since we were stupid enough to follow long behind the first time." I turned to Sir Julian. "I miss anything?"

He shook his head.

"We'll be in the field shortly," said Sir Julian, "and I can assure you we will find the Boer, and we shall both bleed."

"It's that kind of war," I said.

"Winston," said Byng, "your kind of war went out with Agincourt."

Winston pouted. I wanted to crack him over the head with a stout chunk of stovewood.

Finally he stalked away, to sulk I supposed.

"He'll either be hung or Prime Minister someday," said Sir Julian.

Both Winston and Theodore were sure they were not like other men, and if they gained power other men would die at their bidding. They felt themselves fit to dictate destiny. I'm not like that. I never have enjoyed telling anybody else what to do.

The next day I wandered around Cape Town picking up odds and ends of things might come in handy, and I happened to be down at the wharves when one of the cranes unloading a cargo ship lost a brakeblock and the load fell. It was barbed wire, huge balls of it, and they crushed the wooden planking and went on into the sea beneath, all but a couple of five-hundred-pound rolls that stuck to the wharves like burrs to cloth.

I have a lurch in my body every time I see barbed wire—it carved up my free country like a knife does cake.

I stood there a moment and thought of the amount of wire—it was covered in a peculiar gray canvas—and with a war on I couldn't see why the cattle business was booming so.

I shook my head and went on.

The next morning the horses was loaded and we entrained for the "front," which I have always found very hard to find in a guerrilla war, and this was no different. The actual war was to recover the gold and diamonds of the Rand, it was a mere accident that the Boers happened to be on it. It was an oversight and had England known at the time the Boers would not have been on it at all. Statecraft is solely a matter of correcting such oversights.

The Orange Free State and the Transvaal were the Boer republics, and the Boers was frontier folk so they didn't have a government to speak of, just shouting matches. Behind all of it was Oom Paul Krueger, old, cunning, God-callen, ruthless, and a good judge of generals. His generals had been whipping the British handily and it was getting embarrassing to the greatest Empire the world has ever known.

We off-trained and saddled up and rode the queasy horses around to get the idea through their thick heads that they were back on firm earth, and then we fed them a little and watered them and curried them down.

The Boers was riding out of one or both of their republics and fighting a little and riding on. It wasn't a war, it was a goddamned steeplechase.

Byng supposed we would look around a bit. I gazed longingly toward the south until he got the point and snorted and walked away. Wouldn't do for him to think I was eager for this.

We were living on cold rations because the rest hadn't come up yet—I had four loaves of veldt bread in my saddlebags, a mix of meat flour and wheat flour—and as usual headquarters had only the vaguest suggestions to make to us, because they had no decent intelligence because Buller hadn't any intelligence at all.

As wars go, I have seen ones better run—not many, but some.

We were in the middle of the South African winter, here on to the end of July, and the rains came daily and washed down the dust, and then in early August it got to be spring, and the hot dusty summer up ahead.

The rest of the South African Light Horse was made of young fellers of good family and the scum of the diamond fields—an arrangement much like the Rough Riders. I thanked my stars I had no part in this but to observe.

Byng sought me out late in the day, and he put a hand on my shoulder and his face got mournful.

"What?" I says.

"The Republicans have nominated William McKinley for President and Theodore Roosevelt for Vice President."

I nodded and vomited on my boots.

"God Almighty help us all," said Sir Julian.

Even though you know something is bound to happen it don't sometimes soften the blow when it does. I could look forward in what little life remained to me to an endless succession of errands all over the world, anywhere Theodore could possibly invade something.

More trains arrived at this piece of track—there wasn't even a station here—and it seemed that the British were going to try to chase down cavalry with infantry. Our experience in America trying to chase down the Plains Indians didn't count—Americans lacked British pluck, as everyone knew.

The infantry was coming off the trains in a fine mist of rain and we sodden troopers were watching them from three hundred yards away; all of a sudden there were the high-pitched screams of heavy artillery shells coming at us. The bursts hit two cars of the train and khaki-clad dolls flew loose-limbed through the air.

Our horses were tired and not too skittish, but then a couple 140-pound Long Tom shells burst near us, disemboweling several horses and riders with white-hot shrapnel.

Sir Julian had casually thrown his field jacket over his horse's head, and he was standing there calmly with a compass and two sticks marking the tracks of the shells so he knew about which direction they come from.

"ALL YOU WHORESONS MOUNT UP AND FOLLOW ME!" Byng yelled, he had the loudest voice but for Liver-Eatin' Jack's I'd ever hear.

All the whoresons did and we headed off in the mist NNW. I gestured to some troopers and they fell in behind me—my natural air of command, don't you know—and we cut to the ridgetops and flushed a couple of snipers who couldn't see through the rain either. I shot one while running him down and the horse leaped over him and we joined up with Byng at the bottom of the long shallow descent.

"If we can get some of the big guns," said Byng, "we might have some chance."

The low cloud and mist made it hard to gauge just where the guns was. There was fresh horse sign of a sudden, ten or twelve riders moving fast the same direction we was.

The shells was passing high above. I thought of what they were doing to the train and the men packed round it, and I shook my head.

There was a shot from off to the right up ahead, and I saw a trooper throw up his hands and tumble back off his horse. The way his neck bent when he hit the ground said not to bother with him, not in this life.

Byng called a halt and he motioned me to him. I rode to him and bent over to hear what he had to say.

"I haven't another officer worth a pissed on cravat," he said. "Will you assist me? Take about half and go up that donga, I'll bear left."

My morals wrestled one with another and fled. "Yes," I said.

One certain thing, the Long Toms and Pom-poms would have a heavy guard around them. Without them big guns, the Boers warn't no more than bandits.

Byng moved off and he was soon gone in the soft gray rain. The yellow mud on the trails reminded me of Wyoming. I waved my arm twice and the troopers fell in behind me. The rain pulsed up, hard enough now to splash when it hit the puddles.

I went up a long spur, to try and ear-sight the guns. They seemed to be above and not too far off. I sent half my troopers down to sweep the base of the mountain—here a mountain may be fifty miles long—and I led the rest up and then out over a flat top studded with boulders.

I could see no sign of any Boers, and we went on slow, and the next time we came to the rim there was the sound of a hot fight down below, but we couldn't get there down the jumbled boulders that hold to the mountains like a beach holds the sea.

The guns fired, damn close. I led the men single-file ahead, and then we dismounted and picketed the horses. We walked forward in a ragged skirmish line.

A single Boer sentry stood up of a sudden thirty feet in front of me, a kid, no more than fifteen, and he fired wild, dropping a man behind me. I shot him in the leg and watched him drop his gun and grab the hole in his thigh and look very startled.

We ran for the horses and I could hear mounted troops behind us, coming on fast. I wished to Christ I had a good pump shotgun and plenty of buckshot.

The Boers come out of the mist when some of us was still mounting, me included, and they let off a volley that hit men and horses and turned what would have been a mere undignified rout into a disaster. (I'm a connoisseur of routs, been in so many. Disasters, too.)

My horse was every bit as scared as I was and he decided that my extra weight was hampering him and he tossed me onto a rock and headed out. Smart horse. I shot at him twice in tribute.

I was on foot and alone but for two bodies I thought I'd surrender to the first man or horse that come by. One soon did, and I put my hands high and left my pistols (Theodore's, actually, so it didn't hurt that much) on the boulder. The Boer rode behind me, and I trudged toward the sound of the cannon.

The terrain and the weather fooled the ear. I walked for perhaps five miles before I came to a trench line filled with Boers and then another and behind them the guns and a canvas fly stretched between a couple of blue gum trees that was headquarters.

There was a big black-bearded gent in farmer clothes and a tall gray hat sitting on a log, whittling. He motioned me to the log and went on whittling. The guns stopped firing.

"Well, English," he said, his speech sharp with High Dutch, "I think your war is not going so well for you, eh?" He looked at my khakis, without so much as a single regimental badge on them.

"I'm an American observer," I said. "Colonel Kelly, United States Army." I held out my hand.

Black-beard looked at it like it was something unexpected in the bottom of the stewpot, when everybody'd already et.

"Do you shoot when you observe?" he asked.

"Only when I'm being shot at," I says. One of the Boers who had marched me in came up and rattled off something in Boer, and walked off. I'd been twenty years away and only caught "liar" out of it.

"Why were you leading the troopers?" says Black-beard.

"A friend asked as a special favor."

Black-beard nodded and went on chewing his tobacco and whittling his stick. He put his fingers in his mouth and blew a long sharp whistle.

Half a dozen Boers come up at a run. They was all big men but for one on the far end couldn't manage five feet high.

"Shoot this one," said Black-beard.

"Now just a gaddamned minute," I roared. "I am an emissary of the United States of America, and I . . ." I was drug off and tied to a sapling and blindfolded.

I wanted to live, so I could skin Teethadore alive.

Well, I heard the rifles cock, and the command to aim, and I wasn't thinking on nothing much at all and waiting for the slugs when a good kick caught me right in the nuts. I said what you always say at a time like that—*Whhoooooooffffffff*—and slid down the pole. Some merciful soul cut my hands free and I clapped them over the pain and puked quietly sideways for an hour or two. There is nothing hurts a feller quite like that.

The little Boer and another one come by and they lifted me up and set me back against the sapling, with my knees drawn up and my hands still in my crotch. Red waves of pain danced in front of my eyeballs and my breath was a staggered wheezy thing, but I could actually think of small things other than my mashed glands down there.

The little Boer took off his hat and it was . . .

"Oh, shit," I wheezed. Marieke Uys, once a lovely young girl I had snuck out on. Back in '79, when I had been here being entertained by the Zulu War.

"Kelly," said Marieke, "I just couldn't shoot you till I had a chance to kick you hard in the nuts."

"I understand," I wheezed.

"And this is your son Dirk . . ." she said. I looked over and saw a paler version of myself, except the teeth in his smile were his mother's.

"General Botha has paroled you to us," said Marieke.

"I don't give a damn what they do with you, Kelly," rumbled Botha, he'd been behind me all along.

I got on the horse they gave me, standing in the stirrups, and away we went into the soft wet night.

9

My wounded balls was the best way of keeping me from escaping. Felt like I had a pair of sore cantaloupes down there. I walked like a duck and not all that fast. Better than chains and a dungeon.

"I waited twenty-one years to do that!" said Marieke. She was so happy about it I wanted to strangle her. I couldn't really blame her, but I was sulky about the dirty pool with the firing squad and all. I always exhibit good taste in these matters. (No, I don't.)

Fortunately she wasn't one to dwell on such quarrels—having repaid my perfidy with a straight shot to the nuts she sort of fell right back into deciding what we were going to do and I was expected to foller along with it. Fine with me, long as I had these tender balls. Situations like this I have always proved to be an amiable and rather stupid feller. I play it well enough long enough and they start thinking so, too.

Our son had gone back to shoot Englishmen, the Boers called them "roineks"—rednecks, for they had no little capes over their necks like the French Foreign Legion favors.

Over the days she told me about her life after I'd taken ship and it was just what I suspected—she'd had a suitor or two, but they got the wim-wams and sheared off after a while. Marieke was stubborn as a mule that's found a patch of chamomile. She knew her mind and once it was made up it was useless to argue.

Her little holding was a shallow valley on one of them long table mountains that country holds—she'd been supporting herself and son Dirk for all this time breaking and training horses and selling them to the English who flocked to the Rand goldfields or the Vaal River diamond diggings.

Then when the war come on she volunteered as a scout, and when one of the rough Boers who didn't know her laughed, she lifted up a blacksnake whip and cut him up till he apologized. After that there was no more backchat.

I had my ears out for any hint of what was going to be done with good old Luther. As my nuts shrank and my gait improved I began to wonder just where the lines were. Well, it's my habit when captured to figure on a way out of it—I've done it dozens of times.

Marieke seemed unconcerned. I was sleeping in a little lean-to on her house, on a cornshuck mattress with rough cotton sheets and a big heavy quilt. One night she slipped in bed with me and clung to me, breathing hot and sweet, and she stayed until the morning. Her perkiness returned and I was bothered by it, for I was thinking maybe she thought I was going to stay and break horses or run cattle, all of which I know how to do and don't much like.

The rains got heavier and we even spent some of the days in the lean-to, with the pattering on the shakes and the clean smell of lightning coming through on the breeze.

"I want to have you come with me to look at some things," she said one day. "No one in the world know what the British have done. We are a simple people. Few of us even read well. I want you to come with me, please. You won't have to fight the English."

I was coming up in the world. From the low position of husband I had climbed to journalist. I took her up on it.

"What things the British are doing?" I asked. She put her fingers to my lips and then her body tight and hot against mine. My parts was about back to normal, and she was a pretty thing, a small blond woman with a small body wiry and hard from riding and fighting, too, for she was a dead shot. (The light is so strange in Africa, compared to what I'm used to, that I missed things all the time, shooting high or shooting low. It's funny, but true.)

One day she said we must go, and so we saddled and packed two horses with gear—she'd got my Colts somehow, and then she had a Mauser rifle for me, too, and bandoliers of ammunition. The food was veldt bread and dried fruit, sugar, and tea.

Marieke was closemouthed about what I was to see that angered her so. She came of a bloody clan in a bloody land, and I never was to see her flinch.

She led by narrow paths that skirted the flat-topped mountains, and we come up one morning to a Boer camp with the same black-bearded general setting on another log, whittle-shaping a piece of wood.

This time I got introduced to Louis Botha, who gave me a dry handclasp and inquired about the health of young Winston Churchill.

"I suppose the little shit is in splendid health," I says, "Though it would cheer me to hear otherwise."

Botha laughed, a series of booms, and he went to the saddlebags and got a poster and unrolled it. There was a crude likeness of Winston and some description and the reward was twenty-five pounds. Winston would be having blue screeching fits over the low amount, that's for sure. He valued himself a bit higher than that.

"You could have made it twenty-five shillings," I said.

"He would have known it for a joke," said Botha, laughing again.

"We should not have begun this war," he said suddenly. "We did not know that the strength of the Dutch and French and Germans is only on the land, and it is too far that way from them to us. They cannot help. Heaven help us, then. We cannot go near the sea, the guns from the ships are terrible. So the English will strangle us."

'Twas true. England's Navy was the equal of any three others on the face of the earth.

"Marieke will show you how they do this," he said, looking both angry and sad. "Please tell your country how the English treat Christian white people."

I didn't know, but I could guess.

Crushed beneath the wheel. The Boers were a simple frontier folk; they bought only powder, lead, and cloth and had lived by their cattle for nearly three hundred years. They had a stern Old Testament God. It surprised me that men like Botha would rise up at need, but then I remembered Stonewall Jackson.

My son Dirk was here with the Boer rangers, the men who harassed the English and rode in the night. The boy—hell, man, he was taller than I am and probably nicer, too, he come and shook hands with me and said in pretty good English he was pleased to make my acquaintance. He turned to go. I clapped him on the shoulder and gave him the one piece of advice I could think of.

"Don't make a life of this," I said, waving a hand at the guns and the soldiers.

Then he was gone.

Marieke was ready to go. I swung up and I even saluted Botha, another day we might have been friends.

We made our way south, sometimes coming close enough to a town under siege by the Boers to hear the crump of the guns but not going near—a lot of Englishmen from the goldfields were either fighting or robbing or serving as couriers, the war was a mixed up brawl all over the map. It was easy to tell who was running the British end—Buller's one notion of soldiering was to charge. He was as subtle as a raging bull and just as easily outwitted.

We made a long hook east and come out near to Durban, where I had sailed from twenty-odd years ago. The harbor was packed. We looked down from cover on a ridge to the west, and I suddenly saw a corral of barbed wire, and it was full of people.

"That's what the Roineks do with the families," Marieke said, her voice flat and drained. "They herd them here and put them behind wire and there they die."

"Die of what?" I said. I doubted that the English would go so far as to just shoot women and children, like we done to the Sioux, Kiowa, Cheyenne, and all the others.

There was a big slit trench outside the wire. I saw a couple soldiers toss a child's body into the pit and shovel quicklime after. What you'd do with an unclaimed dog run over by a carriage.

"They die of being packed together," said Marieke, "the sicknesses come on them when they live too close."

It was coming on dark, and we went on, winding up a trail into the Dragon Mountains, the Drakensberg. Marieke knew this country like her mother's face. We stopped at dawn near a spring, hidden by the tambookie grass and the acacias. There was a little meadow for the hobbled horses to graze on, and the high lion-hiding grass would keep them in it.

We slept in the shade near the spring.

Marieke woke me with a poke in the ribs and a hand over my mouth. She jerked her head toward the little trail. We scurried off into the tambookie grass, me thinking my fifty-year-old ears was definitely losing their skill. We watched our hobbled horses all throw up their heads and point their ears forward, and then a man come along the trail on foot, looking down at the tracks. He saw the horses and held up an arm, stopping those behind.

Marieke stood up and whistled. The tracker whistled back, a bird call made to sound like the little honey creeper, and he motioned again to the Boers behind on the track.

There was about a ten-minute pause, and then all of them came out of the grass, they had circled us and would have made very short work of us indeed if we had fired.

Marieke and the leader of the band rattled at each other in Boer. Marieke pointed at me and said something funny and the rest of them had a good laugh on me, which annoyed me some as I could only catch the Boer word for "gelding."

Take it like a man and get even later, I said to myself, when the odds is obscenely long in your favor.

The band of rangers went on, leaving me and Marieke to the hobbled horses and leafy bower and purling spring.

"The British aren't fast enough to catch us and we are not strong enough to throw them out," she said.

We went on this narrow trail, cutting through the foothills of the Dragon Mountains, and then right through them at a pass which was so low I didn't notice it till I saw the mountains to each side of us and nothing up ahead but savannah. We passed whitened heaps of bones left by the Manatee Horde seventy years or so before, when for some reason thirty tribes fell apart and went to eating each other. They passed through and vanished toward the east.

This land was old with death, sure enough. Africa is much different than what I was used to in America, the landscape itself was all horizontal lines, where ours is mostly vertical.

We rode for days south and a bit east, even cutting across rails and highways time to time, and taking care to skirt round farms and the little towns.

We rode one day into a flat country, of sandstone and gullies—they call 'em dongas here—and once or twice we flushed lions from cover.

Marieke stopped and stood by her horse a while, looking as though she was praying. I put a hand on her shoulder and she came close and I held her still for a while, and then she snuffled and mounted up and we rode no more than a quarter mile and reined up on the lip of a gully and I looked down and there was hundreds of bodies—long dead, gnawed by the jackals and the birds—piled in this gully miles and miles from anywhere. I could tell by their clothing that they was Boers.

"The prisoners were too much trouble," said Marieke. "They won't escape now."

I looked down at my feet. Brass from machine gun bullets lay at my feet. There was discarded belts and other litter, all British.

"The Americans don't do this, do they, Kelly?" she asked. Her voice was wound tight, like she might start laughing and not stop till knocked unconscious.

"Yeah," I said, "we do this." I was thinking of Sand Creek and Wounded Knee, where twelve thousand American troops vanquished four hundred unarmed Sioux of all ages, sexes, and kinds of helplessness.

"All the very best nations do this sort of thing, Marieke," I said. "It's the new fashion. And you know how nations is about fashions."

There warn't anything else to say. I supposed she wanted me to do something. There wasn't anything to do.

"After you sneaked away and the Zulu War was over I went with my brothers—the ones left—to get the bones of Papa and Cornelius from Hlobane Mountain. When we found them, we found them back to back surrounded by the skeletons of the Zulus they had killed. We gathered up Papa's bones and Cornelius's bones and packed them in our saddlebags, so they would lie with the others in our own cemetery. We did not dishonor the Zulus, who were fighting to keep their Zulu order, as we were to overthrow it. Years later I met three Zulus who had fought my father and brother and they told me that my men fought like lions. One of the Zulus had killed Cornelius and helped to kill my father and I didn't hate him, somehow he seemed part of my family, too."

We mounted and rode on south, winding down pale gravels in the dongas, our heads turning to look for silhouettes of men against the sky.

I've been at a loss from time to time but never so utterly as this one. What could I say? That I could tour with magic lantern slides and a brass band and no one would care? They'd not be one bit interested.

Civilized nations did not do what was piled back there in the donga. So it hadn't happened.

We camped that night up high and she clung to me and I kept telling her to come on with me, get out of this place, for it will only kill you. She wouldn't talk, and I knew the answer was no. Her son (and mine) would fight till he got killed. She wanted to be around to wash his face and lower him down. She was probably right. Teethadore and Miles would be tossing me like a dart to wherever on the globe they was interested in. She'd be alone with her regrets a long damn way from home.

We come nigh to the sea and rode for miles on the hard-packed sand of the beaches, below the tideline so the tracks of the horses would wash away. It wasn't all that far to Cape Town and I was getting worried.

And the worst of it was I didn't know about what. The sea was shrouded in a fine low mist the sun hadn't burned off yet, all glittery above the yellow-green swells. I couldn't see any sign of travelers and the soft rolling hills were covered in short grass and I didn't see how or why any lookout would be on any of them. There was nothing to guard against, no roads or rails or harbors.

The sun was behind the mist to us and glittery, I'd no notion anything was wrong when there was a sound like a great ripping and a rush like a train makes passing close by you, and then the hillside behind us away from the sea gouted dirt like a geyser does water, and then a second explosion blew me right off the horse and sent it sprawling too. Up ahead I could see Marieke's mare bucking, and a small sprawl of clothes on the sand. I ran as fast as I could, one ear cocked for another shell.

I turned her over and her eyes fluttered and she smiled up at me. My right hand was on her belly and the blood was warm running over it. She went to sleep, it seemed, and then her body, which had been tensed against the pain, relaxed and I knew she was gone and I was glad for that, she was cut up awful bad and at least she had no pain.

I picked her up. She weighed no more than a child, she was so light in my arms. I walked away from the surf, toward the hills. When I came to a grassy patch I sat and waited for the boat. They'd been naval shells, and they could see us and we couldn't see them.

Perhaps it was twenty minutes, I wouldn't know, a longboat cut in through the surf and some Royal Marines scampered up to me, all bearing rifles with fixed bayonets. A subaltern come along behind and I looked at him level and told him my name and rank and to contact the consul's office in Cape Town or Durban.

The boy didn't know what to do. I stood up and carried Marieke to the longboat and stepped over the side and sat on a water-tin, still cradling her.

The subaltern came along, bringing my hat, and the Marines put off and clawed their way back out into the sea.

Two battle cruisers had been laying off, I supposed some lookout marked us in the telescope and they fired at Boers just to test the guns. An eight-inch shell weighs five hundred pounds, a bit large for the two of us, but it had done the job.

When we come to one of the cruisers the oarsmen held the boat steady. I had put Marieke over my right shoulder, had her head and arms hanging down my back, and I grabbed the rope ladder and struggled up to the steel gangway and then on up to the deck. They had put out a stretcher and the ship's surgeon covered her with a sheet and they hauled her away to the sailmaker's to dress her for burial at sea, with a cannonball at her feet.

The captain was a short, wiry feller named Fanshaw—that's how it sounds, the spelling is five times as long. (Featherstonehaugh, so help me.) There will always be an England.

I felt light-headed of a sudden, and the sea motion seemed to grow. I stumbled to a hatch cover and sat, trying to keep what little was in my stomach down.

The surgeon came again, and he looked at my back, and then a couple of his assistants picked me up and carried me to the surgery. They peeled my clothes off and when it come off my undershirt peeled away with a gluey sound.

A small fragment of the shell had come in below my left shoulder blade and lodged somewheres in my chest. It had taken this long to affect me because my left lung was collapsing and the blood was pooling in the space provided. This I all heard later. The surgeon rammed a needle the size of a goddamned pencil into the lung cavity to drain the blood. I struggled a little, so he gave me enough morphia to stun a rhino.

They dumped Marieke off the taffrail while I was sleeping an opium sleep.

10

I was told later that I almost died of one thing and another that the doctors did to me on the battlecruiser or on the *Maine*, Lady Randolph Churchill's steam yacht with bedpans. I carry a few arrowheads, bullets, and bits of shrapnel and I will by God crawl off and heal up my own self, it's safer. The medical profession is largely made up of them as flunked out of Divinity School.

When I woke up there was a cool hand on my brow which proved attached to the arm of Jennie Churchill, one of the great beauties of this world.

"Luther," she said. "Behave yourself."

"Wha?" I said.

She pointed at a tremendous hard prick I had and hadn't so much as noticed yet.

"Waste not, want not," I says, grabbing for her bodice. She brushed my hands away, laughing with her head throwed back, a big laugh.

I looked around for the other ill and dying, who was probably hale when they come on board. I was in a single suite in a double bed and there was fresh flowers everywhere.

"What happened," I said. "Was I promoted to general? Did Teddy get caught in a spasm of guilt and order this up?" There was her lovely breasts under that cloth. I made another grab.

"Luther! I'm a married woman!" she said, still laughing.

"First I knew that ever bothered you," I says. "I'm hornier than a five-antlered elk and you got to quibble about title deeds. Jaysus Kayrist." She didn't fight me off quite so hard.

"Oh, all right, Luther," she said, flouncing off and locking the stateroom door and pulling the curtains. They was a pale silk and muted the light nicely.

I watched her slipping off her clothes and thought what a beautiful thing a woman is, and I thought of all the ones I had held, and screwed with, and I smiled.

I was still weak and bandaged, so she got on top and while we thrust our hips at one another she looked at me, eyes half closed, and a smile on her lips.

After, she lay with her head on my throat and ran her hand over the bandages on my chest.

"So many scars," she said. I raised my eyebrows. Almost all my scars was in back, taken while departing and fast at that.

"I have to go," she said, sliding away and standing on the cold metal floor. "I have other sick and wounded men to nurse."

"Maybe you ought to have them buttons replaced with zippers," I says, grinning.

"Luther," she said dryly, "I am the captain of this vessel of mercy and you will do well not to vex me. Either I shall have you hung from the yardarm or perhaps make you walk the plank."

"I'm a wounded man," I said. "I couldn't walk the plank."

"I shall push you in a wheelchair."

"Come back soon," I said.

"There could be scandal," she said, smiling.

"So?"

"So yes, I'll come back. Poor George is at the front somewhere. Winston is at the front somewhere. If I have to eat one more wretched Cape Town boiled dinner I'll puke. Of course I shall come back."

She went out, leaving the door far open so I could get some salt breeze. I was suddenly ravenously hungry, and I wondered what time the grub came round.

I was feeling pretty good, so I shrugged on a robe and went out and leaned against a rail and looked out over the harbor, full of vessels. Warships, including one hulking battleship, coasters, and coal lighters and merchant ships of every size and shape. Down close there were the big fins of sharks, eating the garbage.

The bandages pulled the hairs on my chest and I itched and wanted a bath. I went back in the room and opened a curtain to find a smallish bathtub and when I fiddled with the faucets hot water come and there was soap to hand. I took a razor from the little possibles chest and cut off the bandages and freed up I got in the tub and relaxed.

I suppose I was soaping and soaking for an hour, and I got out and found some clean clothes my size said "C-W" in them, and told myself that Jennie's new husband wouldn't stick at lending me some duds, man to man. The other I wouldn't bring up myself.

A nurse come in and looked at the bed and at me and inquired as to where Mr. Kelly was.

"That's me," I says. "Feeling much better." I eyed her up and down—a bit heavy for my taste—and she blushed and run out. She weren't screaming, which I took for a good sign.

Not long after a doctor come in and I took off George's shirt and he looked at my wound, humming and smelling of rum, and then he went out without so much as a grunt.

There was a steward's bell somewheres at the end of a tasseled silk rope near the bed, and I hauled and yanked until two young matrons wearing the same sort of Piccadilly nursing get-ups that Jennie favored come in about half breathless.

"I just wanted something to eat," I says. "I'm starving."

The two was one blonde and one redhead and the blonde went out and the redhead ordered me sternly back to bed.

"You are unwell, Mr. Kelly," she said, "off with your clothes and into the bed." I shrugged and undressed, while she stared off somewheres toward Antarctica.

The blonde returned with a little cart packed with food—good stout chicken soup, roast beef, steamed spinach, and I ate like a wolf. The blonde took the cart away and the redhead and I had tea and chatted. It was getting on dark and she got up and closed and locked the door and came over to me. She sat on the bed and began unbuttoning her high shoes.

"Jennie had to go to a dinner on the battleship," said the redhead, "will I do for a bit till she's free?"

I nodded. "What about the blonde," I says.

"Greedy, greedy," said the redhead. "She'll be coming in about two A.M., to quicken your pulse. And my name is Anne."

She was slipping off the yards of tulle and unlacing her bodice, a redhead with a skin pale as milk and big breasts and narrow hips.

She turned, naked, in the great pile her clothes had made. I was healing fast, and no mistake.

A few days and nights later—they sort of blended together into one pleasure, mighty different from being shot at, Jennie was eating a bon-bon in bed and she idly asked me if perhaps she should cable Teethadore, who would be worrying about me.

"Don't suppose you could cable him and tell him I'm *dead,*" I says. "Died valiantly at sea of . . ."

Jennie didn't suppose she could do that. It would be a lie. Found out, Teethadore could perhaps cause difficulty for her son Winston.

"Mother!" come a voice, very like young Winston's, "Mother! Where are you?"

"Shit," said Jennie, grabbing for her clothes. She was adept at getting them on in a hurry. Winston didn't make but about two circles of the ship before she was all bricked up to decent. When Winston sounded again on the other side of the ship Jennie calmly stepped out of the door, the heat of our lovemaking shimmering in the air. She had sand, that one.

I dozed off, the work had been delightful and heavy and I needed my rest.

Which I didn't get much of. In less than an hour Winston was barging through the door of the cabin, all smiles and smarm, ready to clasp me to his manly bosom, a wounded hero, and better yet one that he knew.

"Yellowstone!" says Winston, his lisp making a gumbo out of my hated nickname (a pox on Ned Buntline). "Felled by a treacherous enemy bullet! You live!"

I was mumbling cusswords and smiling. Also wondering what in the hell a *treacherous* bullet was. They go where they're sent.

I wriggled and cuffed him till he unclasped me from his manly bosom and then I politely asked just what in the fucking hell he was so cheerful about.

"War is glorious," he said, smiling and happy.

I thought of the murdered Boers in the donga and Marieke bleeding to death in my arms and I almost lost my temper. It wouldn't have done no good. Men like Teddy and Winston never get wounded bad and they never die and I suspect if you cut 'em they wouldn't even bleed. Bleeding is for the lower classes.

"Are you recovering?" said Winston, remembering why I was here in the first place.

"Slowly," I said. Jennie had come in. "Every night I run a fever and I'm spent and exhausted for most of the day. One of them comes-and-goes fevers, I hear they can last for months."

Jennie smiled at me, but her eyes wasn't.

"I'm sure that you'll be ready to march on Kimberley," said Winston. "We leave tomorrow to relieve the gallant garrison."

I was about to list all the serious unhealed physical ailments which would prevent my going.

Jennie was waving a long yellow cable at me.

I grabbed the damned form and read it. It said get off my philandering arse and to the field, signed Nelson Miles, General, USA.

"When did this arrive," I snarled, waving the damned death warrant.

"Just arrived," said Jennie, looking innocent. I believe that I knew what had prompted it—a cable from Cape Town, from her.

"I ain't got spit in the way of gear," I says. "And I don't plan to wrap one of these here sheets around me and ride Roman."

Jennie went to the closet and hauled out my money belt, heavy with gold, and tossed it on the bed.

"Way things been going round here," I says, "it's a wonder any coin at all is left." I got out of bed then, so Jennie turned away. I put on my pants and boots and jacket. The shirt was long gone.

"I'll escort you!" said young Winston, beaming.

"Lady Churchill," I says to her as I passed, "thank you for your many kindnesses."

"Fuck you," said Jennie, real low.

"That, too." I tipped my hat and wandered up the promenade after Winston.

The Bay was full of garbage and sewage and dead horses and mules being chewed on by the sharks. There wasn't a heavy stench yet, though there would be if the transports sat there much longer.

We walked up the quay the ship's boat took us to and on into Cape Town. I spent the afternoon buying good stout clothing and good stout guns.

"All American," I said, pointing to the twin Colts and the two Winchesters, one a .30-40 and the other a ten-gauge pump gun held eight shells and could be fired off in under thirty seconds if you practiced a little. I got five hundred rounds of double-ought buck and leather scabbards and had the saddlemaker sew the scabbards high and pointed back of the skirts, where they was easy to hand.

"Unsporting," Winston sniffed. He meant the shotgun.

I looked at him, wishing I could drag him by his fat neck to the donga where the butchered bodies lay, and inquire of him which noble Englishman ordered that carnage, and which noble Englishmen obeyed that order. And then I thought that he wouldn't see it, he could stand up to his hips in the rotting dead and speechify about the glorious Empire. He reminded me a lot of Teethadore.

Bungo and the glorious South African Light Horse was already up the rail line, and our train would leave at midnight and get to them at ten the following day. I debated getting drunk and gave up on it because tomorrow I'd have to ride sick and I had done about enough time at that.

We et a good dinner at a hotel and saw our gear on the train and then we walked up and down the platform not speaking till the trainmen called us aboard.

Winston was subdued; ordinarily he was bouncy and babbling enough to drive you to homicide.

I asked him what the matter was and he said that his birthday was coming on in about one minute.

"Well, happy birthday," I says, thrusting out my hand.

He burst into tears. "Oh, the shame, the shame," he said.

"What shame?"

"I shall be twenty-five! Oh shame!" he blubbered.

"Look here," I snarled, "you shouldn't be crying. All the rest of us should."

"Beg pardon?" he said.

"I should have shot you when I had the chance, in Cuba."

"Why would you have done that?"

"Fun," I says. "Now what's so awful about being twenty-five?"

Winston heaved a great sigh and looked at his plump hand and mumbled something so low it couldn't climb over the lisp.

"What?"

"I said that Napoleon had taken Toulon by age twenty-five."

Well, I sat back in my seat, goggle-eyed. This little shit was crying because he hadn't sacked a city yet.

"Don't be so hard on yourself," I said, reaching over to pat his hand, "Alexander of Macedon had conquered Greece, Asia Minor, Babylon, and everything else but India by age twenty-five. So you're definitely second rate, like the rest of us."

Winston busted out bawling. I looked out of the window, wondering what caused mental defectives to flock to me like stink on shit. All my good friends were cast-iron sonsabitches and my women all far too tough and smart for the likes of me. Life was unequal, but this was ridiculous.

Winston had recovered far enough to hide most of his snuffling in a monogrammed silk handkerchief—a sight better than my shoulder.

We pulled off at a siding in the dead of night, and sat there for an hour. A hospital train come past, brightly lit, I could see the wounded men stacked in it.

Winston didn't notice. They were inconvenient to his dreams.

Finally the train pulled on and we come to a tent city about noon—the headquarters of the force relieving Kimberley. It was surrounded with barbed wire and trenches, revetments and gun emplacements and a nice graveyard in the far corner.

We got off and a sharp-looking adjutant took us immediately to Bungo, who was slapping a riding crop into his palm and staring off north. The enlisted men impressed as porters doffed our kit and went off. We picked horses issued by the veterinary surgeon and prepared to ride—Bungo finally had a job to do and were I the Boers, I'd get the hell out of the way.

"I sure hope this turns off better than the *last* time we went hunting their artillery," I said, voice low.

"Fortunes of war," said Byng. "The odds are neither for nor against us."

Sir Julian was dressed nondescript, as were his men. A few troopers had decorated their pith helmets with long gaudy feathers—fine by me, I have always strived in warfare to go unnoticed by all—and I looked at Winston staring at the bobbing plumes, turning beet red for not having thought of it.

I could hear a faint thump of exploding shells—miles north—so this wasn't any gentlemanly brawl of an afternoon, there was heavy artillery and where there was that there would be machine guns and trenches and wire and terror. For you crouch in cover and hear the shells whistle and zip, wondering if the next one's for you.

We rode off up the rail line, crossing a small river and coming over a saddle between two mountains, and then we could see up ahead where they was mixing it up. Bungo picked up the pace and the troopers fanned out beside him, they was South African boys mostly, used to fast riding in country full of ant-bear and warthog holes.

The Boers had the Tommies jammed up some, hard by some big broken rocks. The artillery wasn't doing much, but there was some snipers above pouring down fire and taking an occasional man. The heights would have to be swept. We off-mounted and picketed the horses.

Bungo ordered me to stay behind—wouldn't do to have TR's spy killed in a skirmish with some rebellious subjects. The South African Light Horse struck a path that went toward the tabletop mountain the snipers was on—it wasn't all that big, unlike most here.

I watched for a couple hours—the mountains screened where I was from artillery—and then I saw a line of khakis cheering and the top seemed to have been cleared.

Something about this wasn't right. I untied my horse and led it away east, and found a hiding place under a cut bank for the animal and I crept back and looked down at the picketed horses and piles of stores and the soldiers waiting on the heights being cleared. Then

Boers started boiling out of every shadow and donga and hole to the west, pausing to fire and coming on. There was easy a thousand of them.

The soldiers in camp made a hasty retreat to the winding trail that led up to the mountaintop where the Light Horse was.

About half the troops that had been in the laager were near to the top of the trail, and they began to move out to help the Light Horse. I felt an icy finger go down my spine. The Boers who had been threatening the camp and stores withdrew. All of the troopers were up on the tabletop, which was flat as piss on a plate.

The artillery started, rapid fire. I could imagine what was going on up there, no cover and the shells falling every few seconds. They'd be minced up fine as sand, and then the Boers would stick up their heads, do a little counting, and wipe the whole business out, in not that much time. Them as could get down would get down and fall back on the camp, I figured. I rode like hell south, along the trail I had just come up.

It was an even shorter distance than I had thought, and I raised hell till I was brought to Pauncefote, General Commanding, and he screwed his monocle in another couple of cranks and barked a few orders and his subordinates hopped to and I never seen an Army get down to business that fast, at least a British one.

Troopers loaded themselves down with spare ammunition and took off at a gallop, sorting themselves out on the fly, and the infantry, battle ready, set out at a fast clip not long after. They was going to save brother soldiers and that fires up troops like nothing else.

Even I rode back.

Now, I know I'm not brave, no hero, not even a good fourth at bridge, but I sort of thought that I should fetch Winston out as unscathed as possible, on account of his mother, who would chase me to the ends of the earth if her boy was killed while I was on the same continent. You know how mothers are, they are fond of their offspring. (The more monstrous the better.)

Time I got back to the battleground the wounded was being carried down by stretcher-bearers in turbans—Indians, from India, calmly hauling the maimed off the mountaintop and not even flinching at the fire when it was close. Once in a while the bearers would stop and hide behind boulders if the barrage was bad, then they'd get up and go on.

"All volunteers," said Bungo, at my elbow. "Pacifists. Won't lift a finger to harm another man, but they do this so bravely."

That was a new one on me. I looked at them little wogs hauling the stretchers and wondered why they warn't extinct.

A flying column of troopers had gone on some time ago and we could sure on tell when they got to the big guns, because the shells stopped coming in, cut off sudden.

I decided I'd better go on up and look about for Winston, and no sooner had I got to the foot of the trail than I saw him on one end of a stretcher, talking a blue streak at the little Indian on the other, who was smiling and shaking his head and laughing at times.

I walked along with them to the stack the doctor was working on. They rolled their bloody hero off on the grass and began to walk back toward the bloody mountain.

"Indjah is no more a country than the Equatorhh," said Winston.

I gathered they was deciding the fate of millions to pass the time.

"Ach!" said Winston. He hopped around a bit holding on to his boot, and then he fell on his arse struggling with it. He pulled it off and I saw one of them big velvet ants—a wasp actually—run off through the grass stems.

Winston was cursing and pulling off his sock. He looked at a red spot swelling rapidly on his instep.

"I'll make a trip with you," I says to Winston's chum. He nodded and laughed, delighted-like. He held out his hand.

"Mohandas K. Gandhi," he said.

"Luther Kelly," I said, and shook it. It was dry and very small, like a child's.

"Are there many more wounded?" I asked.

"I don't think so," said Gandhi. "I think we merely need to gather the dead. So you are an American?"

"Yes," I said.

"Tell me about America."

Well, that threw me, but I took a stab at it anyway.

11

By the time the dead was rolled into a common grave on the top of the mountain it was coming on light again. I'd worked all through the night, talking with this little Indian lawyer. He reminded me of Crazy Horse. There was something not quite human about him.

He'd graduated, if that's what you call it, from the Inns of Court and could therefore practice law anywhere in the Empire—that is, anywhere that wasn't put off by his skin.

We made one last round, checking the crevices and such for dead men, but we found none, and the chaplain read a short service and the grave was filled in, and then the soldiers went to piling stones on it to keep the jackals and hyenas out. The carrion birds circled overhead until the rocks went on and they lofted away. They do well in wartime. There would be horse carcases to eat as soon as we left.

I got to talk to Mohandas a lot as we got ready to pull out and head on up the railroad line to the next place the Boers would fight a spoiling action. I remembered Marieke's saying the Boers was too fast for the British and the British too strong for the Boers, which was how it had been with the Injuns I'd scouted on—until we cut off their food by killing the buffalo. All these small out-of-the-way places to fight wars like that, there should be decades of work for the soldiers.

I shook hands with Winston, who thought I was "a coward and

poltroon" for leaving, and I told the little fool I was sent to observe and I had done observed and I could tell him the rest of the story, if he'd like.

He smiled then, a canny smile, and said he was here for a way to Parliament. He wanted honors, and battle scars.

I wished him both.

The train south held wounded and them as was dead and had commissions and so couldn't be expected to be dead with the common soldiers in the mass grave.

Mohandas looked me up—he was going back down, and on these special trains the usual color sortings didn't seem to apply, and we talked all the slow ride down to Cape Town. He was sure he had the key for all men to live in peace, and I told him having the key was one thing, he needed an Army so the key would be used. I think he thought more of folks than I do. I suspected he'd go back to India and preach till the British got tired of his yammering, and then they'd hang him quiet-like and that would be that. Not my problem, thank God.

He also felt that most of life's problems stayed away from them as owned goats. This conversation was getting a little rich for my thick wits—no more so than Theodore's babblings about Manifest Destiny and America standing forth in the world (meaning we can knock the teeth out of anybody) and Taking Our Rightful Place in the Sun (where we likely will get burned). I never had trusted these folks with prescriptions for all the ills of man. Me, I was trying to find a decent seegar and a warm, willing woman.

Finally Mohandas went too far and allowed as how I was a better man than I let on. This gave me a chance to beller some about how I was not, I was infinitely worse than anything he could imagine and two Guardsmen come up and plucked Mohandas out of the seat and tossed him out the window into the weeds that grew so thick by the train line.

"Sorry the little wog was exercising you so, sorr," said one, snapping me a salute. I was goggle-mouthed for a moment, and then I lost my temper.

"Stop the train," I said, flaring up like a match.

The guards didn't know what to do. I did. I went to the coupling and shot out the air lines. The train commenced slowing down then.

I jumped off and ran back up the right of way, hollering "Mohandas" at the top of my lungs.

I cussed and hollered for a while and the longer I did the worrieder I got—the fall could have broken his neck.

Finally I heard him, saying in a normal tone of voice that he was all right and not to worry. He come up through the weeds, limping a little and smiling like he always did. He put his hands together and bowed to me.

"Are you sure you are . . . . . . the hell you are. What happened to your goddamned ankle?"

He went on insisting it was all right. I finally threw the little man over my shoulder and walked back toward the train. I could see the Provost Marshal and some guards poking in the grass up ahead.

"Who the hell else did you throw out?" I snarled. I was about ready to shoot several of them, social gaffe or not.

"Kelly," Mohandas said weakly, "please. No violence. If you commit violence I'll shoot myself."

I have been a gunrunner, which is fairly silly, I got froze into a buffalo hide once and had them big jocker wolves almost chew my ass off, I been an interpreter for the Sioux against the Americans, I have often cut a ridiculous figure or been somewheres without a real good excuse for it, but standing there by the railroad line in South Africa with a demented wog over my shoulder and me about to go to war on a hundred Brits was maybe the low one. (I ain't dead yet. We'll see.)

"Shoot yourself with what?" I says. He waved one of my Colts at me. I set him down and snatched my pistol back.

"That would be theft," I snarls. "Them bullets is expensive."

"WOOOINTHABLUIDYHELL IS GOINOINNN HERRRR?" said the very large Scot at the head to the troops.

"Yer arseholes threw my friend out the window," I says, "and you're in luck he ain't hurt."

Not much consideration was given to us, for we was roughly handled and clapped in irons for the rest of the journey. Portions of the irons was attached to the same seatback, so me and Mohandas got to chat as the train went along.

"You are a turbulent man, Kelly," he said. "I fear you have killed many others."

"Not enough yet," I says. "I'll let you know when I'm happy with the score."

Mohandas sighed. He sighed sort of exasperated-like.

I was expecting further lectures but when I looked he had his eyes closed and seemed to be praying.

"Please don't do that on my account," I says. "I don't want the Heavenly Attention. I plan to keep on bein' a small and movin' target."

"Bugger off, Kelly," he said, smiling, and on he went. Odd little bird-man, risking his neck for Englishmen who had their boots on his neck at all other times.

We pulled into the military depot at Cape Town and Mohandas and me was hauled off the train and then they took off our irons—had to account for them to the quartermaster, I suppose—and then we was marched off to the stockade and put in a fenced pen with the drunks and other petty offenders.

We sat there all night, and in the morning a couple lawyer-looking types follered by two—my gut jumped—officers of the American Navy come stalking up behind a guard, who inserted a key in the gate and beckoned to us.

"Kelly and Gandhi arf' out!" he said. The naval officers was taking an unseemly interest in me, I hate being stared at.

"Captain Forrest," said one, looking at me like he'd rather not. "What in Christ's name did you shoot up the train for? Fun?"

"Fun," I said. "Much fun."

The lawyers was talking a mile a minute at Mohandas, who was waving his hands and jabbering, too.

"You're ordered to the Philippines," said Captain Forrest. "And we have a destroyer waiting to take you there."

"I ain't going," I said. "I can already tell you what's there. My being there won't change it."

"Kelly," said Mohandas, "God go with you!"

"Mohandas," I said, "I'd druther God went and I didn't have to."

I thought to ask if he was going to be all right and he said I shouldn't worry, which wasn't an answer and I knew I wasn't going to get much better out of him. Why this little pain-in-the-ass wog with his continual praying and stubborn refusal to quit doing whatever it was that he thought fair and right should bother me I purely did not know.

Some guards—British Regulars—had commenced gathering around us and it made me nervous because I couldn't see a reason for it. A leftenant came up to Mohandas and began reading off from a list of charges, treason heading it.

The Brits hang folks for treason.

"I'll go if we take him," I said. "I ain't leaving him to be strung up by these lime-sucking sonsabitches."

Well, we had a pretty good shouting match there for a while, till it dawned on the Brits that I was offering to deport Mohandas free of charge, thereby saving the overburdened British taxpayer the trouble and expense.

Or shock if Mohandas was found dead of hanging in his cell.

So Her Majesty Queen Victoria did deliver her subject Mohandas Gandhi to Captain Forrest to take wherever he liked, and it was hoped burial at sea would be necessary. If not, sigh, then India would accept him.

"We will have to coal in Goa anyway," said Captain Forrest. He was beginning to see the humor in this, his mouth was twitching as he wrote out a receipt.

So we went at a slow pace down toward the harbor. A bit over half of the way there we came to the Indian quarter, streets of shops and tiny houses, where the women wore the sari and the curry scent tickled your nostrils.

"Kelly, my friend," said Gandhi," I must . . . . . . say goodbye!" And he dashed into a narrow street packed with people. He disappeared in the time it takes for one breath.

Forrest let off a string of ripe cussings, and then he shrugged his shoulders. The three of us could hardly surround the quarter and search house to house. Less said about it the better.

The destroyer *Kiefer* was loaded and coaled and ready to sail—it was one of the fast new four-stack ships. I was coming up in the world if this ship was here just for me.

We was piped aboard and I was shown to a roomy cabin big enough for the bed and me—all the rest of the room was taken up with cases and cases of canned goods. In half an hour we'd slipped the cables and were on our way.

Captain Forrest invited me up to the bridge. Right as I got there the ship wound up to cruising speed—I was impressed, never having gone so fast on the water before.

In a few hours we hit the hard ocean and set a course east, and I felt the familiar pangs of seasickness coming on. The good Captain Forrest sent me back to my cabin, and I cleared the canned goods off the bed and commenced feeling very sorry for myself. This was easy to do because every time we were hit with a following sea a couple cartons of pineapple would drop on me. I was too weak to cuss much.

I laid there on that damned bunk for three days, and then one morning I got madder than hell and the sudden burst of rage settled my stomach. I stomped out on the deck and put foot to a flying fish—oily devils, they are—and I slid half the length of the ship, bowling over a couple officers, and fetched up against a railing that bent considerably from my hitting it.

Captain Forrest come and looked down upon me crumpled into his ship's works and shook his head some.

"What?" I snarled.

"Just thanking God Almighty you didn't run away to sea," he said, offering me a hand.

I snarled something about being happy to go ashore the next shore we passed—I warn't particular at all.

After that we got on fine, and though it's against regulations for anyone but the ship's surgeon to have liquor, that worthy had enough to keep the whole ship's company medicinally spackled for the whole journey.

Forrest never touched a drop, but he was good company to me and we talked over the Boer War and when I mentioned the concentration camps for the women and children, and how they was dying of camp diseases, he looked sad for a moment and then he said war had gone from glorious to squalid in a generation, and he wondered if it was worth waging under those terms.

"That's the way nations settle those questions," I said. "I don't think it'll wither away because it's bloodier. I wonder if it can ever get bloody enough to not pay out."

And I told him of the slaughtered prisoners rotting in the donga.

The weather grew stormy so we didn't go to Goa to coal but on round to Ceylon. We were two days in Trincomalee, and I was happy to wander around the town, risking my health on the food from the bazaar stalls and knowing for certain that I would have another vile bout with seasickness as soon as the *Kiefer* hit the open ocean.

Ceylon is a grand place for gems—about half of the island is digging for rubies, sapphires, moonstones, and the like, and the rough gems were dirt cheap. I bought quite a few for a couple hundred in Yankee gold. They were wrapped in a piece of chintz and tucked in a compartment of my money belt.

I had a couple wicker-wrapped carboys of the local rum delivered to the *Kiefer.* All I had for company in the cabin was the rum and a couple cases of chutney.

Coaled up and running the *Kiefer* made better than twenty knots, and before long we were winding our way through the green islands that hang down south from Asia all the way to Australia. Them islands is pretty to look on, and deadly to walk upon. Snakes, bloodsuckers, leeches, and tropical fevers can kill you in a couple of days. The natives is cannibals often as not.

As soon as we passed through the Straits of Sunda we bore north, toward the Philippines, and I got testier by the hour.

The Filipinos, like the Cubans, had looked to us for aid, and after the Spaniards was thrown out we stayed; they had not fought their bloody war to change one set of conquerors for another.

Cuba would have been hell to administer, and there was enough common sense in Congress to avoid annexing that one, but the Philippines was a thousand times worse and far away and so the damned fools thought it was practical.

I never have had much use for my government or any other, because they are forever buying a bad horse and commanding me to break it.

Kelly, I says to myself, here you go to another tribal war, where the one side's too weak and the other's too slow.

At night the wake glowed green from some sea creatures churned up by our passing. I drank rum and longed for a seegar.

12

Manila Bay is one of the world's best and largest harbors. There's a tadpole-shaped island in the mouth of the Bay called Corregidor and beyond the water the deep bright green of the jungle crawls up the mountains. All the navies of the world could anchor in the Bay and ride out a typhoon with plenty of room to swing on their cables.

A fair part of the Pacific fleet was anchored, and all their guns was trained and pointed north—to give fire whenever the enemy got within their reach. If the Navy has to protect the Army for more time than it takes the soldiers to storm ashore it ain't a good sign. It means the two sides are fighting different wars, and there won't be conclusions.

My traveling gear was mighty light, and I stepped up on the quay wearing it, only to find some pip of a second lieutenant waiting for me. He saluted me, distaste showing in his every gesture. I returned it real sloppy and then asked what witless peckerwood of a general had this unhealthful command.

"Major General MacArthur," said the looey, "who is expecting you."

"I doubt he's expecting what he's getting," I said. "But you lead on anyway."

"Sir," the youngster said, "he believes that he knows you. Did you interpret for the Sioux chieftains at a peace conference?"

"I made sure all the lies was translated good," I said, "but I don't recall a MacArthur."

"Very good, sir," said the looey, "but I'd suggest you act like you know him. He's . . ."

"Thin-skinned and gives hell to subordinates," I said. "I know the kind. I'll take care of it."

We walked down the quay and got into a horsecab and headed into the city to Malacañang Palace—it was a fair drive, took an hour of the horse's slow feet to bring us under the porte cochere. The palace itself was ugly and too big, which delights the Spanish eye for some reason, like the German.

General MacArthur warn't out front to greet me. I was led down long noisy halls and into an office. The doors was easy fourteen feet high, and to heighten the suspense I believe he had the servants pack sand in the hinges. The damn things sounded like the last page of an Edgar Allan Poe novel.

I threw a miserable excuse for a salute to him and flopped down in a handy chair. The legs was so long my boots barely got a hold on the floor. Everything in this stupid room was designed to belittle MacArthur's guests or subordinates. His desk was large enough to pasture a mule on and there wasn't a damn thing on it but an inkstand and a blotter. MacArthur sat in a huge wingbacked swivel chair, and he gave me a start, for he looked uncannily like Teethadore.

MacArthur stood and come round the desk holding out his hand, his dress sword beating time on his kneecaps. I smiled, too.

"Kelly!" he said. "Delighted. Been a long time since the Sioux delegation of sixty-nine, eh, what? We've a few years on us, eh?"

I allowed modestly that we did have a few years on us.

He offered me a drink which I refused on account of the heat, and then a seegar which I did have.

"I'm being mediatized, Kelly," said MacArthur.

He then launched into an extended aria full of long words I had never heard even rumors about, and finishing with a flash of anger at McKinley's administration, which had failed to supply him with enough troops to subdue the *insurrectos*. Seventy-five thousand was a police force, not an army. The damned nerve of it all. Stick him the hell and gone out here without the means to achieve the desired ends.

I took all this to mean that he was fighting a guerrilla war and I supposed if you put every man in America aged eighteen to sixty in the Army and brought 'em here things would be about the same only more so.

MacArthur went on at length about the vile plotters who were sabotaging his every attempt to wrest peace from the jaws of defeat.

I drew in the seegar smoke and wondered if perhaps he'd get to the point sometime before dawn. I was getting light-headed of the rhetoric. I never heard such loads of goddamned bombast in all my life, and ordinarily I'd have suggested he go boil his head, evil critters was sprinting through his brain. I still wasn't sure what Teethadore and Miles was so all-fired enthused about my seeing. The one good look I had at the jungle, I wondered why *anyone* would want these humid and festering eyesores of islands. I'd bet there was funguses out there so big they could walk and eat hay off the top of the stack.

MacArthur finished with ruffles and flourishes and boo-kays of words cobbled together and I looked at this pompous ass and wondered how quickly I could escape his clutches.

"Drinks are served on the terrace," said a soft voice, another lieutenant risen to butlerhood.

MacArthur led me there. I was still wearing high boots and twill pants, and though my shirt was cotton I was fair roasting. It was early evening; I could feel a sea breeze and took pains to stand in it. Someone gave me an enormous planter's punch with lots of ice in it. I swallowed it eagerly, and the considerable rum made my ears ring.

I was a mite uncomfortable, but I felt real pity for the ladies, who was lashed into whalebone corsets, and though their clothes was all pure cotton there was a lot of layers of it. They dabbed continually at the sweat streaming down their foreheads.

The folks there was grouped into two bunches and not many went from one to the other. Curious, I took myself down the long marble terrace and wiggled in far enough to see the main attraction; it was William Howard Taft, all three hundred and fifty pounds of him. I knew him well, he was one of the kindest men ever born but terribly shy, had a fine legal mind, too. With all that fat he was carrying the tropics could kill him. He was dressed in soggy linen and two shrewd blue eyes.

"Luther!" he said happily, motioning me to come on over. "So good to see you! Nelson Miles cabled that we might expect you! Have a drink! Have a chair! Tell me of your life!"

We talked and such, remembering, for a while, and then Bill Taft—he was a man utterly without vanity and loved telling jokes on himself—related an exchange of cables between him and Secretary of State Elihu Root:

" 'It's rumored you are not feeling well,' " Root cabled.

" 'Feeling fine and went horseback riding today,' " Taft cabled.

A pause of a day, and in the cable traffic the next morning:

" 'Excellent news. How is the horse feeling?' "

Taft roared with laughter, shaking his big belly and doing a merry jig—like so many huge men, he was some light on his feet.

"Who do you report to?" he said, suddenly serious.

"Teddy."

"Good." He nodded. "I'm afraid not much of what goes on here escapes the ears of our overornamented friend down to the other end of the terrace."

I shrugged. Petty politics did not concern me and anytime anyone wanted to throw me off the islands I was more'n happy to go.

MacArthur was surrounded by shoals of underlings and their admirers—I was struck that those around Taft wanted to be there and were having a good time, and those around MacArthur were grim and silent as so many stones. Since I was to go out in the jungle and take a look at what was actually going on there, I supposed I'd be sociable enough so they wouldn't bushwhack me first chance they got. Things had got very rough here, I could see the drawn looks of the junior officers who'd been out in the slop and were doomed to going back in.

"You seem to know Commissioner Taft," MacArthur said, the words hacked out of block ice. "Whatever is he so amused with now?"

"An old private joke of ours," I said, tweaking the popinjay.

I imagined the cable to the War Office: HE WON'T TELL ME THE PUNCH LINE! I'm used to epic displays of childishness in the mighty, but this was a bit rare even for me.

"Captain Tennant will escort you to the lines," said MacArthur.

"I'll find my own way," I says, thinking I'd better get this settled right now.

"What?!" MacArthur shrilled. "Why you insubordinate bastard, you'll go where I send you and with whom!"

"General," I says, "let's go cable the War Office. I wouldn't like to see you cashiered at your age."

MacArthur was looking like a walrus with apoplexy.

So we sent a cable off and in half an hour one came back, to MacArthur, who went from mauve to deepest purple.

"I was a bit hasty," said MacArthur. "I ah um eh off ummm . . ."

I just nodded and walked away. He was one of them fellers who reads about himself in the newspapers and acts accordingly.

"We all know which chair to sit in?" I says.

He nodded, looking sick.

I went back out to Taft. There was a number of lovely women around Billy—he liked the good things of life in large and frequent portions. One or two of the lovelies was giving me the eye, and I thought Manila might not be unbearable after all.

We was called in to dinner, there was places set along a refectory table a good seventy-five feet long, and the bunches of flowers each five feet gave off cloying aromas—I swear I could've spooned up limburger cheese and not have smelled it. When we was all seated the two halves of the tables turned away from one another, like kids over a jigsaw puzzle that wasn't coming out right, and from then on there was a bellering match so it could be figured who had the best din.

Billy had thoughtfully seated me between two lovelies and across from two more, but in this case he'd done me no favors, as they was all trying to catch my eye and I only got so many. I decided to stick to this side of the table, and when I asked the one to my left what she thought of the evening she said "crap" very soft and ladylike and for some reason it struck me as so funny I roared till I damn near fell backwards out of the chair. I said it was my thoughts exactly.

The one on my right had decided the next feller up the line was more interesting than me, and all I could see of her was a tulle-swathed back and one earring, emeralds and diamonds.

"My name is Lucretia," the lady said. "Mrs. Donald Sams, for the record."

"And Mr. Sams?" says I, not having time for to pussyfoot.

"At his mistress's house, no doubt," said Lucretia. "You know how men are."

Matter of fact, I did. This was some funny lady, smarter than whips, too, likely.

"Are you Yellowstone Kelly?" sez Lucretia.

"Only when I'm alone," I said, feeling anger hot in my face. "I should have shot that little bastard Ned Buntline. I didn't. I suffer some for it. He nicknamed me 'Yellowstone,' frinstance."

"I read only one of Mr. Buntline's books about you and it did not seem to me possible that it could be true. That, for instance, you killed fifty-six Indians in one day, one battle."

"While reading Keats to my horse," I says, looking sheepish. I always feel such a fool when anyone brings up Buntline, goddamn the little shit.

"Does your fair Indian princess wait for you?" said Lucretia.

For a moment I thought of Eats-Men-Whole, dead near forty years, but it wouldn't have been fair to get angry over it.

"No, ma'am," I said, "nothing like that."

We talked through the supper, which was excellent, a curry of chicken and cashews and fish broiled with green peppercorns and fresh lemon. That was this end of the table; I supposed they were eating mulligan stew in the heat down there.

There were not, mercifully, any speeches after supper. The ladies filed out to the conservatory and the men went to one of two parlor/salons where there was brandy and seegars.

Bill come up to me, his merry eyes twinkling, and we strolled outside where it was a bit cooler.

"I'm ashamed of my country," he said. "For the first time we grab land and the people on them when it isn't necessary. We defeat the Spanish and the Filipinos love us as liberators. Then we announce that we are here to stay and extend the pleasures of democracy to our little brown brothers. Stuff and nonsense. We want the Philippines for the markets of China and to block Japan from taking them."

"Japan?" I said, for I knew virtually nothing of Japan.

"Make no mistake," said Taft, "Japan is soon to be a power. You know that Teddy told me of the first Japanese student at Harvard. The young man had won over ten thousand others, to come to Harvard. He studied himself to death. He wouldn't eat or sleep. He studied till he died."

"Purely crazy," I says.

"The whole nation is crazy like that," said Taft. "They have the fifth largest fleet in the world, and probably the strongest after America and Great Britain. For a people who didn't know spit about what was going on in the rest of the world, they have come a long damned way since Perry opened the gates in fifty-six."

By the map the Japanese were closer than anyone to the islands. I supposed I'd best look out for defensible positions, too. A map of the islands floated up in my mind, and I thought the only way to defend them at all would be the Navy. Once on land, an invader would be too dug in to dislodge.

"And this war is unspeakable," said Taft, dropping a long ash from his seegar into a potted palm. "Our troops are sent on impossible missions, they watch their comrades die every day, and soon they are killing every Filipino within reach. It is a moral quagmire."

He went on about how disgusted he was and what this was doing to the morale of the Army, and further what it was doing to America. We were supposed to be the great hope of nations, what with our democracy and free public education.

"I fear this place is going to teach us no end of a lesson," he said, and then caught himself and apologized for his rude dwelling on the unpleasantries of the islands.

"Do you speak to any highly placed Filipinos who might have truck with the rebels?" I says.

"All of them do, I'm sure," said Taft.

We were called to join the ladies. I had seen the biggest damned moth I ever have diving around one of the torches on the lawn, I swear it was a full foot in wingspan, and there were giant bats flapping by, about the size of beagles. Strange *thrwarks* and *grooooiips* and such sounded from a thousand throats hid in the shrubbery. And this was *tame.* I wondered what it was like out in the jungle. I suspected. I wondered for a moment if I couldn't slither out of this, and then I thought, no, Miles and TR would just find a worse place to send me to.

After some idle chitchat with a couple other guests I come up on Lucretia who smiled and made room for me to stand, and she went on with her anecdote and bowed at the titters of applause from a handsome gray-haired couple.

They was the Martins, he banked and she painted the viscid jungle blooms. We chatted for a moment and then Lucretia and I went out for some air and an exchange of vital informations. She would call for her coach and go home. I would walk a mile or so in an hour, and the coach would be waiting for me on a side street.

Mrs. Sams went, and I wiggled through the throng to MacArthur and thanked him profusely for having invited me, twisting the screw since I had set up at Taft's end of the table.

"A bit of advice," I says to MacArthur. "I once was in a poker game with Bill there, and he won twenty-seven straight hands. He warn't playing against nursemaids or fools."

The general blinked and looked like something wet had just crawled up his leg.

William Howard Taft was beaming like a happy moon over the guests at his end of the room. I shook his hand and he gripped mine sudden hard.

"Not to pry, old friend," he says, "but am I right in thinking you have a bunk for tonight which I don't have to provide you with?"

"Yup," I says, "why do you ask?"

"I had a wager that you would arrive ragged and lonely and by evening you would be in one or another bed, invited, shall we say?"

"Who was this here wager with?" I says.

"Our Vice President, Theodore Roosevelt," says Taft.

We went to the cable room, and Taft sent a terse I WIN to Washington. I waited fifteen minutes and sent another cable: PAY UP. DELICIOUS HERE. MAY NOT RETURN.

The horse was snuffling and jingling the tack right where Lucretia said it would be. I got in and the driver chirred to the horse and off I went.

13

Lucretia's husband must have been clean out of his tiny mind, all I can say about it. I began thinkin' that Manila wasn't so bad after all. And that it didn't matter what I wrote in my report, no one would pay it much mind anyway.

I sat up on the edge of the bed, heading for the water closet, and felt her finger tracing the scars on my back.

"I felt them last night," she said. "You've been badly hurt many times."

"I lived," I said.

When I got back she was laying there all naked, the sheets tousled around her. She looked very beautiful and I said so.

She nodded, thanking me, and when I lay down she turned me over on my stomach and started tracing the scars again.

"Where did you get this one?" she said. I said it was so long I couldn't remember which one was which, some was of fighting Indians, some fighting Zulus and Shanganes, some fighting A-rabs, some fighting Mormons, some fighting outlaws, and a couple from being thrown through windows. Nothing particularly special about the collection, I could name fellers had lots more, even had lost hands, feet, and what-have-yous.

"You can't convince me you're a coward, Luther," she said. "You are too much of a piece."

Now what in the hell she meant by that I'll never know, even if I'm told. I've run faster farther from more mean people than any other man on the face of the earth. All I got in my front is one bullet wound and a few scratches. I sang that song full-throated for a while and Lucretia kept silent until I had run down.

"Bullshit," she said.

I was unused to Victorian ladies had mouths on them like that. Ah, the hell with it, I thought.

"Lucretia," I said, "I'll tell you something and deny I did if you repeat it. I enjoy it. I like it out there near off the edge. Chance will get me one day, not foolhardiness."

"You and I are going to my summer house, up in the mountains where it's cool," she purred. "And from there I can put you close to any of the Filipino *guerrilleros* you want to talk to. I have just found you. Don't think of going away. I'll shoot you."

I was full of the perplex. Usually they offer to shoot *themselves* for careless love. This is unsporting, says I, this one is dangerous. When I meet a woman who is a good deal smarter than I am—there are plenty, let me tell you—I strive to get to the window and then I jump. No good for this one, she'd be waiting down below with a pitchfork.

She come up to me, where I was by the window, and folded her long body into mine and found my lips with hers. For someone as cool gold and frozen sapphire as she was, her body was uncommon hot, and it made mine the same.

Afterward we lay in each other's arms while the day's heat rose upward. The birdsongs fell silent and the air got dead still and every little sound was magnified—the creaks of the old timbers in the house, the distant sound of a servant washing—all stuck out, not noisier, but alone. You could separate them sounds easy.

We dressed and after a breakfast of melon and coffee I made to go when Lucretia stopped me.

"For your luggage?" she said, teasing.

I had what I was wearing and that was it. She rang for a servant and sent him to fetch a Chinese tailor and bootmaker, and after a couple of for-show shrugs I gave in. It was easier than having it rammed down my throat.

Also I sent a short note to Taft telling him I was in the way of making contact with the rebels and I added a postscript suggesting he should learn how to ride two horses at once.

I was measured in about two minutes flat by the Chink tailor, who went off saying the things would be ready early the next morning, and then the messenger boy who'd taken the note to Taft showed up again with a note from Taft to me.

"Are raffling off chance to tug on your feet at your hanging. Do come. Black tie. WHT"

"He is a nice man," said Lucretia, "unlike that pompous horror of a general."

"You have contacts and ways of reaching the rebels?" I asked, sorry the words were flown instantly.

"I could hang you from a beam end over the garden, and someone would be round to see about it," she said. "The *insurrectos* are everywhere. They want their country to themselves. A not uncommon urge among peoples. Not to be condescended to. Not be taxed to support those who they don't want there anyway. Not to have murder a national sport. Those things."

The best thing to say at times like this is nothing. I doubted that she'd buy my holding that we was here because if we weren't it would be the Japanese or the Germans. (Diplomacy is easy, all you have to do is follow the money.) Nations don't have moral principles, they can't afford 'em.

Anyways, I would a sight rather take off from her mountain house than from here, since I figured only about half of Manila was full-time spying on whatever went on for someone or other. I didn't feel exactly right going up to Lucretia's house feeling as I did, and then I thought the hell with it, don't piss against the wind.

The servants was around but you never saw them. A cart with meals and whatever arrived shortly after the order was placed and we were sort of like honeymooners, lost in each other's flesh and asking silly questions with sillier answers just to hear the other's voice.

I was just getting up from one of our protracted bouts of screwing when I turned and saw a curtain bulge where it ought not to. My Colts were on the floor by the bed, and no sooner did I grab one than there was a fearful great beller behind me and a Malay with a sharp cane knife come at me. He was yelling and charging and I squeezed off a shot took him square in the chest—I crossnotch all my bullets, makes 'em dum-dums—and I whirled and shot another feller holding a sword. They was both dead 'fore they hit the marble floor and I quick picked up the cane knife and poked the other curtains to see if they had chums, but nothing there.

Lucretia didn't scream or nothing, just gathered the bedclothes around her and stayed out of the way. I admired that.

There was distant cries and hollers and in a few moments a couple military policemen came busting in and they looked at the bodies and at me and wanted to know what in the hell happened. I told them what I knew and ordered them out of the room, for Lucretia was still in the bed and had had enough rudeness for the moment.

Some Filipinos in khaki come in, rolled the bodies up onto stretchers, and off they went quick-time; I supposed they was practiced at getting them in the ground in a hurry on account of the climate.

I waited while Lucretia dressed—I was not to let her out of my sight after this—and I talked hard to the two American soldiers for a bit but they didn't know any more than I did. They was filling up Bilibid Prison with belligerent folks but it didn't seem to slow it down any.

There was bloodstains all over the walls and floors and a couple of chairs would have to be put back together—them dum-dums pick a body up and carry it quite a ways, no matter how hard they are charging.

"They slipped in while we were in the bath," said Lucretia. I didn't know, it would be hard to think of them standing behind those suffocating drapes all night listening to us fuck.

Well, they weren't after Lucretia, she'd been here living the same for a long time, it had to be me. But who would know I was here and want me dead on behalf of the *insurrectos?* I had nothing they wanted, my report was already wrote—get out and do it now—and I began to get hellishly angry at whoever wanted me dead without even a proper introduction.

The servants was all being lined up in the main hall and the two American military police were trying to shout at them through an interpreter. I had enough Spanish to get on with, and I listened and then I walked up and down the row and when I got to the end of it there was something bothering me and it took a moment to grab on to it.

The servants' feet, they was all good honest peasant feet that lived in sandals but there was one pair of feet belonged to a slender feller—I can't tell age on these people—about halfway down the row. I grabbed the nearest military policeman and he whispered to his chum and they walked back down the row casual-like and when they was to him they grabbed and he was up in the air with a giant American on each arm 'fore he knew what the hell happened.

"Who's this one?" I said to Lucretia. "When did you hire him?"

She shook her head. She'd never seen him before.

I trussed him up good and tight with sash cord and hauled him up under one arm like a haybale and went to the bath. There was still bathwater left in the tub, so I dipped him in it and held on while he struggled and when he went limp I lifted him out and asked a few questions but he warn't ready with the answers I wanted so I ducked him again.

Finally he allows as how he'd like to tell me anything I cared to know. I asked him questions I purely cared to know. Well, it was the Germans, they was afraid I might get too knowledgeable on the matter of the Philippines since I had been giving them fits elsewhere, like South Africa.

And how much did it cost to buy an assassin?

Ten dollars U.S.

I thought the chances of this skinny kid causing further trouble was slim, so I cut him free and told the soldiers that the man knew nothing.

If the Germans wanted me dead they could have had that a hundred times in Africa and no one the wiser. It made me wonder.

"What's this summerhouse of yours look like?" I said. Lucretia drew a crude layout of the place, up on a ridge of a mountain to capture any breezes, and not so awfully big as this place. I figured it a fair go for three men to hold 'gainst all comers didn't have cannons in their dittybags. Only problem was where did the other two come from.

I explained to Lucretia how I planned to keep us safe. She nodded and went to packing, saying that my clothes could be sent on when the tailor reappeared.

We spent that day packing and every hour on the hour a cart would pull up and another load would go on up to the mountains near

Baguio. It was getting on to late afternoon and we would have to leave pretty damn soon. I still hadn't come up with how to get the other two fellers we'd need to sleep sound.

Then a lieutenant come up on a lathered horse and says to me please come there is an awful problem which needs me. I says that's terrible, but I just had a couple fellers try to murder me and I wasn't going and leaving the lady unprotected.

The kid calmed down some as we walked down to wherever his problem only I could solve was, with Lucretia riding sidesaddle on his horse.

What this problem was was there was some drunks barricaded in a saloon and they threatened to shoot anyone who come in. To let everybody know they could, they kept throwing bottles out the door and shooting them before they hit the cobbles.

A local priest had gone in to pray with them and come out so staggering drunk he didn't walk, he poured from place to place.

"Why at a time like this are you on a fool's errand to a couple drunken soldiers," Lucretia bitched. "Isn't that a matter for the military police?"

"They keep demanding Luther Kelly by name," said the military police lieutenant.

"By name?" I says.

"Yessir," said the boy. "They said they saw your name in the newspaper. They claim to be old comrades-in-arms. If we can get them to disarm . . . . . . they were apparently excellent muleskinners once, before they . . ."

"Got bored and decided to stir up the town a little," I says, "As cowboys is wont to do, they being easy to bore."

"I understand that," said the looey.

"I think that I got a good guess about these here drunks," I says. "Was they by any chance reciting poetry?"

"Uh ah uh yes," said the shavetail.

"Anything like 'he was dirty and lousy and full of fleas and his terrible tool hung to his knees'?"

"Yes, sir, exactly," said the lieutenant.

"Lucy," I says to Lucretia, "I do believe our problems is solved."

There was a couple half-moons of people on the outer quarters of the front of a cantina which had all manner of chairs and tables piled up as barricades and a lot of busted glass out front. I heard feminine squeals and more verses of the Bastard King of England.

I let out my best wolf-whoop and everything went quiet. I allowed as how I was born on the Powder River and I slept in a rattlesnake den at night 'cause it made me feel warm and cuddly. My arm was longer than a Kansas well-rope and my fist hard as a banker's heart. I saddle-broke grizzly bears and et my hay from the top of the stack. Picked my teeth with spud bar and milked the moon for my whiskey . . . and I went on a lot longer than that, for I was getting cheers from the inside.

I walked over to about a battalion of military police.

"I'll be responsible for these men. Go away. If they see one of you when they come out they'll shoot ya. I take all responsibility. Git. And it's Major Kelly to you."

They cleared off in a hurry, and I walked back by Lucretia and she reached down and grabbed my shoulder.

"Drunks?" she said. "We don't need drunks."

"We need these drunks."

"You know these people?"

"I hope so," I said. "If I'm wrong piss on my grave once a year in memory of our love."

I walked slow back toward the cantina and kept my hands out where they could be seen. All the hoo-rah inside cut down, and I stepped into the cool dark and blinked for a moment.

"Kelly," says Butch, "what the hell are you doin' here."

"Yah," said Sundance, "whassa doin' here?"

"I need you bastards for some help. I got my lady out there and someone's trying to kill us."

"Why the nerve of the sonsabitches," says Butch. "They can't do that, can they, Sundance?"

"Nope," says Sundance. They had both gone cold sober like that. I led them back out to Lucretia, and they doffed their hats.

"This here's Smith and that's Jones," I says to her.

"And I am the Queen of the May," says Lucretia.

"Lo, May," they chorused.

"You know these people," said Lucretia, pointing.

"Well," I said, "yes, and they are just what we need."

"We'll be sober tomorrow," they chorused.

"You're out of your goddamned mind," said Lucretia.

"Sundance," I said. "See them pigeons?" There was a flock on the wheel and coming our way.

"Tschup," says Sundance, staggering away.

The birds come on and when they was about overhead Sundance drawed and began firing. I never seen anyone so fast ever. Twelve pigeons fell to the cobbles, and Sundance walked round to them and shook his head disgustedly at one. It wasn't nothing but a strip of skin and the wings.

"Luther," says Sundance, "I apologize. I'm off my form today—didn't get the head on this one."

We rented a cart and a cab and put our drunken warriors in the cart, all bundled down with the straw, and went back to her house.

"Jesus," said Lucretia. "If I hadn't seen that with my own eyes I wouldn't have believed it."

I nodded.

"What do we do now?" says Lucretia.

"Have some supper. Bed these boys down in the room we was in—there is another room in this pile got a bed in it I'm sure— and get under way first thing in the morning."

We feasted on lobsters and cold white wine and salads and piles of shrimp cooked with flaked red pepper and told stories on each other. Lucretia let rip with a couple raunchy tales very artfully constructed and Butch actually blushed, he didn't know whether to laugh or go blind.

Sundance was getting more and more vague, and his face seemed about to slide right off his head and into his baked Alaska.

Lucretia and I saw the boys to the room we had so lately been much one with another in, and they fell down any old place, but I did notice that each of them drawed a gun and had it close to hand.

When we were in a big room on the next floor up—had no way to it but the one door in the hall—Lucretia dropped her clothes off and stood outside on the balcony, naked, to feel the evening's breeze. I soon joined her. We could see the far-off lights of Manila's square and the cathedral. The land below us was dark, and there was no movement in the shadows.

"Are those really the bank and train robbers?" she asked. "The outlaws that gave such trouble to E. H. Harriman?"

"Yup," I said.

"How do you know them?"

"Well," I says, "there ain't that many folks in the West and so you tend to meet them if you are in any way a convivial person."

"And how did you meet these two?"

"Them two? Oh, I was, ah, I sort of forget, back in the middle eighties I was . . . . . . it must have been a saloon."

Lucretia was looking at me out from under one eyelid and tapping her bare foot on the parquet.

"Ah, I don't see why I got to dredge up embarrassing things from my past," I whined. "We robbed a bank."

"Well, thank God," she said, "for a moment I thought it might be something shameful."

"They's good boys," I says. "It's just they aren't much at ranching or ordinary work. They'll have to keep on headed to raw places as can stand 'em."

I didn't like what that last meant. It wasn't that it touched me, for I'd get by, but them other two would go on being bright and murderous children till folks killed them in self-defense.

I was getting more than some interested in Lucretia, who was as fine a woman as any I've known.

We made love on the sheet, it was too hot for even a single layer of cotton over us. Then we murmured things, nothing of importance, and drifted off to sleep.

In the dead dark middle of the night all hell broke loose downstairs, a quick rip of gunfire and shouts, and then silence. Lucretia slipped on a long robe and I pulled on my pants and down we went, me with a Colt in each hand.

Butch and Sundance had killed six fellers and winged two more—whoever was after me was some serious.

All the dead carried cane knives, machetes, and weren't a one of them looked over about fifteen.

"They are pretty serious about this," I said. "Maybe you ought to ship home for a while." I was looking right at her. Her blue eyes flared up and she said she was going with me, and that meant into the jungle, too. And no mistake.

"Well," I says, "everybody's up, so let's us pack and go, we can figure this out off in the mountains."

So we did, and was on our way within the hour.

14

I never was sure just what kind of business Donald Sams was in, but he had a room lined with metal in the basement just full of modern weapons, all oiled and gleaming, and the cases of ammunition that feeds them. Butch and Sundance was soon festooned with bandoliers and grenades and big Luger pistols that fitted into the wooden holster one way and the holster made a stock for it the other.

Lucretia had a line of carts and buggies fetched, each one with a smiling driver, and the household help was busily stuffing most of the mansion into the carts.

"They'll finish," said Lucretia, climbing up beside me. A policeman came up and bowed and handed her a flower. He wished her a pleasant journey. No mention of the six dead and two mostly there in the house. It seemed that this was old hat, and nothing to get in a lather over.

I was in a lather over it. I am used to being shot at at range, not having to wonder if the next shrub or drapery is full of assassins waiting on a chance to leap out and make kebabs out of poor old Luther. It occurred to me that maybe I was getting old for this. Then I thought of what I might do otherwise and then I figured I'd die when I'd a mind to.

It was still fairly cool as we clopped away over the cobbles and headed up the avenue. The mountains was a ways off, behind rain clouds, and we wouldn't see them close until the evening, and it was a two-day trip up to the mountain house.

Butch and Sundance was slouched back to back in the cart behind, having an eye-opener and ready to let the broadsides fly if they saw suspicious wiggles in the bushes. I expected that after last night's set-to there would be a few days before a rematch and I hoped by then to get to whoever was ordering this and convince them that it warn't us. All the while hoping that it really *warn't* us.

"I like it when you call me Lucy," said Lucretia, putting her head on my shoulder. We were both bushed, and she went to sleep immediately. I followed. Butch and Sundance were good for many hours and I wasn't. They were so damn drunk you could've brain-shot the pair of 'em and they wouldn't have died till they sobered up. Like all good cowboys, they feared neither God nor man but was terrified of Bennington Schoolmarms. Talking to Lucretia every other word was ma'am and they was continually correcting each other's etiquette. They'd knocked over the eight that come to Lucretia's house in about four seconds. And then apologized for making such a mess, ma'am.

I didn't dare to laugh at them, though I grinned a lot as they blushed and stammered.

The buggy we was in had deep, comfortable seats all plushed in dark brown velvet, and we sort of laid back and held each other while drinking cold white wine from a canvas bag full of ice and bottles. I idly pitched one of the bottles toward the side of the road and a horde of brown children were fighting over it at once. And fighting hard, they was kicking and using sticks, any old thing to get that prized green bottle, worth about one cent U.S. Lucretia saw my stare.

"The country people are so poor an ordinary glass bottle is wealth to them. They sell their daughters to the whoremasters for money to buy rice with. They never have enough to eat. They wear rags. That's the Philippines, Kelly, the crowd around that bottle. They have God, but can't eat Him."

We passed skinny farmers walking with carabao, for here the family water buffalo is a pet, too. They has acquired some of the habits of dogs.

"Tell me about the Yellowstone," she said. "Tell me about Cody and Liver-Eatin' Jack and Tom Horn and all of them." She put her pretty head on my shoulder. I resolved not to cuss out Ned Buntline so much.

So I did, as we moved slowly along in the rising heat. We stopped to change horses and use the jakes and went on. Butch and Sundance was pert as ever, they'd found another bottle of Panther Sweat, which I supposed Lucretia had stuck in their cart. She was a superb hostess.

For that afternoon I told her true and funny stories of my friends, and I had a potful of both. They'd as soon get a laugh as get a drink, those friends.

When I told her of meeting Cody when we was both cinched up to the eyebolts in the Hitchfoot Hotel she laughed so hard she slid off the seat. I told her about me being the Great Crepe of the Northern Plains, and my first meeting with Spotted Tail. I ain't never been rich enough to afford much dignity anyway.

There was a huge inn at the halfway mark, and we stopped there for the night, and looked the rooms over good and finally took a big suite away from the main building, over the carriage house. There was only one stairway up to it, and the walls was three feet thick. I figured we could do watches.

Lucretia tried to send down for food but I shook my head and we went down together and picked up food from the kitchen pots. There was a couple hundred other guests and more coming on every minute. I didn't figure anyone would try to get us by poisoning everybody. We had plenty of white wine, iced tea, and I took four bottles of arrack for my two fugitive chums. It's Malay rice brandy and shaves yer gullet down to bedrock.

"Why are these people trying to kill you?" she said later, when we were soaking in a huge tub of cool water. I said I purely didn't know but expected that I wouldn't allow it. I tried hard never to interfere with someone else's fun but in this case I was going to be obnoxious about it and never mind why.

We had come up some in altitude and it got cooler quicker, and we sat out on a broad balcony and ate and talked, and kept an eye on the foot of the stairs. We'd told the inn we was not to be disturbed by anyone and those that did could find themselves shot pretty much to death. One moment I looked at the plates of paella and the cheap silverware, and then at the guns all about like makings for another kind of feast.

At dusk them huge bats flapped past and I guess I must have flinched a little, for Lucretia laughed and said they were fruit bats and didn't attack anything that could move.

This island was the most dangerous place I had ever been in, where murder was cheap and there was so many people needy for so many things that they confused it all and I couldn't tell just who wanted me dead. If the war was the kind of war I suspected it could even be American troops, who'd been killing everyone out of frustration and didn't want the word to get back.

Well, I thought, if they want to try me and the other hardcases good luck to 'em.

Nothing at all happened over the night, and we took off long before dawn. The hostlers had slept with the stock and near the buggies and carts, and they didn't see anything either. All of them were Lucretia's family's retainers and had been employed for forty years or so.

The jungle is beautiful. I have never seen flowers like there was beside the road again. The Philippines also has thousands of different kinds of mosquitoes and millions of each one of 'em, and a feller could go reasonably insane in a short time without loose clothes and citronella. Me, I didn't mind smelling like Aunt Maud's Christmas fruitcake.

We got to Lucretia's summer house without incident, and the maids and butlers and all was lined up out front, and they didn't flicker an eyelash when Butch and Sundance and me run right round them and in the front door and through the house, guns out, finding only one elderly drunk passed out in a clothes hamper. We come back out in a few minutes and we was clanking in our armaments and looking like fools. Lucretia was explaining us in rapid Spanish and the staff was nodding at double time.

The house was light and open and airy, a pleasant place surrounded by lawns and ponds. I saw fish turn in the ponds and asked about them, they was ornamental carp, from Japan. When I walked up close there was a swirl of reds and oranges and whites and blacks—and

I stood there musing on pinto fish for a while. Jesus, what some folks will do for fun.

Full of the perplex, I went back to the house. I heard a soft whistle, and there was Sundance on top of the roof, just having a look, and armed like he was going to take Manila alone. I suspect he could, if he'd wanted it some.

I was still in my same old clothes, and Lucy and the other folk had gone through the closets and found me some light cotton shirts and loose, light trousers which I put on gratefully. It was hot this time of evening even up here, though I could see the breeze beginning to move some of the trees. I put a gunbelt over the pants and thought that this was the first time I'd ever fought in goddamned pajamas.

We had a late supper, just three of us, with Butch on the roof at first and then I went up and took the watch for a while. There was three automatic shotguns loaded with buckshot, I figured I could about stop a brigade with rapid fire.

Lucretia come up to join me and we sat together, me scanning the grounds. I did not think we had worries, but I wasn't sure. She got impatient with my head turning and kissed me for a long time and then I went back to it and she said "Jesus!" and flounced off. I knew it was inconvenient to be doing what I was doing but I thought we all might live longer this way. The events of the last few days had me hard spooked.

Sundance showed up right quick and though I thought I was due for the night watch apparently Lucy had made her vexation known and I was being given a chance to smooth it over.

Time I got to the bedroom she had recovered herself and she apologized.

"I just want to spend every second with you. It's foolish," she said, her arms wrapped around herself.

I heard Sundance whistle and I run to the balcony and looked up. He was pointing out on the lawn. I could see someone with a white banner standing there.

"I'll go out," I said to the Kid. "Keep an eye on me."

"I'm going with you," said Lucy. "And don't try to stop me." There was considerable steel in her voice and I shrugged. I got a shotgun and my Colts full all the way round and then I padded down the hall and stairs in my bare feet—my boots was too hot—and then I started across the cool clipped grass, which felt good on my feet. Lucretia was right behind me to the left, so I could swing and shoot in a part of a second.

"It is not necessary," the feller with the flag said. "I am not armed and there is no one with me." The Spanish was a soft dialect, I could sort out some of it but not all.

"What do you wish?" says Lucretia, and she and the flagbearer rattled at each other for a few minutes.

"This is Mrs. Maria Aguinaldo," said Lucretia. "The Americans have captured her husband and their infant son."

"And is in hot pursuit of the mother," I snarls. "Well, that's about right."

I waved to Sundance and saw him back away from view. He'd had a shotgun pointed this way all along.

"Come, come," said Lucretia to the tiny Filipina. "Come inside, we can talk there and no one will bother us."

Not for long anyway, I thought, my mind resting on my chums. I felt a sight safer than if the entire Fifth Cavalry was riding close order on the lawn.

Butch and Sundance was at the dining room table, eating quick, pistols by their plates like an extra fork. They finished quickly and went on out, to become two more shadows in the bushes. I hoped Mrs. Aguinaldo wasn't lying about being alone, for if she was we'd soon know it with God alone knew what effect upon our conversation.

Lucretia gave Maria a glass of wine and we sat down at the dining table and listened to her story. It was simple enough. The *guerrilleros* had fought the Spanish for as long as anyone could remember, and the Americans had come and been greeted like the liberators they was only they then settled down into the chairs so recently vacated by the Spanish and announced they liked it here and it suited them.

So the rebel soldiers took two deep breaths and began fighting the Americans, as they did not want *anybody* bothering them. They would like their own country free and clear to make their mistakes in and as for a corrupt government, they were sure local talent would easily equal anything available elsewhere. They did not enjoy shooting Americans any more than they had enjoyed shooting

Spaniards, but they felt obligated to do it so why didn't we just up and leave?

And who the hell were the goddamned Americans to refer to Filipinos as "little brown brothers," the ill-mannered sonsofbitches?

Maria's husband, Emilio, was on Bataan, and their two-year-old son captured.

They felt that stronger nations was making a war for their own purposes, but the Filipinos were doing most of the dying and it was very real and close to them.

Maria didn't cry, she had a glittery air about her, and when she said modestly that if she was a general things were desperate, no? I laughed uproariously and shook my head.

"Luther!" Lucretia scolded me. "You are being rude!"

"But what do you want me to do?" I asked, raising an eyebrow.

"Come with me, see what the soldiers do in the name of your country."

"Who was trying to kill me in Manila?"

"The Japanese," Maria said.

"Why?"

"Ask them." Well, I had about half a mind to do just that, but Lucretia shook her head at me and looked dangerous. "Don't think that. Quit," she said, so I did.

"Why do you think this will help—my seeing it, I mean."

"No one knows," said Maria. "We are a poor country. For most of us, life is all lived within a few miles of the huts we were born in. Most people think that the earth is flat and the sun a god. Most cannot read. Yet strange soldiers come, huge men stinking of raw beef, and kill them, call them rebels when they are not, kill, rape the women sometimes to death, kill whole villages. Is this your democracy?"

Pretty much, I thought, remembering Sand Creek and Wounded Knee Creek and the Bear Paw battle.

All hell broke loose outside. I blew out the candles and grabbed my guns and peeked through the bamboo screens. There was spurts of flame out in the jacaranda and I heard the crump of grenades and wondered if Butch or Sundance had any or was that the others? Then I could see them coming across the lawn, flicking a shot backwards from time to time. They dove through a window and crashed on to an end table, scattering porcelain Buddhas and ashtrays. I was looking hard across the lawn but didn't see anything coming on.

"Who was it?" I says.

"The fucking Altar Guild canvassing for a new rag," says Butch, who was not a patient feller, "or maybe it was the Doan's Little Liver Pills man. Orientals."

"Since we are in the Orient that comforts me," I says. "It would be unnerving if they was niggers or Eskimos."

Butch held up a handful of bloody papers.

"I cain't read it," he said.

Neither could I. The characters were swift penmarks. I stuffed them in my shirt.

"I think maybe we should leave," I said. "You know, go somewhere and leave no forwarding address. Somewhere remote and not much traveled upon."

"Suits me," said Sundance, smiling and looking for someone to kill.

"I got money," I said, "if we end up anywhere that uses money."

Maria Aguinaldo was laughing, quiet-like, I loved her for it. Lucretia was snickering, too.

"It's just a game to you, isn't it," she said.

"Philosophers make my teeth itch," said Sundance. "All my life I been looking for a place where everybody's as stupid as I am.

"One thing though," says Sundance, "I got to ask. I don't mind the jungle, I don't mind the leeches that reminds me of lawyers, I don't mind the shrubbery and the mud, I don't mind the birds that sound like they escaped from the bughouse."

"What?" Maria said.

"Republicans," said the Kid. "We ain't going where they got Republicans, are we?"

"No," said Maria. "No Republicans."

"Well, thank God," said the Kid. "I was worried."

It was still outside. No movement in the bushes, maybe, maybe not, maybe someone was there, but we'd have to find out sooner or later.

"You ready?" said Lucretia. I was struggling into my knee-high boots.

"Yup."

"Yup."

"Yup."

"Yup."

We followed Maria out the back way and filed into the jungle. She found a path and led us on. We walked for maybe three hours and come to a ridgetop, and when we looked back Lucretia's house was burning brightly.

I shook my head and so did she.

"This is serious business," I said. "You can leave if you want to."

"Fuck off, Luther," she said, smiling.

15

Goddamn it," said Lucretia. "They burned up my Turner and the Hiroshige prints. I don't mind being hounded and shot at but that makes me mad."

There was a sudden whirl of sparks, from an explosion.

"There went the dynamite in the basement."

We was both tired from the long day and all the excitement and the long walk, where we'd been lashed with branches had leaves that cut you a little.

"Eeeeh! Come on!" said Maria. "Far to go." We follered our general right along.

Butch and Sundance was bringing up the rear, with a practiced routine. If they each didn't have a thirty-thousand-dollar price on their head they could've gone on to vaudeville.

"When we find the pink-spotted snake we can go."

"I just saw it last night."

"Why didn't you call?"

"Wrong time."

(In a few months time they was to go to Bolivia, steal a big herd of cows, and drive them clear through the Amazon to Argentina. How they did it, no one knows. Keeping yourself alive on that journey is a miracle, to keep two thousand cows alive is beyond all the hopes of men, cows being as dumb as they are.)

"Sundance, look? A little paint and it'll do? Right?"

"You call that a snake? It ain't big enough for a damn bootlace. Jesus."

Maria kept up a stiff pace through the gloom, that pale green-gray light of the jungle. Critters crashed off through the jungle, and once or twice I saw the huge coils of constrictor snakes tighten around something as we passed. There wasn't a breath of wind, and the high whine of mosquitoes in their millions was enough to send you mad—like having a dentist's drill in your ear.

She left us in a glade by a small river and went off and she come back in a bit with balls of gluey rice, and that was lunch. We crossed the river, which was fairly deep, and picked the leeches off each other on the far bank.

"Modesty is for people don't have leeches on them," said Lucretia. We all stripped and plucked and then dressed and went on. I was watching every move Maria made, for this was all new country to me and I didn't know its ways or dangers. There were different ones that I wasn't used to. In the line of work I'm in time to time a sprained ankle or a missed meal can be a death sentence.

We walked till dark and finally come out into a small clearing with little thatched houses up on stilts all the way around it. I heard pigs grunt and the bawl of calves—water buffalo, I guessed—and a couple men slid out of the shadows and Maria hugged them and then brought them and introduced Juan and Diego, her friends and fellow rebels.

We was all exhausted, and Lucretia and I was led off to a hut on the far edge and gestured into it. I let the cloth door drop and looked at my beautiful, bedraggled love, who grinned out of her tangles of hair and sank to the floor, exhausted.

"Used to be all I did was take tea and lovers," she said. "I don't know how a girl gets used to all the excitement."

I pulled off my boots and took off my clothes and Lucy did the same. There was a faint coolness coming up from below the grass mats we was laying on, and we both settled down and then I looked at her and she me and we fell to it as though we had just woke up from a long sleep. I damn near expected sparks when we touched.

Too tired to sleep, we lay there murmuring things of no value or weight—foods we liked, wines, childhood stuff—and went to sleep in the middle of sentences.

No one woke us, the little village went about its business like it had for the last ten thousand years or so, and after the worries of the days before the sleepiness of the place was like a medicine.

In the late afternoon it smelled of rain, and tall black clouds was piled up coming in from the Pacific, and there was a little wind. We dressed and come down to find Butch and Sundance and Maria playing poker. She was winning.

Butch looked up and smiled as sunny as could be, while Sundance furrowed his brows and glared at his cards.

"The Kid and me is heading to South America," said Butch.

"Damn right," says the Kid. "I know I'll end on the gallows but I'll be damned if it's going to be for rustling water buffalo. The goddamned things is the family puppy dog, and I ain't gonna hang for stealing the family puppy dog. These Filipinos sure knows how to break a badman's heart."

"We're overspecialized, I told the Kid. Here, I said, 'Kid, we own plain old hidebound skulduggery.' Said we ought to have gone into the whorehouse business or making matches or something," said Butch.

"We're what ya come to you don't get an aim in life early," said the Kid. "Just like my mother said, if I didn't buckle down to them schoolbooks I'd turn out like me."

"But we hear in South America they got real cows to steal and banks and even a few trains, for a change of pace," says Butch. "And at our age we don't really have the wherewithal . . ."

"The *what?*" says Sundance.

"Money."

"Well, why the hell didn't you say so?"

"I did."

"Shit."

"Anyway, we can't see anything we can do for you and if you can think of something we'll stay for sure," says Butch.

"Till Wednesday," says Sundance.

"You don't even know what day it is, goddamn it!"

"There you go, picking on me for my lack of education," says Sundance, looking grieved. "I done the best with what I got."

Lucretia was about on the ground, she'd laughed out so much air that her tight chest wouldn't get it back.

"Which way is South America, anyway?" says Sundance.

"Over there," says Butch, pointing.

"How far?"

"Ten, twelve thousand miles," says Butch.

"We gonna swim?" says Sundance.

"Naw, we'll take a boat."

"I was lookin' forward to the exercise," said Sundance.

"We'll get exercise stealing the boat," says Butch.

Lucretia gasped her breath back and said, "I have a boat you can have. It's in the yacht basin, and I'll give you a note to the harbormaster. You'll have to learn how to navigate."

"What's navigate?" says Sundance.

"Tellin' where you are."

"I'm here."

"Sundance," says Butch, "I'm gettin' tired of your goddamned act. Now, draw a line in the dirt and step up to it and then tell these nice people where you went to college."

Sundance drew a line in the dust and stepped up to it and put both toes of his boots on it.

"Princeton," says the Sundance Kid.

"What in," says Butch.

"Mathematics," says Sundance.

"And how did you graduate?"

"Mongoose come loudly," says Sundance. "I always wondered what it was that they did to that poor mongoose."

They hitched on their bandoliers and picked up their guns and Lucretia handed them a note and she hugged and kissed each one of them a long time. They was both grinning like walruses, and happy for me, which they expressed by warning her what I did to dogs and poultry if I was let loose without a keeper.

"You need money?" I said.

"Money's in the bank," says Butch. "We know all about it."

And they walked down the path that went down the mountain to join the main road. They waved once at the bend in the trail and then they were gone.

"Marvelous," said Lucretia, over and over.

"Those boys is better behaved than most," I says. "Some of my friends ought to be welded into cages and left for the birds."

She laughed again.

"Nice of you to give 'em your yacht," I said.

"Sams won't use it," she said. "And I'm glad to be rid of it. I wonder if they will turn to piracy before they sight South America?"

"They'll turn to piracy 'fore they get out of Manila Bay," I predicted.

It was damn lonely without them. We were at the mercy of the people in the village, and whatever form the *guerrilleros* were taking now.

"It is easier for them to come to you than for you to go," said Maria, "but there are some things I want you to see here." I expected bullet-riddled children or amputees but it wasn't anything like that. She took us to the village school, where twelve children were studying on one tattered book and doing their alphabets in the dust.

"If the Spanish found a village school they would shoot the teacher in the stomach, so they would die in great pain over many hours, and then cut off the left hand of each of the children." The kids all had stumps on the left.

We walked away, toward a little brook that came from high up, starting near what looked like the cone of an extinct volcano. There was fifty kinds of orchids I could see, and hibiscus and frangipani. Bright birds dashed around the green trees, their songs were ones I had never heard before. Huge butterflies with metallic wings hung sipping nectar from flowers shaped like flagons. The jungle seemed to breathe, to throb visibly, all one creature. It scared the hell out of me.

The islands had fifty kinds of snakes, forty-eight of which was poisonous, and them damned tiger hornets and insects the size of shoes that lived on fresh meat. I saw a spider would've hung off a dinner plate leap out and grab a bird out of the air and all manner of leeches was squirming and trying to get to us, like they could smell us even though they was underwater.

"El Tigre will come in three days," said Maria. "Until then you should rest, there is plenty of food in the village and you must eat and drink well. I am going back to my warriors now, all you must do is stay, do not try to leave, the people of the village would have to kill you."

"I think we should stay," said Lucretia. "I think they really want us to."

We fucked a lot, and walked around hand in hand, and looked for different colors of butterflies and lived in each other for days. The heat was just bearable, and we could bathe in the stream if we got the leeches off before they was dug in good.

The villagers went on about their business as if we weren't there. The meals was communal, but they brought a big leaf all piled up with food and a weak warm beer and looked hurt if we did not finish everything at once.

Lucretia's undone hair fell almost to her knees, and she bade me cut it one evening. I had only my killing knife from my boot and it was sharper than a razor, and I cut her hair off short as mine all round, and a lucky thing I did, for I found a big tick in her scalp, all swollen up with blood. I lit a candle and heated my penknife blade in it and got the tick to back out—it's bad when you jerk them out and they leave their heads in—and I smashed the bugger and had her look me over good but I hadn't any. Them ticks have an ether in their saliva numbs the skin when they burrow in, I guess.

It rained every four hours, and we'd lay together in the hut running our hands over each other. Lucy had a grand smile, white and quick.

The *guerrilleros* came on the fourth morning, we were sitting on the lashed bamboo staircase when these small brown silent men came out of the jungle all around us, and the leader come walking toward where we sat, with his machete in his hand.

I damn near burst out laughing. He had tiger-stripes tattooed across his face. El Tigre, indeed. I must have smiled wide, for he smiled, too.

"I was drunk," he said, in good English. "You know how it is when you have too much fun."

"Luther Kelly," I says, extending my hand. He took it in a firm, dry grip and shook twice. He was still smiling.

"And Lucretia Sams," I went on.

"Did you have to mention that son of a bitch?" she said, smiling at El Tigre. Butch and Sundance had left her a shotgun and a pair of ivory-handled thirty-eights ("we took them off this bank clerk and they was too small to use and too purty to throw away") and she did look ready for war. I aimed to keep her as far out of it as I could.

"We go now," said El Tigre, and he and his men split halves, one group going in front and one behind, and off we went into the wet green dark of the jungle.

The path was cleared and flat, with only an occasional liana or strangler fig across it, but they was big enough to see good. The quiet was eerie, and any sounds of birds or animals came from high above, two hundred feet, in the tops of the trees. As green as it was and as full of life it felt old as sin.

We come to a fire clearing, where some folk had burnt out the undergrowth so they could raise one or two crops of whatever before the tired soil gave out. There was a death stench in the air and I pulled Lucretia behind me. I doubted that she'd ever seen a corpse bloated from the heat and I meant to spare her. There was several, in American uniforms, and Lucretia took one look and choked and stuck her face in my shirt. I led her away and to the trail and she sniffed twice and was fine.

"I'm sorry," she said.

"First time it's hard. And the forty after that," I said, telling her no more than the honest truth. I don't see how a human could ever get used to it.

A couple of hours farther down the mountain she come up beside me and said, "It isn't a game, is it?" and I said no it wasn't and it could get very rough real quick, especially fighting in the jungle, where everybody was fighting like they had blindfolds on and Bowie knives in a darkened room, like the stories.

We crossed a pretty good road in a hurry and the ones in the rear brushed away our tracks and on we went, swinging with the same rhythm, silent and sinister. Killers in front, killers behind, killers looking for us, and who knew when we would stumble blind one into another. I wished to Christ that Lucretia had stayed. I feared for her, and, damn it, I had begun to fear for myself, and wondered how much of my life had been misspent because I did not really care what happened to me at all.

When we stopped for the customary ball of rice glue Lucretia got near me and whispered, "What are you thinking so hard about?" and I said I was philosophizing on an empty head and not to take it too serious.

"They won't let anything happen to us," said Lucretia. "We are the ones who tell the world."

Assuming that they'd listen, which I doubted deep.

Early that evening we padded into a big clearing with many large bread loaf–shaped huts spread out around the edges of the forest. We stopped for the night, and Lucretia and me was steered to a small hut back behind one of the big ones. One of the *guerrilleros* beckoned to us and led us to a tall tree all hung with big green vines. He slashed one open and water sluiced down and he left us the machete and a double handful of leaves that had soap for sap. We got clean and washed our clothes some, and though there were fifty men about not one gave us so much as a glance as we walked to the hut, leaving our clothes to dry as much as they would on the bamboo staircase.

We coupled like leopards, full of some urgency we felt, and lay for a while till the sweat dried and then went at it again. Her fingers dug into my back and I moaned once, and thought I have never done that.

In the early light we went on, along a wider trail, and the troop was much more relaxed. The dangerous territory had been crossed, it seemed, and we were closing in on shelter. I had a quick sight on the stars when I had first got up, and we seemed by my reckoning to be moving out on the peninsula on the west side of Manila Bay. I couldn't remember what it was called.

I whispered the question to Lucretia, who said "Bataan," and I shrugged and went back to watching the bushes. I wondered if you sat off in the jungle twenty feet if anyone could see you, the colors was such a riot to the eye.

We went up a steep slope and along a narrow razorback ridge, and then through a cave that went right through the flank of the mountain. I heard a crashing off a ways and lifted my gun, but it was just some wild pigs.

The pace slowed and we come through a narrow gully and to a clearing shaped like a willow leaf.

The troops filed off left and right and there was Maria, and next to her, unless I missed my guess, the often captured Emilio Aguinaldo, patriot, busy cleaning his house.

16

El Tigre and eight others with stripes on their faces just like him stood behind Emilio and Maria, grinning like sots at a wake.

Lucretia put a hand to her pretty mouth and then she burst out with that booming laugh.

"Every once and so often the Americans kill or capture El Tigre. They brag on it. And a new one comes forth. El Tigre cannot be killed. El Tigre is immortal. Bravo Bravo Bravo." The nine bowed.

"Did you hear what your Speaker of the House Reed said?" Emilio grinned and kissed his fingertips. "He said to the full House of Representatives that the valiant United States Army had captured Aguinaldo's two-year-old son, and was presently in hot pursuit of the mother."

Tom Reed, now there was one to conjure with. I'd been near when Teethadore had asked him if he'd plans to be the Republican presidential candidate. "No," said Reed, "I expect my party can do worse, and they will."

"I got a fool letter promising amnesty, so I could be with my son, from that General MacArthur—he's pretty good general—so I wrote back and said I was fighting so my son wouldn't have to be kidnapped by bastards like him, in his own country," said Emilio.

Aguinaldo had some dry wit, I'll tell you.

The peninsula we was on was so jumbled and jungly it was a defender's dream and an attacker's nightmare. The Americans would win hands down anything fought where they could maneuver, but they couldn't do much here but get lost and wear themselves plumb out chasing noises which was usually wild pigs.

Maria took Lucretia off, I supposed for a bath, and Aguinaldo got me a gourd half full of rice brandy and we found a dry old log to set on and we talked.

"These Spaniards, they were cruel," he said. "But you Americans are just greedy. Your merchants want to milk my country for as many years as you can get away with. We don't deserve that."

I sipped the brandy. All true so far, for all the good it will do you, Emilio. Under all the fancy talk about democracy you are just another nigger standing on the gold to them. I have known these people a long time.

"Also, I worry because I am beginning to love war. It is a sin, but I do. I love the battles, afterward is bad, but the battles are good. Do you know how many American troops there are here trying to catch me and my five thousand men? One hundred fifty thousand. Most of them are lost in the jungle, feeding the leeches. If some get shot or have their throats cut, they kill everyone, little babies, everyone, in the next two or three villages. They run around looking for me and I let them fight me when I want to. I can't take Manila, the MacArthur, he's a damn good general. He can't find me in the jungle. I'll stay here until he leaves and the troops, too. You tell them go home?"

I explained that very little of MacArthur's ears was hanging on my every word, and that I could scream in MacArthur's face and he'd just wave a hand to have me thrown out and go on with his correspondence. In short, I was not likely to be real useful.

"Then I will have to wear them out, let the bugs and the boredom of the jungle destroy them."

I nodded. There wasn't anything wrong with his tactics save I knew he didn't have no notion of how far greed will propel a country of businessmen if they don't have to do any of the dying. Also he didn't think much of Germany or Japan bothering him. One or the other would be coming right up the walk the moment the last American troopship was hull down on the horizon.

So we sat there and I told him all this and he looked at me like I'd had too much sun, wondering what on earth those countries would need from the poor Philippines.

We watched a couple battalions of his soldiers drill. They was wearing ragged peasant clothes and sandals, but the guns all gleamed with oil and the men drilled right smart. The bandoliers was full of cartridges and everything had been lifted from the Americans, adding to MacArthur's fury. This war could go on for a long, long time.

Maria and Lucretia come back, Lucretia all aglow from her bath, and I wanted one, too, but would have to wait. She tried the rice brandy and screwed up her face and grinned and drank the rest of it.

"Waste not, want not," she said. "That's very good. The jungle seems *greener* after a few snorts of that. *Mmmmmmmmm.*"

Maria laughed with her hand held over her mouth.

Just then a runner burst out of the jungle and he looked around and saw Aguinaldo and raced over, spewing out a string of the bastard Polynesian that everyone in the Philippines knew but me and I thought Lucretia, but she was listening and taking in the words and nodding.

"What?" I asked.

"Americans pushing into Bataan. Aguinaldo said we'll go give them a bloody nose."

I rose to go with Aguinaldo, but he shook his head.

"We talk more when I get back," he said. "You stay with the pretty lady."

Lucretia was glowing, her skin was some transparent anyway, but now she looked pale and hot. It worried me. I had her turn round and I looked at the place where the tick had been, but I couldn't even see it. She felt warm to my hand. This was no place to have a fever in. I gave her quinine and the bitter taste wrinkled her nose and then she laughed.

"I don't think I have malaria," she said.

"Everybody in the tropics has malaria," I said, smiling, my heart in my throat. If the fever would just go down I'd not worry.

An hour later she was burning, so hot I took her to a hut and stripped her and bathed her with cool water, got by soaking a rag and whipping it through the air.

"Don't make such a fuss, Luther," she said. "I'll be all right." She smiled and comforted me. I was getting more worried by the minute. Her lovely blue eyes got dark half moons under them, and once in a while she shook. She was so chilled I took off my clothes to hold her and give her my heat.

Finally I decided that she had to go to Manila and damn the cost. There were a number of *guerrilleros* in camp and I said I needed a dugout and I'd paddle her to Manila across the Bay, and I offered gold, which they smiled at and wouldn't take and in ten minutes flat we was racing down a trail to the east. The Bay was only a couple of miles from the camp, and there were several dugouts hid back from the shore. They picked the biggest one over my protests, and launched her and I carried Lucy in my arms and stepped in and eight of these boys who knew my kind only as killers and usurpers bent to the paddles and we shot across the water right quick.

Without their belts of cartridges and guns they looked like Filipino peasants. I quit worrying over them.

It was a good fifteen miles across the Bay to Manila, and we got there in three hours, with Lucretia protesting a little more feebly each time that she would be fine.

The boys dropped me off and turned and went along the shore, they had fishing nets up on poles now, and I carried Lucretia till I found a horsecab and told the driver to take us to the best of the hospitals. It was one run by a couple of Swiss physicians that catered to the traders and planters.

They was good. Lucretia was getting weaker by the minute and I suddenly realized that she was being slowly paralyzed. I was near on to hopping up and down in fear, but I mentioned the tick I had taken out of her scalp and both docs said "WHERE?" and I showed them and they shaved a patch of Lucy's hair and then dug round with a scalpel and bodkin and come up with a little black speck on a square of gauze.

"These ticks leave part of their head in the wound," said the doc, shaking his head, "and after three to six days it leaks a very powerful poison. If it is not taken out the patient will suffocate, for it paralyzes the breathing muscles, a horrible way to die."

"I feel better already," said Lucretia, grinning brightly.

"Balls," I said. "How long will she have to recover?"

"We would like her kept here for two weeks. The toxin will attack the liver next. She will be very weak."

"Two weeks!" yelled Lucretia, "I will not be stuck here for two goddamned weeks! Luther!"

"You want to see me again?" I said, glaring. "Then you stay put. I still have a couple things to do."

"Bully," she said. Her face went pale and she vomited off the side of the bed.

I stayed with her that night, bathing her forehead or holding her as the chills and fevers went back and forth. I left before dawn, buying new jungle clothes from the Chinese stall merchants, the Jews of Asia.

I bought two pairs of light cotton and rubber shoes, and let my boots find a new home by just standing them against a wall and looking away.

I barged into the palace demanding to see MacArthur, and a shavetail lieutenant said that would be difficult, he'd been relieved and that General Merritt would be in at ten. I didn't like waiting four hours and said so, and then from the high main hallway a few doors away I heard Bill Taft.

"Don't molest the peacocks," he said. "Come and talk to an old hack Ohio politician never made an honest dime in his life and proud of it. What you need, my friend?"

"A few things," I says. "Like a willing ear to start."

I told him the Filipinos were a lot more determined than anyone thought to have their country to themselves. It was going to cost a hell of a lot of money and a great number of lives, and I didn't think it was worth it.

Taft nodded.

I'd done my job and wanted to go back to America, and take Lucretia Sams with me.

Taft grinned.

"All in good time," he said. "I have a message from Theodore, says send that damned Kelly to the Igorotes."

"Islands?" I said.

"No," said Taft, "tribesmen, in the hills north of here. They are proving an uncommonly resourceful foe. Killed two brigadiers and six colonels so far."

"Hire 'em," I said.

"You are to go look them up and chat," said Bill Taft, a goddamned beaming walrus.

"Why is it always me," I whined. "Always me."

"You have an uncommon ability to come back," said Taft. "And when you don't come back we'll find someone else."

"Who's gone to the Igorotes?"

"Six volunteers."

"And."

"They were sent back in installments."

"I see."

"Tongues first," said Taft.

This sort of set me down, what with my love in the hospital maybe or maybe not doing well, and now I got to go look up a bunch of maniacal thugs probably lived on rat brains and fubu leaves, for Teethadore. I was unhappy, and said so by kicking a spittoon halfway to Macao.

"What the hell does he want with these damn Eye-gorotees? Why don't he just have them all shot and save me the trouble."

Taft steepled his fingers and rumbled like a big fat tiger. He smiled and slid his fingers in and out, like nested pitchforks.

"We plan to stay here a good long time," said Taft. "Until our little brown brothers have the fruits of democracy and have forgotten that there were ever other fruits. Japan is a serious rival for the markets of China. Trade follows the flag."

"These here Eye-gorotees sound unpleasant. If they live in the mountains why not leave 'em in the mountains?"

"They live by hunting, piracy, and banditry," said Taft.

"Just like Americans," I says. "I refuse to go."

"One moment, while I summon the Provost Marshal," said Taft. He rose.

"I'll go."

Taft sat back down and beamed at me. "Where was I before I was interrupted?"

I rang off a stream of cusswords in their pure and hybrid forms both. I cleared the record on Teethadore's ancestors, and mentioned Taft's lard.

Taft beamed, he complimented me on my blasphemies, and then allowed as how he was a busy man with much more to do than listen to the complaints of a National Disgrace like the one in front of his desk.

He asked if the Army could help me find the Igorotes, and I said, Gawd, no. I'd check on Lucretia and then be on my way, and I'd be back when I was done.

"Failing that," said Taft, "I shall await your tongue, which I assume is black."

I left, muttering imprecations.

Lucretia was pale and wan, lying there in the hospital, and I kissed her and we talked a bit. I said I'd be back in ten days to three weeks, and then we'd go to San Francisco and up to Chico, where old General Bidwell had given me a thousand acres of orchards and pasture. I was going to damned well get out of the trade I'd been in since the Civil War.

"I'll miss you," she said, reaching for my hand. I could see the blue lines of the veins in her palm.

I planned to go at dark, so I had time to fetch her flowers and some loose clothes and fruit and such, and at impulse I bought a pair of caged birds, mynahs, and a bag of seeds for them.

We talked of this and that through the afternoon. I wished that I could stay till she was well, and then reflected she'd want to go with me and there would be no stopping her—the fever had took away a lot of her bullheadedness, she was reasonable only so long as she was about half dead. I asked about Donald Sams and Lucretia said he was no problem. Off selling Krupp arms to the Chinese. Neither one of them could recall just why they had got married, it was like a railroad accident that your memory is hazy on.

Dusk was settling, and I kissed her long and hard and then went away quick because my eyes was burning, must have been the citronella candles in the room, for the driving away of insects.

I struck up the road north, figuring on walking all night. I'd have rented a horse but the less bother and trail the better. The Igorotes would be easy to find—find the mountains and walk in and they'd be by right quick.

In the black middle of the night I rounded a bend in the road and saw a single figure standing there, and the gleam of starlight on the honed machete. I whipped out a pistol, and was checking behind me when the figure waved a hand and said, "Kell-Eee" and motioned me out of the road.

It was one of the eternal El Tigres, and he and his men had been watching me and I had some folks following me. He asked if I had arranged for it and I said, hell, no, I need to go and talk to the Igorotes and I don't need no help with that.

El Tigre #5 or what have you whispered to one of his men and the feller scooted down the shadows and in five minutes or so I heard one yell, cut off. So that was that. Pretty soon a half-dozen *guerrilleros* come up, and they said the fools that was following me was Army officers, young ones, and all six were dead. There was not a lot left for discussion the way this war was going and I'd be damned glad to be out of it.

We went off the road and had us a conflab about this and that and El Tigre said he'd take me to the Igorotes himself, they knew the tiger-striped faces as friends, and me being white going up there alone would just mean my slow dismemberment. The soldiers had killed entire villages of Igorotes, shouting orders in Spanish, which the Igorotes did not even understand.

The Igorotes were a warrior people still enjoying their ancient religion and occupations, which was piracy, banditry, and lately kidnapping, politely asking if the relations of the victim wanted the whole contiguous victim or a prized part the first of every month. They was a jungle version of Sears and Roebuck.

A couple days later we rented burros and headed up into the North Luzon mountains, a place loud with parrots and other birds.

17

El Tigre #5 and me left the others down below, as the Igorotes was known to dislike crowds descending upon them of a sudden. All sorts of arms, legs, heads, torsos, and innards was hung from the trees and black with kites and crows. I knew I would never be able to look at a bird feeder quite the same from this trip forward. The Igorotes was ugly customers and advertising it. If Lucretia hadn't been back in Manila I do believe that I would have bought a canoe and paddled toward China and taken my chances on the pirates and the sea.

After we passed the trees all hung round with vulture food we come to a trail cunningly decorated with human skulls, each in a little niche hacked out of the trunk. Several of the skulls had gold teeth.

A couple miles past that we come to the shrunken heads. These was strung on twine much like children string cranberries for the Christmas tree. It warn't Christmas. It warn't festive at all. The hides of trespassers with interesting tattoos took up about a half mile of trail, them hides having been fashioned into lanterns.

"These folks aren't at all mild-mannered," I says to El Tigre #5.

"Oh, no," he says, laughing. "Mean people. Hate whites."

This information did not soothe me.

"I got letter from Aguinaldo," he says.

"Good," I says, hoping it'll do.

"Only problem is I can't read."

"So?"

"I don't think Igorotes read either."

"So?"

"Maybe they don't believe letter sent from Aguinaldo if a white reads it."

Just no end of cheerful babble from this fucking tour guide. I was beginning to look about peckishly, one hand on my Colt. I was not in a good temper, I shouldn't have come, I was going to turn this donkey around and take my chances on . . . . . . and about fifty little fellers in bones and grass leaped out from everywhere. I went sideways off the burro like I'd been backhanded by a gorilla, and I hit the ground and they all landed on top of me. They slit off my clothes, tied me up like I was a goddamn bobbin, and hung me upside down from a tree limb. An industrious Igorote was demonstrating how to make fire a foot under my hair. Others was demonstrating how sharp their knives was by slitting strands fine as frog hairs off leaves.

"El Tigre, gaddamn it!" I snarled. I was turning and I got a full round view every once in a while, long enough to notice El Tigre #5 trussed up like me, with the same damned show-and-tell going on.

El Tigre was talking a mile a minute in a lingo I couldn't follow. The fire-building demonstration under me had worked, a pungent plume wound round my head and I sneezed and couldn't stop.

Finally a headman cut El Tigre down and sliced off his bonds. I had some hope. Then I caught "gringo pig" and thought things were taking a bad turn.

I kept up with my slow revolving, and listened with real and honest interest to the conversation El Tigre was having with the chief or whatever.

The headman shouted and jumped up and whacked through the rope holding me and I thumped down on my head, fortunately the ground was matted in leaves, and then I crashed flat. More conversation while I watched a centipede a foot long go by an inch from my nose.

Jaysus Kayrist, Kell-ee, I thinks, about to give up. There are times when hope is simply painful.

I felt a cold knife run up my back, and the ropes fell off. I sat up, rubbing my neck, which had taken a bad crick. El Tigre thrust the letter in my face and stood ready to translate. The letter said I was not to be harmed, that I would be helpful, and the Igorote must tell me all the crimes that the Americans had committed.

The little headman sat down and began reciting a long list and El Tigre #5 translated it for me.

The Spanish had never bothered the Igorote after the first time that they crossed each other. Something about boiling a dozen priests alive. But the Americans had come, and they were marching along the big road, and saw Igorote women washing clothes in the river and they just shot them, dozens of Igorote women, and since then things had not been good between the Igorotes and the Americans.

So after the women were shot the Igorote warriors crept into the American camp and they slit the throat of every other man. When the camp woke up it was most enjoyable to watch how excited the Americans got. The Igorotes were very amused. The Americans weren't, and they sent many soldiers and the Igorotes fought them but there were too many. Since the Igorotes never war on women and children, they sent their families to a small valley. The Americans shot them, and then dynamited the mountain down on the corpses.

"Imagine," said the headman, "women and children. And they laughed while they did it."

I'd heard this conversation more times than I liked.

I was plain flat furious, and not at the Igorotes who had been minding their own damned business. Days my country makes me want to puke.

"What I need to do here," I said, "is find that place where the mountain was dynamited down on the bodies. I need to know just exactly where it is."

So off we went, me in loincloth, Colts, and canvas shoes. It was maybe four miles from where I had been hanging around waiting on the chief.

Half a small mountain had been scooped out, leaving a reddish-yellow scar on the mountainside. The blasted earth had dumped down on a little bowl below and I knew I was in the right place because when I looked down at the ground between my feet there was a child's mummified hand sticking out, and a few feet away a foot more adult-sized.

"El Tigre number five," I says, "let's us get back to Aguinaldo, I think I got a plan."

My honest face and holy demeanor had charmed the hell out of the Igorotes, all they did was wave absently and go back to crying for their dead. They seemed real attached to their families, I said to myself, for niggers or wogs or whatever they are. And I goddamned the whole human race and I much wished to go render down that fat Yale lawyer in Malacañang Palace. Grease the wheels of Empire. We hadn't been at this business two years and we was as bad as the British, which is as bad as it gets.

Me and El Tigre #5 ran fast downhill—the trails was good—and no one had bothered with my money belt, as the Igorotes had no use for money and would have thought it a crude and foolish invention.

I expect I was something of a sight as I stalked into a trading store, which unfortunately had a number of bombazined missionary ladies in it, all of whom shrieked and fainted and then kept opening one eye or the other as I bought some clothes and seegars and trade gin.

Since El Tigre #5 had a price on his head I bought some food—smoked meat and such—and some of the coarse black chewing tobacco that he favored. I put the pants and shirt on right there at the counter, nodded to the trader who ain't batted an eye all the way through this, and went out, to the sounds of the black-clad ladies reviving.

We trotted through the jungle till we come to a mountain spur had a rill of pure, clear water coming off it and we sat and ate and drank and smoked and got drunk as clipper hands just made port. After a few rousing choruses of something or other we boldly passed out beneath the tropic moon, and we woke early because the roots of our hair was growing and it hurt like hell. We stuck our heads in the rill and let the cool water stop the throbbing.

"No more gin ever," moaned El Tigre #5.

I seconded that, plunging my head back into the stream. We got tired of moaning and whining and started off on the long trail back down to the Bataan Peninsula and Aguinaldo.

We run on to our first American checkpoint and patrol station at mid-afternoon. They was on a broad highway with too good a view both ways for us to sprint across and take our luck in the bush. We hid in some reeds in the barrow ditch and waited. There was quite a lot of firing on the other side of the highway, but that meant nothing at all, since the Americans were rich and would send a thousand bullets after a bush pig made too much noise.

Rather than stay there while the leeches piled on twelve deep, I waited till all that was visible was a shavetail looey and then Major Luther Kelly, USA, on a mission for Governor-General Taft, emerged from the swamp and faced the kid down while El Tigre #5 scooted across and signaled his safe arrival by trilling like a honeycatcher.

At my abrupt farewell the lieutenant saluted and I did, too, sloppy like as befitted my irregular status, and I found my tiger-striped pard across the way tapping his foot.

"Plenty soldiers in here," he whispered, "we go slow, eh?"

We went slow. This was the real jungle, never been cleared, it was hot and close and sticky and full of mosquitoes, but the forest floor was bare. Everything that fell off above got et 'fore it hit the ground.

That eerie unreal play of light and sound that is the mark of jungle everywhere took hold, a dream-like fever. I swear that we passed six terrified troopers but we seemed to agree not to see one another and didn't.

We soon passed the troops flung farthest in and took up a good fast pace, getting close enough to the Bay so we would be on the Peninsula late tomorrow afternoon.

Why after a lifetime spent genteelly snuffing out the lives of folks less heavily armed than we was I got so flaming angry is like most of them things, a mystery. After all, the Igorotes was prepared to dress me out and make walkway decorations out of me—no tattooes but lots of scars—and normally I would take implacable offense at that, but I was mad clean through and at my country, government, that Dutch Dwarf Teethadore, Taft, and I could go on for days.

I wanted all this dirty business over and done with so I could go to California and raise rutabagas or some goddamned thing, with Lucretia to wipe the sweat from my brow and tumble on the grass at night when the stars was big and clear.

Not much of an ambition, but I am a modest man.

I had turned fifty sometime recently, and since I wasn't at all sure of today's date I had no idea when my birthday had been but I felt a lot older.

We camped up close to the road that cuts all around the Bay to the Peninsula and I went shopping in a little village, buying barbecued goat and trade rum, seegars and tobacco, and even a loaf of bread. I had got out of the habit of bread so long away from a bakery that I had to recall how good it was before I'd think to eat it.

A close-ordered group of soldiers came quick-timing by our little camp—we'd no fire and were careful of noise—and a half hour later there was a spatter of rifle shots and not long after that the soldiers come trudging back, skylarking and telling jokes, so no one had shot back.

There was maybe a hundred of them, and they wasn't much past us when there was a rip of rifle and shotgun fire and the crump of grenades, and the long orange and blue muzzle flashes cut up the night.

"Go with God, Kelly," said El Tigre #5, laying a gun butt up alongside my skull, the thin part. I reeled from the pain and passed out and I'd no idea how long I was there before I woke, bleeding from the head wound, and stiff from the funny way I laid fallen.

I groaned and sat up and looked around and saw several pairs of soldier legs.

"Get up!" one of them yelled, kicking me. I grabbed his foot and separated his damned ankle for him. The others started in for me but I bellered my name and rank and managed to stand up. One soldier reached for my guns, I brushed him off like you would a fly.

"Get me to Taft," I says. "Any a you shitheads get cute I'll see you patrolling the back of this stinking jungle all alone and painted white so they can't miss you."

They was just privates and so they walked me up the road—I set the pace—until they come to a captain who looked at me a moment and said he recognized me from a Wild West Show playbill of Cody's.

"But you weren't there, as I remember," said the captain.

"Bill time to time would do that to try to shame me into joining, him having advertised it, but I told him to go to hell."

They'd taken seventy casualties in about as many seconds, four big patrols coming in at once, and the *guerrilleros* had waited till their fire could plow through soldiers three and four deep. Many wounds of four men were from one bullet, and then the soldiers of Aguinaldo, of the Philippines, melted back into the night and were gone. The place where the fire had come from was searched, but there wasn't a single Filipino body.

The captain, a 'Point man, was slamming his fist into his palm, seething with fury over how badly they had been cut up without a single enemy corpse to show for it. They took roll and counted bodies and came up one short, so back into the black they went, in case it was a wounded man. Someone stumbled over the body, the count was full, and the survivors carried the wounded with them, some on stretchers, as they retreated, because that is what it was.

I walked with Captain Martin, whose jaw muscles looked like they might burst out the skin over them. He'd politely asked me to empty my sidearms—he could have put me under close arrest, so I was only too happy to oblige.

"The damned thing about it is we don't even belong here," he snarled. "If Washington is worried about the Krauts and the Japs, then garrison Manila because this is one of two places they can land troops, and let the Filipinos do the rest. Christ. Forty dead for nothing at all."

He kept on like that—God knows he couldn't have talked that way in front of the men. Sickening, that almost none of this has to happen, not anywhere. Sure, the Igorotes would have to be told piracy and banditry were things of the past, but slaughtering four hundred women and children was not going to bring them round to Bible camp, let me tell you.

I half heard him. I was seeing Lucretia, hoping she was well and waiting, hoping that we could make it to California, by God I'd shoot the first interloper who threatened the dull calm of my little spread. The second one, too.

We had a ways to go to Manila, and I was full of the itch to get there. Leaving her bothered me. I thought of Eats-Men-Whole, so long ago, more than thirty years. I still flinched at that wound.

The captain was the best of American professional soldiers—a humane man, who would not obey illegal orders (shooting noncombatants is illegal, and in poor taste, too) and who was most concerned with the plight of his men. He had a wry humor that I liked, and he didn't have to raise his voice to give orders.

About dawn we could see Manila some miles off, and picked up the pace a little.

I told Captain Martin that my wife was in the hospital, it was too early to talk to Taft, and after I saw her I would hotfoot it to Malacañang Palace.

"Your word, sir?" he said.

"My word," I said.

"Then there will be no problem," he said, holding out his hand. I shook it warmly, and loped off, my hunger to see Lucy lengthened my stride. I had a sick feeling that she had died and I ran faster till I gave out and wheezed along till my heart quit galloping.

She wasn't there. The doctor on duty said she had left me a note.

"Am home and waiting, L" it said. I had to ask the doctor for the address, and hire a cab, but when I got there she had heard the horseshoes on the cobbles and was standing in a gown on the balcony, with the wind plastering the silk close to her lovely body.

"Kelly," she said, "you need a long bath. I'll scrub your back."

I took the stairs three at a time and hit a rug on the top landing and went flat on my ass and slid to the feet of my love.

18

For three days we hardly stirred from the bed, and slept fitfully, and et there, and let the world go hang. I had nothing of importance to say to Taft or General Merritt—at least they wouldn't think so.

Arrest soldiers for the murder of Igorotes? Preposterous. Bad for morale. They're brown, and you don't try white men for murdering brown ones.

I told Lucretia all about my years scouting and how I was only hip-deep and to-the-elbow stained with several thousands worth of blood.

Lucy run her finger over one or another of my scars and come on the bump where the Cheyenne arrowhead had lived for twenty-five years, and I told her about the fight in the Sand Hills. The arrow had been shot at me by Crazy Horse, and it ain't every feller can point to a gen-u-wine Crazy Horse arrowhead in the hide of his back.

Our lovemaking took a long time each time and we rocked like a boat in the chop.

Finally I sent a letter to Taft describing my sojourn with the Igorotes and recommending that they be left alone, as when they got modern weapons they'd whip just about anybody. I told of the families of the warriors buried alive and said warriors who have lost their families is the most dangerous of all.

I didn't hear from Taft for a long time—hoped that maybe he had forgotten me—but it seemed the guard had tossed the Filipino messenger into a dungeon and forgot him for five days, and my letter, too.

Taft had his note delivered by soldier and the note summoned me and ordered me to be damned quick about it.

"I'd just as lief not go," I said, looking at the friendly scrawl, "but Bill's one of them affable men who always seems to get his way, affably. He has a chortle of iron."

Lucretia laughed—one of her best qualities was she laughed at my jokes—and I bathed and dressed in cool tropical linens and sandals. I'd always hated the heat but found like cold it was bearable if you were dressed for it.

There hadn't been any rumor of the *guerrilleros,* so I just supposed that they was waiting on some big piece of nefariousness, one that would kill a lot of Yankees and embarrass the ones who survived.

Malacañang was ringed with gun positions and sandbagged revetments and there was five hundred soldiers on duty around the clock, protecting Taft and his lackeys from their just desserts. There must have been fifty freighters in the harbor being loaded down with sugar and rare woods. The Sugar Trust had come in and drove sugar prices down so far the plantation workers had to harvest the cane to *starve.*

I waited out front with a small band of soldiers, bayonets fixed, of course, while them as was inside figured on whether or not I had a landmine up my ass and was just a clever ploy by Aguinaldo to get at fat old Bill Taft.

Finally a couple guards patted me all over to search for hidden broadswords and boar spears and satisfied that my hands was too small to go round Bill's neck they led me into the palace and past yet more soldiers in sandbagged rifle pits and finally to the office of the Great Expanse His Own Self Yes Sir.

"Luther, you rascal," said Taft, coming round the desk and beaming at me like some long-lost brother. "How did you fare on your journey?"

"I got shot at a lot and almost skinned alive," I says. "And I am too damn old for this business."

"But no permanent scars! Come, have a drink." He waddled to the sideboard and began tucking ice cubes in a glass.

"The scars is permanent, Bill," I says, "they're just where you can't see them."

I told him of the Igorotes and Aguinaldo and that I'd seen some bad country to fight a war in but this was the worst on the damn earth and the Filipinos would win anyway—it was *their* country and they knew the jungle very well.

"MacArthur dealt them some very smart defeats," says Taft. "Drove them right back on their line of march."

"Aguinaldo made the mistake of fighting the U.S. Army like he was another U.S. Army. He won't do that again. He'll gnaw and peck and set off bombs in the city and pick off unwary soldiers looking for a whorehouse with a skinful of rum. He won't line his men up and charge again. He'll bleed us to death."

"Kelly," says Bill, his eyes flat and gray, "we are here to stay. However many Filipinos killed it requires to make that point, we will manage. You might comfort yourself with this: the Germans and the Japanese would only be worse. I don't have to explain Manifest Destiny to you, do I? That is a euphemism. The strong nations of the world feed upon the weak. It is a natural law. If not us in the Philippines, then it is another. Don't bore me with trifles. The Igorotes can be crushed, Aguinaldo killed or captured, El Tigre hung, a common murderer. Fifty years hence no one will remember, not even the grandchildren of the slain."

I looked at Bill, who apologized for the speech.

"I ain't going back out there," I said. "I am fifty. I won't do this anymore. I got Lucretia, I want to go raise turnips."

Taft shrugged and said it was hardly up to him.

True enough. Don't let the smile blind you, Teddy was as ruthless a character as ever was hatched.

I found my own way out and walked toward Lucretia's house, some miles away, and I come upon a street bazaar and bought some cheap jewelry from India, full of jangles, and a big armload of flowers.

I come close on to her house and she was out on the balcony smiling down at me.

"Hey, sailor," she said, "want to come on up?" Jorge, the gatekeeper, let me in. There was so much theft and thuggery in Manila that the well-to-do had watchmen—armed, of course—and huge iron fences topped with razor-sharp spikes and barbed wire. Soldiers lost in the poorer quarters were murdered for their shoes. For poor folk America had nothing to match this.

Trailing blossoms, I went up the outside staircase and into the bedroom and Lucretia got a batch of vases and filled them and the scent was so sweet in the room it near on to made you light-headed.

"I've told them I have had enough," I said. "I've told them that before, but I fair enough mean it this time."

Lucretia nodded, and said the sooner the better.

"You want to pack this and send it?" I said. "I got a house and all."

"No," said Lucretia. "Let's just go with a couple of suitcases and start over. All this is is money, and I don't care about money."

I sent Jorge out to the steamship offices and he found us passage on the *Warnecke* to San Francisco, leaving in two days time with the high tide at nine in the evening. We should be on board by five. I sent Jorge back with the money and me and Lucretia lolled around the bed in the flower perfume and had idiotic conversations meant nothing even to us but we didn't care.

That evening we packed the few things that Lucretia valued—two paintings, some letters in a pigskin lettercase, and a few photographs of her family.

I'm always itchy to get going anyway, and my worries about being frogmarched out to the war again was real enough. Taft was shrewd enough to know I would be more dangerous than helpful out there, but I wasn't so sure about him taking on Teddy. He was only the Vice President, to be sure, but McKinley had "no more backbone than a chocolate eclair" to quote Tom Reed, and I was fair sure McKinley did the ornamental appearances and Teethadore did the imperial duties.

Taft invited us to supper and we went and had a fine time with the man. He was a wonderful teller of stories and most of them on himself, and General MacArthur's son Arthur was a guest, too—he was a lieutenant on the battleship *Texas,* which had come to wave its huge useless guns at the *guerrilleros.*

We were pretty drunken and merry and as we got out the front gate headed home I got one of them prickles on my neck said we was watched, so I had the horsecab take us to the biggest hotel in the city and I rented three rooms under my name and a fourth under "Holtz" Krupp S. A. and when we finally slept I did so with a gun under the pillow, and I kept snapping awake all the night but it was just the unfamiliar city sounds.

We had a breakfast on the hotel terrace and I had sent a feller off with a note for the luggage, to take down to the ship.

We were still sitting there drinking champagne when the feller who'd gone after the luggage come on back jabbering about murder and fire.

I dropped Lucretia off at Malacañang Palace, leaning on my budding friendship with Taft, and much over her loud protests which I didn't listen to even when they got ripe about my parentage.

The Samses' house was blackened and there was seven corpses laid out on the sidewalk waiting on the cart from the morgue. The police were mystified and so was I, until I come on a sword-tip in a hard to see place on the gray marble flags. It was Japanese; I could see the laminations made when they fold the sword blank over and over and over, sometimes as much as a thousand times.

I shrugged and slipped the piece in my pocket. I'd no idea why the Japs were after me, or if it was someone unlikely, like maybe the Swiss leaving sword shards to foul the scent. I'd soon have us aboard the *Warnecke*—an honest tramp steamer with six staterooms—and I figured I could keep us alive till we cleared the harbor and after that it was up to the ship's captain. The pigskin letter case and the paintings had survived—the fire was just furnishings, since the house was stone and stucco—and I carried them down and back to Malacañang where my lady love had been working on her pronunciations of ball-jointed cusswords. She run them by me and I grinned and she came close and said she was worried and if anything happened she wanted it to happen to both of us.

Taft and Captain Martin asked me for my opinion on both the Igorotes and the *guerrilleros* and I told them that my opinion was that we ought to leave, they didn't want us here and the country was theirs. Having wasted my breath on that I said that the only way to fight them was like they was fighting us.

"We plan to move the inhabitants of the plain into fortified villages," said Taft. "This will give them security against the bandits."

Faced with such imbecility I smiled and wished them luck.

Lucretia and me went down to the dockage with four soldiers that Taft insisted on sending—I always do like being conspicuous—and I hurried Lucretia up the gangplank and into the cabin—the few things from her house were in it already, and then I ran down the captain, one l'Heureux, a Cajun, who turned out, not surprisingly, to be a cousin of Deleage. Only one other cabin was rented, by a pair of missionary ladies whose husbands had been turned into decorations by the Igorotes. The ladies seemed to be *very* happy.

Lucretia shivered when I described the skulls and whatnots up in the mountains. "Awful people," she said.

"I like 'em," I said. "They got a nice, conservative foreign policy and they want to be left alone to pursue the good life. They ain't never bothered by salesmen twice and they avoid the strain and uproar of importing a fresh religion and thus causing arguments. Fat grubs on every palm leaf, I say, and no foreign entanglements."

I had a couple Colts and a shotgun, and I had agreed to turn them in to the captain as soon as the gangway was up and the tugs was hauling us round. He promised a thorough ship's inspection as soon as we were under way.

When the tugs tautened the cables I took the guns to the captain who locked them away and went back to fetch Lucretia and we watched the Manila lights recede. The ship's main engines were pounding though the screws wasn't engaged yet and as soon as we was out in the ship's channel the tugs slipped the cables and the ship—a good-sized freighter full of sugar, teak, green cow hides, and wickerwork—was under her own power, loaded down, and outward bound.

"Luther Sage Kelly, Turnip Herder," I said to the sea breeze.

"You can't mean you grow turnips on your ranch?" said Lucretia.

"Great big turnips," I says. "They make no noise, they don't shit, and as they can't walk you don't have to brand them."

Lucretia's laugh was a booming thing, a lady laugh you could hear good at a thousand paces. She threw her head back and roared. I wanted her suddenly, and grabbed her hand and we ran down the deck to the cabin.

So it went like that for a couple days, the ship's crew would go past us stony-faced and then if you looked at their backs they was shaking with collared mirth.

I was out on the deck early one morning, I'd woke up bothered without knowing what and when the dawn came it was blood red to the east, where we were going. The old sailor's rhyme run through my mind, and I shrugged it off, and then saw the captain scowling at it, too, and I began to worry. The seas were not big, but they had a peculiar brown-green tint to them and the tops of the waves looked oily. An albatross scudded west over us. I waved to the captain and he motioned for me to come up on the bridge.

"A bad one ahead," he said. "I don't know whether to cut north or south."

"How 'bout turn round and steam flank speed for Manila?" I says, only about half jesting.

"It would catch us, and bad as they are with the bows into them, it is worse a thousand times to be caught by a following sea. The wind strips paint off."

Typhoons could blow two hundred miles an hour, I'd heard.

The entire crew was turned to, securing the hatch covers and storing anything loose in the lockers and checking on the water kegs in the lifeboats. The storm was a ways off but when it got here there wouldn't be any time for tidying things up.

I went to the cabin and found Lucy still asleep, her hand moved over to where I had been laying.

"Where you been?" she mumbled.

I sat on the bed and petted her.

"A typhoon ahead. I was talking to the captain."

She yawned and stretched and sat up, the back of her hand to her mouth and the coverlet fell away from her breasts.

"Anything to do?" she said. "About the storm?"

"Nope. Crew's got it."

"Well, come back to bed," she said, grabbing at my flies.

We had finished and were lying half asleep when the first of the winds got to us, and there was a low hum in the rigging and then the ship dipped into a swell and the tone changed. We listened to the soft deep hum, like an organ note almost too low to hear at all.

When the storm hit it happened in a flash second, and the

rigging screamed and there was a sound of metal ringing—I thought a bucket left out had been battered along the deck. Rain so thick the damn boat could about float in it came, too, driven by the high winds and with such force that it seeped in through the seals of the portholes and the door.

"We're stuck here!" I hollered. Lucretia grinned at me and came at me with her whole body, laughing while she did but I couldn't hear a damned thing but the wind and the water. The storm was so loud we couldn't have heard a damned cannon if it went off between us. There was enough water on the floor now to slosh a bit—maybe half an inch.

Twice I staggered to the portholes to look out—no clear idea how in the hell I would do anything about what I saw—the door opened out and the wind wasn't putting more than two or three tons of pressure on it.

Lucretia thought it was wonderful fun. She laughed and whooped—I could tell which by the shape of her mouth—and she pointed to various belongings flying back and forth across the cabin.

I thought sort of idle-like that there was nothing at all to do—if the ship went down, we went with it and no argument. Death could be very close, and our dice was rolling on the wind.

Around midnight the wind died and we come into the eye of the storm. I got up and went out and looked at the sea, there was rafts of seabirds on the black water, silent, waiting.

Captain l'Heureux was trimming his fingernails with a bosun's knife. He was rumpled and tired-looking, but the bridge was neat and he had a thick sandwich to hand.

"Mr. Kelly," he said, "there is no extra charge for the excitement. Everything is fine below and we shall have another twelve hours of an interesting nature. But we shall be fine. The galley is closed, we cannot have a fire, but the steward will be happy to bring you sandwiches."

He couldn't have made it plainer if he had pointed, so I left and went back along the deck and found an unpadlocked locker full of kapok life preservers. I took four, and underneath there was a "Clemm's Patent India-rubber Boat" and so I took that, too. Something was amiss and I warn't being told about it. I used an air-cylinder to blow up the boat, it was small but plenty big enough for two, and it had a cover-fly to keep out the waves. I put the life vests in it and then I lashed it carefully to the inside rail, so I could cut it free with one swipe of the knife if the occasion demanded.

Lucretia got dressed and come out with me. I pointed far off to the east and said that we'd hit the storm there and this time the winds would be coming from the opposite direction.

"What's wrong with this ship, Kelly?" said Lucretia.

"I don't know," I said. "Maybe nothing, but I like havin' my bets hedged."

The steward brought the sandwiches and a couple bottles of Saratoga Springs mineral water.

"Ain't been there in forty years," I said, shaking my head.

"Where?"

"Saratoga Springs. I was raised up near there."

"In *New York*? Hell of a place to raise a scout."

So she pestered me about my childhood and when I told her the true story of how I come to join the Union Army I thought she'd bust a gut laughing, and then I told her about Spotted Tail and Washakie and Jim Bridger and all. I gassed on so long the storm hit before we got everything nailed down.

Suddenly there was a horrendous shuddering jar, plates screeching even above the storm. It could only be one thing: we'd run smack into another ship adrift in the storm.

"Come on, come on!" I yelled, dragging her to the door. The water was coming over by the ton and I got a glimpse of a red-lead hull—we had hit a capsized vessel.

For a fraction of a second there was a lull in the wind, and I slashed the raft free and dragged it and Lucretia to the lee and I threw the raft over and when the seas fetched up again I shoved her off the rail into the raft and went after. I got the cover fastened and then I reached out for Lucy to hold her.

She wasn't there. I felt and felt but she was gone.

19

I just kept screaming and hollering and the storm paid no mind. I kept running what the last things I'd done before I thought I put her in the raft was, I thought on it till I thought I'd go mad. I raged and screamed and there was no help.

The storm raised hell all around me, and I hardly noticed, since I was passing my time by going insane. The wind died down and the sea got a little calmer, still fifty-footers but at least the top halves wasn't being cut off and carried by the wind.

In time I opened the cover up and breathed real air and not the foul rubber-scented muck I had been torturing my lungs with for hours. The stars was out, and I thought we were coming on the morning. The eastern sky was soft and gentle, and it made me weep to see it. I tormented myself with all the whys and ifs I could think on. What the hell, it passed the time.

I was about half delirious and I looked round the little boat for water—wasn't any, which I thought was fine as I planned to die as soon as possible. I began stropping my knife. A couple quick slices deep across the wrists and neck and I'd be gone like White Bear, the great Kiowa, how he escaped the prison. And over and over I kept saying to myself that I screwed it off. What had gone wrong?

No answer to that. There was a big puddle of rainwater, at least mostly, and I drank it warm from the rubbered cloth. It tasted like I was gnawing old galoshes, but water was water. It set me up a little, and I commenced into wondering where in the hell I was. The *Warnecke* had gone down, sure enough.

Time to time I would see a piece of dunnage or a scantling or a sail, eerily spreading under the water, but nothing on my close and narrow horizon looked like land or ship.

The seas died as the day grew, and it got hot enough so I put on a shirt. My lips were chapped and the skin between my fingers was splitting. It hurt like hell to put my hands into seawater. There were no medical supplies at all. If I could have coaxed a bird down I could have killed it and made the fat do for dressing.

The first day went past, sun glare on the water burning my eyes to where they felt like they was covered in hot sand. I knew it would just get worse until I went overboard to swim down to my love who would call me to the depths.

It got cold in the night, and the wind freshened and several flying fish fell in the boat. They was oily and greasy to chew but I et 'em. I had begun to have thoughts upon living, what will always perk me up is thinking on the list of folks I am going to shoot before I go down in a hail of lawman gunfire. Teethadore, John D. Rockefeller, J. Pierpont Morgan—it keeps a man alive to have a purpose and promises unkept.

There was enough rain for me to drink all I could hold.

The dawn was calm.

I saw a black speck on a wavetop. It was another raft. There was a flash of golden hair, cut short. It was Lucretia. Not quite believing my eyes, I commenced hollering and paddling with one of the ridiculous paddles the boat used for oars.

Lucretia turned and saw me and we did the same thing, jumped up and down in a leaking rubber raft. I damn near ruptured myself when I come down.

When she was close enough I leaped across with a line and pulled my raft to hers and lashed them together. We just kept looking at each other and laughing and then crying.

There had been two rafts bobbing in the storm and I had put her in the one and then got in the other. Things had been some confused and it was easy to see how it was done. Awfully easy. I still don't understand it.

She had two bottles of mineral water and a bottle of brandy so we toasted our luck and though both of us was covered with saltwater sores and our mouths was cracked all round we were mighty damned glad to be one with another. We might starve or die of thirst or drown but it wasn't much, not to worry, we'd go out together.

From the top of a wave I saw a freighter, and there was a flare gun and two shells in a pocket in the rubber boat. I fired off a flare and a moment later I saw one come up off the freighter, out of sight, but they'd seen us.

The ship hove to and come round and there was a boat down the davits in no time and a crew pulling like hell for us, the bosun calling out the pace. They hauled us in and rowed us back and we were going up the Jacob's ladder when a familiar voice come to my ears.

"Ya look at this, Butch, why we are always the ones save him from the pay of his own mistakes like the fools we are. All he did was manage to give us a goddamned yacht . . ."

"She gave us the yacht," says Butch.

"Well, here they are again."

"Is the bridal suite empty?"

"I moved out the sheep, yup, yessirree. The cut flowers and Spanish Fly will take some doing but we will manage."

Lucretia and I come up to the deck, much torn and worse for wear, and there was Butch and Sundance all duded up like they was on the way to the whorehouse.

There was an unholy stink of cow everywhere, billows of it come up from below.

Lucretia was laughing and her lips were bleeding and Butch told Sundance to shut off and let's get the lady taken care of. We were led forward to the main cabin, where there was a hot bath for Lucy and clean seaman's dungarees and shirts and a Filipino steward who smiled and said there would be food brought up in a moment.

Lucretia bathed for a long time and I got in after her and we put on the clean clothing which felt like silk since it wasn't all crusted with salt.

"That's genuine Kansas City tailoring," said Sundance through the porthole.

"All the best derelicts are wearing it," said Butch.

"Come eat now, we have raw fish and seawater!"

We caught the steward as he was wheeling a cart for us out the door and he wheeled it back in and we was set down and served about forty courses of Chinese food and lots of pale Philippine beer and we felt the much better for eating. Every minute a new pulse of life would shoot through me.

The steward brought cognac and when we all had a glass he poured one himself and sat down. A nice, democratic ship. I sort of wondered how these two crazy sonsofbitches had come into possession of a cattle freighter.

"They want to know why we're here, Sundance," said Butch. "And no doubt some explanation of the . . . . . . accident . . . . . . with the yacht is in order. I believe it was hers."

"Of course," said Sundance. "My college years are bright in my memory . . . . . . but my mathematics was a little rusty."

"Rusty," said Butch, pointing to Sundance's head. "I could hear the screek and scrawk as he thought on his math."

"So we were several days on a course when we came across a freighter standing still upon the waters, and a boat was loaded and the captain himself came over and asked us where we were headed."

"Pleasant man," said Butch.

"We said Santiago, Chile," said Sundance. "And he turned off very rude. He said that they were not in the fucking Aleutians."

"Neither of us knew where the Aleutians was," said Butch. "But the good captain was kind enough to point out that Santiago was not in them."

"In who?" said Sundance.

"Copernicus here almost got us froze to death."

"So then this captain asked us whose yacht it was we was going to the North Pole in."

"We said Lucretia . . . . . . Lucretia . . . . . . Lucretia . . . . . . but we could not for the life of us remember your last name," said Butch. "And we poured our hearts out to him."

"We told him our names."

"He'd heard of us."

"He turned pale."

"And the cows started bellering in the holds and we looked at each other and . . ." Butch said, "I said when we get to Santiago what are we going to do by way of professional practice? Be yacht brokers?"

"So I said, 'No, by God! We'll be PIRATES!' " said Sundance. "I have always longed to climb over a taffrail with a cutlass between my teeth, or I did till I found out how goddamned heavy a cutlass *is.*"

"So," said Butch, "we told the captain that we were new at the pirate's trade, but we'd rustled a lot of cattle, so this was by way of informing him his yacht was waiting for him, and any who wished to join him."

"Two did."

"The rest have thrown in with us. We are bound for Santiago where we will sell the ship and cows, and go over the Andes to Argentina where we will go back to robbing banks and trains," Butch said. "If they have trains."

"The whole crew is coming with you?" I said.

"Yes," said the steward, "it is a great opportunity."

Lucretia had her face in her hands and she was laughing so hard tears was running out between her fingers.

"Butch," said Sundance, "do they have money in Argentina? I'd feel foolish if I walked into a bank and told them give me the money or I shoot and they didn't know what money *was.*"

"There wouldn't be banks if they didn't have money," said Butch.

"Well," said Sundance, "I'll worry till we get to Argentina and I see a bank and I steal money from it."

"How did you ride out the storm?" I said.

"We prayed," said Butch.

"Threw out a sea anchor and prayed a lot," said the steward.

"I hope your yacht didn't sink," said Sundance to Lucretia, afloat in her puddle of tears.

"No matter," said Lucy. "It was all worth it."

"We're bushed," I said, lifting Lucretia up. "See you tomorrow."

"Need anything?" said Butch.

"Sleep," I said.

And we slept like the dead, straight on through for fourteen hours, and when I got up Lucretia was still out cold. I kissed her shoulder and I went out on the deck, unsteady on my feet.

The seas were mild and the day bright. I felt strong again, and marveled at my luck. I really had thought that Lucretia had gone in and drowned.

Who the hell had pumped up the other boat?

It was warm and brisk, and I took off my shirt and tossed it in the cabin, and saw my lady yawning, and stretching, so she would soon be up.

There was measured gunfire off the stern, and I wandered that way, to find Sundance practicing by shooting the sugar cubes that the steward was throwing out with a slingshot. I watched for a bit—it's boring to see someone perfect do the same damn thing over and over again.

We et solid sea fare for lunch—I could see how a person would get damned tired of canned vegetables on a haul across the Pacific. The crew ate in shifts, and I thought they all looked more or less like folk escaped from Devil's Island. A couple was so scarred up they might have escaped three or four times.

Lucretia and me walked around the deck—for some reason my seasickness had forgot to take hold this one time. We didn't have too much to say. I stopped to look at a big frigate bird cutting close to the freighter.

"What will happen to them?" said Lucretia. "Those sweet, funny madmen?"

"Shot down or hung," I said. "And they know it."

"Did you ever rob a bank?" she said.

"Once," I said.

"A train?"

"Twice."

"Why so few times."

"I just didn't care for it."

Well, it was true, damn it, I did not care for all the fuss, the women screaming, the clerks soiling themselves, and then to ride like hell far enough fast enough so that the outraged citizens whose money you had did not come string you up or fill you full of buckshot.

"I always wanted to be a cowboy," said Lucretia. "I once told my father I didn't *want* to be a lady. I wanted to rob stagecoaches."

"I hope your father spanked you," I says.

"No," said Lucretia, "he just laughed. He was a banker so he said he was grateful that I didn't want to rob banks."

"Where?"

"Baltimore."

"How did you . . ."

"I married Sams for his money, he needed a beautiful young wife, and I went to Manila and that was that. He . . . . . . uh . . . . . . likes Chinese boys."

Well, no goddamned wonder, I thought, you'd have to be a pederast to leave this woman for a moment.

"Are your parents . . . ?"

"Very much alive. Don't worry. My father's no fool, and my mother has a tongue like a longshoreman's. It will be one more scandal to our account. Hooray."

Butch stepped out of the bridge and come over waving a piece of paper.

"He did it!" said Butch. "He did it. I gotta go kiss him!"

We follered along, back to where Sundance was shooting.

"Sundance! It worked."

"Course it worked."

"What the hell are they doing?" said Lucretia.

"Sundance plotted our course south and I checked it and we are going south."

Lucretia started shaking from laughter.

"He's getting better!" said Butch. "You just got to be patient with these here Princetonians."

"Butch," I says, "do you have someone who *can* navigate up there on the bridge?"

"Yes," said Butch, "but don't tell Sundance, he's jealous of his knowledge. He keeps saying that in the country of the blind the one-eared goombaw turns left. I don't know what it may mean, I never got to go to college, but where the hell else but a place like Princeton would you hear such bullshit?"

And on he went.

The steward come to us and motioned for us to follow. He pointed at another freighter coming across our bows and he said it was an Australian ship bound for San Francisco and they would signal presently.

Flags was run up and presently the freighter hove to and we steamed for it. Lucretia and I didn't have anything to carry on board, for sure, my money belt had enough to bribe one captain if he weren't too greedy.

Butch and Sundance piped us down the ladder, joking as they always did. (I never saw Sundance again, he died in a shootout over cards somewheres on the Pampas. Butch stops by to see me every now and again; he had his face altered in Paris and he lives on "income from a good gold strike in South America," which is one way of putting it.)

The Aussies leered at Lucretia—they have funny habits about women—until I paid the captain a couple hundred in gold and said there would be more in San Francisco—if his crew of morons kept the hell out of our way.

Six days of bad food and a cramped and airless cabin later we lurched through the Golden Gate and it took the whole damned night for the tugs to berth us. We went down the gangway and off up the street to the hotel.

The clerk didn't even glance up and I took my key and the porters brought up the three trunks with my clothes and such in, and I sent a note out for a seamstress to come by and take Lucretia's measurements. She would have to be redudded top to bottom.

After the seamstress left and the boy from the bank brought money I thought that Lucretia and I could spend a week or so here and then maybe go off to the Colorado Rockies and laze around Glenwood Springs or something.

There was another knock at the door and a porter brought the customary silver tray piled high with all my mail. I'd have stuffed it in the fireplace if I had one.

Lucretia laughed, came over, put her arms around me, took a short look at the pile, and opened her eyes wide.

"Who the hell is Gussie?" she said.

"A professional dowser," I said. "Thought I'd have him site some wells on the ranch."

"Paulonia?"

"She's a refugee Baptist Russian keeps a borscht pot boiling, little place down near the docks, I eat there sometimes."

"I can fucking well imagine," said Lucretia. "You are a terrible liar."

"I'll swear off," I says. "You come along unexpected-like."

"Umm hmm."

She sorted through the mail, unerringly tossing the letters from old lady friends into a pile.

"You going to burn them?" I says.

She shook her head.

"What?"

"Write them thank-you notes," said Lucretia.

"Thanks for what?"

"They'll know."

I gave up and went to bed. I wasn't alone for long.

20

Lucretia and me had an idyllic couple of days in San Francisco—there was a pretty good earthquake at midnight on the second day and it broke a lot of glass and made the chandeliers swing and the peacocks in the park screamed all night.

The uneventful passage across the Pacific had rested us so much we was in the habit of sleeping about sixteen hours at a stretch, and what with being in my own home country that I have served so . . . . . . served, anyway I had an attack of the stupids and thought myself reasonably safe.

Lucretia and me was locked in unwedded and illegal bliss when there came a fearful pounding at the door and bellers of welcome and while Lucy dashed to the bathroom to hide and dress I got up naked as a jaybird and walked across the carpet to admit the President of the United States to my suite. Before he kicked the door in.

I flang the door open and Teddy, in soup-and-fish and a top hat yet, bounded in, scattering felicitations like shit in a hen coop.

"Marvelous work," said Teethadore. "Marvelous, marvelous."

"It is six goddamned o fucking clock in the morning, you walrus-brained bastard," I yelled. "Come back at noon."

"I ordered coffee and croissants," said Teethadore, "for we have much to discuss."

I slammed the door in the faces of a couple of Secret Service fellers, who were right in thinking I was dangerous to the President.

Teddy tossed his hat on the bed and unbuttoned his vest and stuck his hands in his pockets and grinned.

"Capital work you did, capital," said Teddy. His eye fell upon a feminine undergarment and his right eyebrow rose accordingly.

"I ah uh," said Teddy.

"Cousin Theodore," said Lucretia, coming out of the bathroom wearing a tightly wrapped blue velvet dressing gown, "You sound just about as obnoxiously bullheaded as when in the good old days you tyrannized us on the tennis court."

"Lucretia?" said Theodore. "Oh, my God. Lucretia, ah um . . ."

"Do you still pull the wings off flies and shoot cats with an air-gun? Put firecrackers in beehives? Steal those awful Ned Buntline books from drugstores?"

The President was shrinking before my eyes, and I had hopes that Lucy would keep it up till he disappeared entirely.

"Lucretia . . . . . . Lucretia?" Theodore piped, sounding forlorn.

"So get your fucking carcase out of here and send a letter or I'll tell all the world about . . ."

Theodore was making tracks in his spats. I threw his hat after him. The door closed and I shot the bolt.

"I stand in awe," I said. "I have been kicked around the entire globe by that ivory-bearing bastard and you run him out flat in four sentences."

"I'll tie that twerp in knots," Lucretia muttered. "Nerve of the man."

There was a soft knock at the door and a bellman wheeled in a tray with the coffee, croissants, and newspapers. I tipped him good and he went out.

We sat in the bed like the swells we was having a decent breakfast—the raw flying fish and rubber-tasting rainwater was still good and fresh in my mind.

My eye fell upon a news item.

> Entire ship filled with cattle and carrying a sizable shipment in gold went down, apparently with all hands, in the great typhoon three weeks ago . . .

"Maybe Butch and Sundance," I said, showing her the paper.

We wondered, and went on. Nothing to be done.

"Teethadore wants something," I said. "I don't know what. I had better find out."

"We'd better find out," said Lucretia.

"He's actually afraid of you," I said.

"I have a hell of a right cross," said Lucretia, "and no scruples."

Every time I looked at my darling she seemed more wonderful than formerly. I also made a note not to cross her.

There was a meek knock at the door and when I opened it a Secret Service feller handed me a letter from Theodore, in his spiky manly masculine script.

"Critical need for your thoughts on situation South Africa and Philippines," said the note.

"Critical my corns," I snarled. "Leave them all alone."

"His trouble was always that he enjoyed *doing* things," said Lucretia. "He never was much good at them and he never has believed that the bad consequences are his fault."

I nodded. Theodore had always seemed to me to be about age six.

"He can toss me in prison and have me hanged," I said.

"Not now he can't," said Lucretia. "Let's just go up to your ranch and I'll take care of Cousin Theodore."

"It's frying hot now," I said. "Let's go up to Yosemite and Hetch Hetchy. As soon as the fall rains come, we can go on to Chico."

So we packed and caught a train that would take us to another narrow-gauge train and we rode in comfort up to the big lodge and rented a room and bath with a balcony.

The lodge had horses for the guests, and we took two and went through Hetch Hetchy—it's a prettier valley than Yosemite, and we et a lot of trout and huckleberries.

We was lying in bed one morning and Lucretia propped herself up on an elbow and says, "We need to go to Washington and Baltimore."

"WHAT?" I said. My eyelids had flown so far back in my head I wasn't sure they'd come out again.

"We can settle all the petty matters there and then leave for California when it is cool and nice to be there."

Well, it made sense, for damned sure. Lucretia felt that given her husband's tastes she could get a quiet annulment and if I very docilely writ out reports for Teethadore he would not consider me so much of a challenge.

God knows I longed for Teethadore's contempt like Parsifal did the goddamned Grail.

So back down we went and picked up our various duds and bought trunks and took the train the long six-day trip, and even though we had a Pullman suite it was wearing.

We stayed in Washington a couple days and then Lucretia took a train for Baltimore. Waving goodbye to her was actually painful, my chest hurt.

I sent a message to Teethadore and another came back fast as a ball caroms off brick. Teddy had arranged and furnished an office for me on the backside of the Department of War building, and there was prominent maps of South Africa and the Philippines up on the walls and boxes of little toy soldiers on pins should I care to reduce war to a kid's game, like Teethadore did. Like a child, he was unaware of the pain he caused. The chance for greatness was all.

I settled in and commenced writing out my reports on foolscap so TR would get the point. There wasn't much to 'em, in South Africa the British were making sure the Boers hated them for five hundred years.

The Philippines was another matter, and I pointed out that fighting a war of extermination, for that is what it would take to solve the Igorotes, to protect a sugar trust, and to open a gateway to the markets of China might cost no more than ten or whatever times the money that could be got back on it.

The first of September come and it was hot and muggy—the capital is built on a malarial swamp—and Lucretia come back from Bawlemohr with that funny accent they got there saying all was well and society was horrified and was there a decent restaurant in Washington?

I took her for some seafood at a small back-door kind of place had three tables and five stools, for the best crab cakes and grilled swordfish I ever et.

We was still walking when I heard the clear boom and Maine

accent of former Speaker of the House Ted Reed, who'd been so disgusted with our national policies of late he had retired and gone to the practice of law.

"Luther!" he cried, getting down from his cab and waving for us to wait while he settled his bill.

Tom was a giant, well over six feet, and heavy, with an enormous moon of a face and a bland and sleepy expression which ain't what he was at all. I'd seen him in debate, slitting up the opposition into strands.

"Our national life seems to have attained the moral fervor of a yellow-backed novel," he said. "And excuse me, ma'am," and he bowed to Lucretia, who smiled at him.

"You have the tragic news?" he went on. "As soon as the inconvenient guerrilla war in the Philippines passes on I suppose we shall invade Greenland and teach democracy to the musk oxen."

"I think," I said, "we could just look at a map of what ain't taken and quit holding our breath, we'll own it a day after the President finds out where it is. Whatever it is."

I suggested coffee and perhaps even something stronger, and we repaired to the escorted-ladies section of our hotel's saloon. Tom was charming Lucretia out of her bustle, as I went to piss. I figured that if they was gone when I got back I'd have to shrug and say "good luck." Tom on full charm was formidable. His mind was the best one I knew, and his speech seemed struck from Maine granite, like sparks off a flint.

Tom was an orator and if he had only Lucretia for audience, why he would call forth his uttermost powers to charm her. I was contemplating setting him on fire but I liked him too well.

"McKinley had but one talent," said Tom. "He knew uncannily when it was the right moment to nail his colors to the fence. Theodore, while a pleasant and ebullient youth, confuses foreign policy with lacrosse. We shall shortly buy ten million Malays, unpicked, and no one knows what it will cost to pick them."

"This man is your friend?" said Lucretia, showing her pearly white teeth. "I've met only the bank robbers."

"Worthy occupations," Tom rumbled. "I am at the moment ashamed of my most recent one. The country has enjoyed twelve decades of peaceful illusion, we shall now either be worse bastards than the Europeans or be eaten by them."

From that man, a cry of pain.

We stayed very late, talking a little but mostly listening to Tom, who, unsoiled by office, still missed listeners straining to catch his every flourish.

We walked outside together and I hailed a cab and asked Tom if he would like to join us. He said no, and he waved and walked away, his cane tapping the cobbles. I supposed he would walk most of the night and end up either on a bridge looking down to the filthy waters of the Potomac, or sitting by them. It's what I do when thinking is mortal painful.

Neither me nor Lucretia was tired, so we sat drinking tea until dawn, and then I pulled the shades and we went to sleep.

I was about dropped off when there was a cattle stampede went right under the window, pursued by howling Minneconjou Sioux. I sat up, holding my head.

"What in the name of Christ is going on out there," said Lucretia, behind a satin sleeping mask.

I'd gone to the window and throwed it open and looked down.

"Texas Longhorns being pursued by Injuns," I said. "And I know some of the Injuns."

"Kelly, you've been smoking that opium again," said Lucretia.

Bloodthirsty war yells and clattering iron-shod hooves and a flap of banners.

"Well?"

"Don River Cossacks."

"I ask the nice man a question, he tells me some damned lie," said Lucretia, going facedown.

Bellers, hollers and whip and pistol shots.

"A lot of cowboys," I says, "follered by Custer's Seventh Cavalry."

"I am going home to mother," said Lucretia, standing up. She was naked and she grabbed a shift from the bedpost.

"Elephants," I said, "and Bengal Lancers." The elephant brayed a couple times.

"In short, Buffalo Bill Cody's Authentic Wild West Show is in town." I shut the window.

Lucretia leaned on my shoulder. "I don't take anything back but I'll stay a couple of days," she said.

"Here come the gaddamned buffalo," I said, eyes widening. Them buffalo is not easy of herding. There was about twenty, including a huge old bull weighed better than a ton.

"I believe that last was a mistake," I said. "I say we don't go out until we have news that they are all penned up."

"MMMMMmmm," said Lucretia, dragging me back to the bed by the ear.

"You know, Kelly," she said, much later, "I know so little about you. Just the wonderful Buntline novels. What a jackass he made you into! Good stock to work from, give him that. And all the people you know who I want to meet."

"Most of the people I know you don't want to meet."

That wasn't entirely true, but when you consider Butch and Sundance was about the best-mannered of the lot, and you think on Liver-Eatin' Jack and Geronimo, who both had their good qualities, and there was far too many embarrassing details out there I'd as soon stayed hid.

"You know Buffalo Bill Cody," she said.

Oh, God.

"You know Annie Oakley."

"She's a very straight arrow and nice woman," I said. "Her husband's a bastard."

"Oh, how I read those Buntline novels when I was a little girl. Yellowstone Kelley! Why did he add an 'e' to your name?"

"So if I sued him he could claim the books was about the *other* Yellowstone Kelley," I says. "Ned's no fool. Then all them columns by the Hartford Rodent. I don't remember him, he looked like an underfed hamster."

"All true!"

"None of 'em."

"Thank God," said Lucretia.

"Actually, my friends are pretty good boys," I said.

"Your former ladies were an interesting lot," said Lucretia.

"You talk like they died."

"They lack the wit to stiffen. I'll provide it."

I was beginning to know what a land claim felt like. Stakes everywhere. No Trespassing signs. Gunfire.

There was a methodical tapping on the door panel.

I walked over and snarled, "YASS!"

An envelope was slipped under the door and the tapping went away. I was growing weary of all the nonstop mellerdrammer in this hotel and planned to register in another as "Launcelot Compote," and as I was airing them objections and criticisms pretty loud when there was a series of thuds, like a mule was kicking the door or something.

Lucretia pulled the covers up to her chin and I threw the door open and a mule backed into the room had a cowboy on it and the cowboy was a nigger and he was grinning, too, and I reached up and grabbed his big old hand and jerked him off the mule and whooped. One of my favorite people in all the world, Bill Pickett.

Lucretia was looking from me to the mule and Pickett and grinning like a dog found a fresh cowflop.

I hauled on my pants and shirt and boots and told Lucretia I'd find us better lodgings and send a note back. The management was coming down the hallway pretty smart and I'd just bet they had the coppers with them.

"I'll be going, now," says Pickett. "See you at the show," and he coaxes the trick mule forward and turns right and there was a sound of muley feet and a lot of boots and splintering doors and I sashayed out to count coup. Bill had rode the mule out the big window at the end of the hall. I went down to look, but they must have landed all right. The sidewalk twinkled with glass.

"We are in mortal danger," I says to Lucretia. "From my friends. What I guess is that the following news has made the rounds. 'Ol Luther's looking serious at that new piece he's got. We need to help him 'fore he hurts hisself.' "

"Piece," says Lucretia, her eyes looking very bright. She nodded.

"So what we need to do is register at a dozen of the best hotels in town."

"As Luther Kelly and 'Piece'?" says my darling.

"I misspoke there."

"They misspoke," said Lucretia. "If you'd said it you'd be dead."

I have had looser escapes from Apaches, with them on horses and me on foot.

"Only way that we're gonna get any peace . . ." I says, halting at the unfortunate reminder, "is do what I said."

"I don't want peace," said Lucretia. "I want war."

She dressed and we slunk out the back way just as the high yips of my approaching friends signaled the arrival of a herd of whatever at the front doors.

21

War raged in Washington between Lucretia Sams and about two hundred no-good out-of-work train robbers, horse thieves, and bunco artists, not to mention tinhorn gamblers and dice shavers.

My admiration for the lovely lady, who kept muttering "piece" under her breath whilst practicing elaborate skulduggeries grew. Admiration, hell, rank *fear.* There hadn't been a military mind like this since Alexander the Great croaked.

All of Buffalo Bill's employees was trying to find where we had holed up—with such fervor that several hotels hung banners out front swearing that Kelly was not registered there and would further be tossed into the street if he so much as walked into the lobby.

She had struck up an instant alliance with Tom Reed, whose boredom with the practice of law was, in his words, perfect.

We three were eating a hasty lunch from the shish-kebab stalls—too dangerous to perch on chairs for very long—and Lucretia wiped her pretty mouth and said, "What did you do in the Civil War."

"I," said Tom solemnly, "was a grocer on a gunboat. It was not strenuous and certainly not dangerous. I knew all the regulations and they did not. I had all my rights and most of theirs."

"What superb training for high office," said Lucretia. "I had wondered what got you to Congress."

"The Representative moved up to Senator and I was next," said Tom. "Virtue had nothing to do with it."

Lucretia put on her widow's black veil and she and Tom went off on some other nefarious errand. I was not told about it on the grounds that "if you should be captured and plied with strong drink you will become indiscreet . . ." as Tom put it.

I had found that a safe place to hide was in my office in the War building. I had had the cubbyhole such a short time that the guards didn't even know I'd arrived.

I knew that Teethadore would wish to have detailed reports on my travels in South Africa and the Philippines, and I scrawled page after page of material that was just a waste of ink.

At sundown we three met at Pratt's for supper. It seemed that the couple hundred friends I had in the Wild West Show sued for peace, begged for it, actually, as Lucretia and Tom had won all of the combats.

"No contest," said Tom. "If I were their attorney, I would advise them to die."

We had a simple supper and Reed joined me in a seegar. He drew in a long breath of Cuban leaf and smiled, happy with his lot.

"My dear," he said, "I haven't acted a complete ass in so *long.* Couldn't do it in Congress, they are too stupid to get the point. My, this was satisfying."

"More than welcome," said Lucretia.

"Speaking of asses," said Reed, "now that Theodore is President, I may tell you what he said to me a couple months ago. We were in Portsmouth Naval Yard, looking at the laid keels, and Teddy said to me, 'Tom, when I'm President I am going to paint our fleet white and send it round the world to call at every major port.'

" 'Theodore,' I said, 'why are you going to do that?'

" 'Paint them white or send them round the world?'

" 'You'll paint them white so that they look like your teeth,' I said. 'Why waste the public's coal on a world cruise for vanity.' "

"What'd he say to that?" I asked, when I'd quit bellering.

"Nothing. Ain't spoke to me since and doubt he ever will," says Tom Reed. "Likely better for the both of us."

Reed of Maine arose and bowed and wished us all good things.

"If you ever have pity for a poor, spavined, bored witless lawyer do call on him. For whatever." And he touched his cane to his homburg and walked away.

"I'd be very content if he were President instead," said Lucretia. I nodded.

"Then you never really know," I went on. "Nations have interests. They seek them fulfilled. They must be absolutely amoral to do it."

"Luther," said Lucretia, "I like you better when you're not so sad and hifalutin'."

I wanted to go for a long walk, now that the war with the Wild West Show was over.

We went slowly all around the town, which was somber for the death of one President and a little giddy over the new President, who would provide excitement, sure enough.

"I think we could safely go to California," I said. "It'll be a few weeks before Teethadore remembers he was sent by God to make my life miserable."

Even though it was September it was hot and wet in Washington. It would be hot in Chico, too, but dry and the fall rains would be along soon.

Lucretia said her annulment would be along no matter where she was.

So we walked back to the hotel and tossed things in trunks and had the hotel carriage take us to the station and by God there was a late train leaving in an hour. We had time to go to the oyster bar and eat a quart or two apiece, washing it down with French champagne. We were feeling no aches or regrets when the engine leaned into the weight and we began to roll.

I'd got us a suite with a sitting room and bedroom and bath—the tub had a furl on the rim just like a whaleboat has, only it was inside.

Going up the Piedmont we went into a thunderstorm, a hot one sending down huge bolts that would light up the land to the horizon and once I saw a flock of geese frozen in flight by the flash. The thunder was deep, sounding like it was under the earth, too. We opened the windows and leaned out and caught fresh rain with our faces.

When we got to Chicago the following evening we had to change trains and there was a couple of hours delay. As we wandered in the station we come on a whole mess of Swedes taking trains to the Dakotas. They were poor people, eating sausage and bread they had brought rather than pay vendors. They were talking with real wonder in their voices—I speak some of their lingo—of how big their holdings were going to be. Bigger than the local baron back home.

I hadn't heart to tell them that the local baron could likely raise on one acre all that they'd coax from a six-forty.

I told Lucretia and shook my head, I'd been seeing hopeful people headed west for coming on forty years. It was a good, raw land, but hard to tame, and harder on the women than the men.

We thought we'd walk outside but the rain of soot and ash was like to turn white cloth black in five minutes. We could smell the steel mills and stockyards. Chicago was booming and dirty and loud.

That night we rocked across Iowa and Nebraska part way, on to a spur to Denver—I never have been able to figure why that city got built where it is—and we stretched our legs on the platform a bit and went on in an hour toward Salt Lake City.

Making love while the train went round the mountain curves was a delight.

"A certain . . . . . . unexpected quality . . ." said Lucretia.

We proudly fucked all through the stop at the City of the Saints. I pulled the blinds down even in the sitting room and did not let them up until we had crossed the Great Salt Lake.

At Sacramento we got on a riverboat that chuffed on up the big brown river, and when we docked I hired a drayman to take us to my little place.

I had a small three bedroom house with a big front room and setting porch, about fine for a retired bachelor scoundrel but I thought it scanty for a lady of Lucretia's tastes and breeding.

"Wonderful," she said. "No place to put all that crap in."

Georgia, my housekeeper, dropped crockery in the kitchen. She was a wonderful lady and I went to see if she was upset, and as I helped her brush all the shards into a dustpan I made some mealymouthed attempt to soothe her.

"Luther," she said, "I dropped the pot in surprise. What does a pretty woman with that much horse sense see in *you?*"

"Georgia, the same has occurred to . . ."

"Some of them women you brought up here, Luther, they . . ."

We both looked over at Lucretia standing in the doorway, arms folded.

"Georgia," I said, "why don't I . . ."

"Luther," said Lucretia, "why don't you take a long ride, and when the horse drops of exhaustion walk on from there . . ."

"I was just . . ."

"Skating on thin ice. It cracked. Georgia and I must have tea and chat."

Holy flat flaming Jaysus Kayrist, I couldn't have been happier if Teethadore had been pounding on a pan in the corner.

I saddled a horse and rode off down toward the river. Chico was a hard place to get a drink in because the Widow Bidwell was a force in the Temperance movement and she owned damn near everything.

So I found a little landing with a couple skiffs tied to it and I went in the cantina and ordered a drink or eleven. I tried to recall all them women Georgia had been so scandalized by. The snake charmer from the medicine show had been unusual. The aerialist from Bailey's circus and her pet Giant Anteater had galled Georgia. Every time I thought I had remembered them all something would jog my memory. After a couple hours of Georgia's recitations (the ungrateful bitch) Lucretia would sigh and shake her head and track me down and kill me and go back to Bawlemohr with my parts in a jar of gin.

One other feller with a hunted look and clothes too good to be drinking in a place like this come in and sat far down at the end of the bar, drawing his lists in the air while I drawed mine. We never traded a word but was so blood close we'd have swore the other was not here if we was being prodded with shotguns.

I had a good skinful coming on dusk and rode back to the house, and I circled it a couple times. Lucretia and Georgia were laughing, and there was a sound of glass breaking every third breath or so.

I'd forgot the chest with the framed pictures of women who came here time to time, as a courtesy I would have their portrait on the bedside table.

I got off the horse and considered my options. I could hightail it to South America and join up with Butch and Sundance. I could plead with Teethadore to send me to Antarctica. I could change my name and live in a cave in the desert. I could go to Alaska and be a squawman and live on fish and memories. I could take this handy rope and find a bridge somewheres.

Thoughts of suicide emboldened me to where I went in my own house and asked if it was all right for me to be there.

"No more of this," says Lucretia, pointing at the barrel of busted photographs.

Georgia nodded, for moral support—and not for me—behind Lucretia.

"How would you explain this?" Lucretia asked.

"Book learning," I said.

"How so?"

"*Poor Richard's Almanac,*" I says.

"Huh?"

"Waste not, want not."

Lucretia let out a beller of pure rage and come at me with an arm cocked and I was so bumfoozled by it she did hit me with her right cross and stars hung 'fore my eyes and I fell to the floor with a thunk.

Lucretia was on her knees beside me in a flash, and she held my head in her hands and asked me if it was all right.

"Of course," I said.

"Good," says she, standing up and kicking me in the ribs hard enough to make one pop, " 'cause I don't want you to forget how your life is different now that I am here. I will not have you pawing down memory lane. Your formerly eclectic tastes . . ."

"Yah," said Georgia, "one them come and stayed a week once. Brought an electric mattress . . ."

I hauled myself up by a post, hand over hand. My rib hurt like hell.

"Yes," I said, "I understand. I have got it in my mind. A thousand apologies for not telegraphing ahead and having the photographs thrown out."

"You did," said Georgia, waving the yellow telegram. "But I was curious 'bout what you were bringing home *this* time . . . . . . and 'sides, if it hadn't worked out you'd a been complaining about the pictures being gone."

"Is this *all* of them?" Lucretia asked, pointing to the barrel like it smelled bad, too.

"I think Georgia would be better at answering that. I don't know where all exactly you extracted those pictures from."

"We got all of them 'cept the ones in the bedside table drawer," said Georgia.

"Jesus," roared my darling, stalking off. She came back with the drawer and one by one she examined the photos and then took a ball-peen hammer to them.

She tapped my chest with the ball-peen and looked at me real unblinking.

"I would not have been surprised to find a portrait of my *mother* in that lot. Now are we done? No choice high-graded collections of your goddamned whores enjoying Shetland ponies?"

"If they like Shetland ponies what do they need with me?" I said.

"Good thought," said Lucretia. "I'll remember that."

"I'm going to bed," said Georgia.

"Goodnight, Georgia," Lucretia and me chorused.

"I did telegraph ahead to have 'em thrown out," I whined.

"Georgia was right. It's all past. How's your rib?"

"I'll live," I said.

"I'll let you."

In the morning I had a black-and-blue mark exactly the size of the toe of her boot up high on the right side of my rib cage, and it stitched when I breathed or walked.

Lucretia and I had a late breakfast, and no discussion of the various outrages of the night before.

The valley was cooling and soon it would rain, them big Pacific rain clouds would come over the Coast Range and dump torrents of water on the parched grass and live oaks. I saddled horses for us—and she looked thoughtfully at the well-worn sidesaddle and then at me.

"I bought it like that," I says. "Jesus H. Kayrist, woman, I surrender, I give up, I'll burn the damn saddle."

"My mother told me men forget," she said. "And I always do listen to my mother."

"Does your mother know about us?"

"Ummhummmm."

"Well?"

"Ummmhummm."

That was the answer I would have to make do with.

We rode down to the Sacramento River to the west. There's miles of marshes and tule reeds, all full of every kind of duck in the thousands. They would be here all winter, and we could eat wild duck whenever we'd a mind. Geese, too.

There was an old coot living out in the tule reeds on a hummock island. He was a strange old man, and claimed he'd come with the Forty-Niners and he damn well might have.

We splashed through some shallow river-grass beds dense enough to take the weight of the horses, and I pointed out the nameless old coot's shack, made of cottonwood logs and canvas. He had only the one luxury, he raised wonderful Labrador duck dogs, big heavy dogs with coats black as the inside of your pocket, able to break through the tule beds faster than a wounded duck could swim.

Old Tules wasn't a hermit. He come out bright enough, smiling and waving and we sat outside his shack and drank good coffee, he spiked his with rum but we didn't have any, the ride home was a fair long one.

One of his bitches had whelped a few weeks before and she was leading eight small puppies like a mother duck leads her brood. Lucretia laughed at the little pups, they are about the cutest things in creation at six or seven weeks, and one little dog, a bitch, come over to her and commenced tugging on her dress, all the while growling in high piping tones that would have been about right for a bird.

I asked Old Tules how much and he said forty dollars—a damned steep price, but I paid it to him. We got ready to go and a couple horsemen was crossing the grassbeds out east.

Coming for their dogs, Old Tules said. One of the riders was a railroad magnate, the other a Senator.

"Raise good dogs," said Old Tules, "that I do, yes."

I put the little pup in my shirt. She squealed once and scratched my belly with her puppy claws, and then decided it was warm in here and she was tired, and she went to sleep and didn't wake up till we got near my house, when she announced her waking by pissing a lot more water than a dog that size could possibly hold. I cussed some in surprise, but of course the little thing didn't know no better.

We kept pretty much to ourselves that fall, not wanting to see any other folks. Other than the hooraw about the pictures we had no quarrels and certainly no fights, I did as I was told, which made things easy all the way round.

Lucy and me took the steamer down to Sacramento to buy her a couple shotguns and hunting clothes.

She was a crack shot, of course, having grown up near the Chesapeake, and she'd sit out in sleet half a day to bag enough canvasbacks to feed us for a week.

One day I realized with a start that I was happy. I wasn't used to it. I thought I'd get more familiar with it.

22

I had the newspapers delivered by mail, so they was four or five days old—longer if I didn't go into town to pick up the pile, mostly letters from old friends who needed money.

In early November I got a big sack—hadn't been into town in three weeks we'd been hunting so much—and the headlines on the Sacramento paper said Aguinaldo had escaped. I was well out of all of it and wished Emilio all success.

Sorting through the pile I come to a letter written on heavy vellum in a spiky script and I tore it open gleefully, hollering at Lucretia to come on in.

It was a letter from my old chum Mark Twain, now a white-haired and prophetic-looking cuss, he amounted to our national conscience.

I was looking for a funny letter but this warn't it. Twain and Tom Reed were enjoying each other's company—their barbs would be a true clash of Titans—and the disgusting events in the Philippines was causing Twain and Reed anguish.

They wanted to know if I would come back and give sworn testimony of the horrors I had seen.

Lucy pounced on a perfumed violet letter from Gussie, and she ripped it open, growling a little, dainty-like, deep down in her throat. The rest was the usual ruck from folk I barely knew, who assumed that I was rich and kindhearted. Fools.

Lucretia was jumping up and down on Gussie's letter, softening it up for the match. It was my profound hope that I would be an innocent bystander in all this. I should have taken a closer look at the sack when I had the chance.

She did not even feel the courtesy of letting me read my own mail was required in this instance. She set fire to the letter and put it in the little kitchen stove and did a sort of war dance around it and when there was just a flat paper of ash she bashed on it with the poker hard enough to bend the haft.

She halted, puffing a little from the exertion but looking most pleased with herself. I was scratching a refusal to Mark, or Sam as we called him, saying I would let this letter be my speech, I don't like speaking and won't do it. I didn't think addressing the Parnassians was in my line of work.

"You know Mark Twain?" said Lucretia, with about the same amazement she'd give if I said I knew Charlemagne. She'd seen the signature over my shoulder.

"Yup," I said.

She tugged the letter away from under my elbow and read it and said "My God! Luther, I am so proud of you! Speaking to the country's men of letters. And women, too."

The sure feeling that I was being completely misread washed over me. This coupled with a sinking sensation in the pit of my stomach, since it seemed I was going to be improved up to what she thought was snuff.

"And the wonderful Mr. Reed! What a fine, funny man!"

And the wonderful Mr. Kelly, the one with the collar around his neck, with the rhinestones turned *in.*

"I ain't doing it," I said, firm as I possibly could, pounding the table and raising my voice to whoop level. "I'll send them a deposition but I ain't doing it!"

"Fine," sniffed Lucretia. She went outside to flee the stink of spinelessness and mopery.

An envelope caught my eye. White House stationery. It seemed the very President of the United States was writing me, no doubt for advice and to pay back the $500 he borrowed of me in 1887. I thought perhaps I should just burn the damned thing and claim I never saw it, which only meant that the next letter would be delivered by a flying wedge of generals and admirals.

Lucretia came back in, sniffing, in the fond hope that I had come to my senses and would now act like a hero. I am here only because I rarely ever acted like a hero—on purpose, anyway.

"If Mark Twain wrote *me* . . ." said Lucretia, pulling a stool over to the stone table, and setting to glare at me.

"I'll write him and ask him to write you. I don't know what the hell Sam has been drinkin' lately, he knows me better than to write with a fool proposition like that."

This sally was met by a gloomy silence.

"This here's a letter from the President of the Ewnited States and points east," I says, tearing open the envelope. It was a short message. Teethadore was demanding that I come along with him and God alone knew what gaggle of congressmen and other grafters and dethroned kings to wreak a great slaughter in the Yellowstone country. Soon it would be illegal to shoot game in the park, and Teethadore was a law-abiding man.

"How can he go hunting when the world is in such distress?" said Lucretia, and it was one of them questions a smart man would not answer.

"He's teaching a lesson to the grizzly bears, who would otherwise sweep down upon Omaha. Teethadore's vigilance guards us all."

"You're afraid to give a speech?" said Lucretia.

"No," I says. "I look out at all them faces, and they always seem to be made of pudding, and I think 'My God, these idiots have come here to listen to me,' and my dicey stomach acts up and I puke over the first two rows. I ain't a crusader."

Besides, a p.s. from Teddy said all was forgiven and I was retired, *if* I came to guide him hunting.

"Lucy," I said, "I've been out where no sane man would go since 1865. I done a lot of things I shouldn't have. I have been through places no other white man has gone to yet. Theodore says if I come, I'm retired. Means I don't have to hope every time I see a letter or a rider that it isn't an order to go to Boola Boola and either watch a war or start one."

"Luther, get out here," said Georgia, a polite housekeeper is a treasure, I always have thought. "It's one of your goddamned red Indians and he's coming right here! You answer the door! Hurry!"

Lucretia snorted and laughed while I scuttled.

I was standing on the porch waiting when he come up and I couldn't quite name him, but he looked familiar. He was Shoshone, and I knew why he had come.

"I am Fools Enemy," the young warrior said. "Washakie lies dying and wishes to see his son Stands-in-the Fire-and-Argues. He sends you this." He handed me a grizzly claw all carved, strung on a horsehair string. I bound it around my neck.

Fools Enemy had turned and gone, the Shoshone don't bandy words at a time like this.

I come hollering into the house and Lucretia and I packed and were rushed into Chico by my neighbor, Tom Clarke. We took the spur train to Sacramento and got on the next train headin' east.

When we were in our suite Lucretia washed her face and found some mineral water and we drank two of the big bottles, so parched we'd got from the heat.

"Washakie must be quite a man," said Lucretia. "You wouldn't go to this trouble for a whole nation."

It seemed my spine, though flabby, was perceived to perhaps adjust to stiffening, if the right goddamned hammerlock could be found for it.

"I'm sorry, Luther," she said, after a moment. "If Mark Twain can't do anything, no one can."

I told her what I knew of Washakie, how he was a warrior so feared by his enemies they made effigies of him to mutilate before going into battle with him. How he'd taken me, a green boy, and plunged me into the warrior's world, what he had taught me of tracking and leaving no tracks, his courage and humor.

"I wanted to be a cowboy," said Lucretia, "and be in the West because it seemed so new. It's gone now."

That it was, that it was.

"Where is he?" she asked.

"At Crowheart," I said, laughing. "He'd want to die in Crowheart, to twit the Crows." And I told her of Washakie's challenge and how he had eaten the heart of the Crow's best warrior and so taken the lands from the Crows.

He'd been born before many white men ever saw the Rocky Mountains. His people had been there a thousand or ten thousand years, and then along comes the likes of Luther Kelly and the next thing you know everything is fenced in, shot, or polluted.

Lucretia listened, laughing, and I told her how Washakie stole the warpoles of the Crows, and how he'd given me a spotted horse to ride who never did buck for spit until exactly five minutes after you mounted—to the second—when the horse fell apart in about twelve pieces, all of which had teeth.

We slept through Salt Lake—everyone does one way or another—and got off at Rock Springs. I rented us horses and tack and we bought canned stuffs to eat and made tracks north, driving two remounts ahead of us. Lucretia was a dandy rider, and she was wearing denims and boots like me.

It took five days to get to Crowheart, and it seemed that half the people in America was there—and a mess of old scouts and trappers—Jim Baker from out in eastern Wyoming, and Jim Bridger's daughter Anna.

There was a cordon of young Shoshone warriors around Washakie's lodge, and when they saw me they motioned for me to come, and I grabbed Lucretia's hand and went on in the lodge. There was a fug of sweat and tobacco smoke and sweetgrass, and propped up on a willow backrest was Washakie, more my father than any other man.

"Stands-in-the-Fire-and-Argues!" Washakie boomed. "You bring me a pretty woman! Perhaps I die tomorrow. You can go now."

Lucretia giggled, and by God, if I'd have turned around I'd bet she would have *stayed.*

"Stands-in-the-Fire-and-Argues is my son," said Washakie. "I tried to teach him how to fight, how to have honor, how to steal horses. He learned how to steal horses." And the old bastard told the tale of my naming, which Lucretia much enjoyed.

"Come here, child," Washakie said. Lucy scooted over and he took her hand.

"You're pregnant! Good!" said Washakie. "Any idea who the father is?"

I looked quick and sure enough, Lucy was blushing red as a holly berry.

Something cold crawled across my heart. I shivered and thought of Eats-Men-Whole. So long ago.

"This dying is tiring," said Washakie. "You can't really die without saying farewell to your friends. I didn't know I had so many friends. I should have been more careful."

He closed his eyes for a minute. They flew open and he looked at me.

"You guiding Teddy?" he said. I nodded.

"God, what a fool that man is. He's dangerous."

He closed his eyes again and I took his hand and murmured goodbye to my father, and Washakie gave a little jerk and he was gone, like that. His jaw dropped and he sighed, with his eyes half closed.

"He waited for you," said Lucretia. We held each other for a moment, and then we walked stooped way over out of the lodge and I went to the grandson of Washakie—well over sixty himself—and said the old man was gone.

The women began the ululations and the men sang. I held Lucretia's hand tightly and we walked away. There wouldn't be but a few minutes before the newspaper reporters and such would be here like flies on shit.

We were a fair haul from anyplace that you could call a hotel, and I suggested to Lucretia that we just ride on up toward the Yellowstone country, hooking around by Jackson's Hole, where we could get proper outfitting and I could meet Teethadore and his beaters and she could stay in the inn at Old Faithful. I assured her that she would not *want* to be along with Teethadore and the rest of his faithful clowns. I don't like trophy hunters much. If you don't want to eat it, why bother it?

I was able to rummage around and find my old sheaf of tricks to keep warm and comfortable, and there was still quite a lot of game. We et antelope a lot, and when we finally come up the last rise and saw the Tetons spread across the sky and the sun on them Lucretia gave a whoop of surprise and joy.

We checked into the Lodge and took baths for hours, and I was able to get a telegram to Chico to tell Georgia to send a trunk of

Lucretia's clothes along. In the meantime she scandalized the toffs who were dressed like they was going to dinner in New York or Paris. I thought she looked fetching in jeans and boots and the big yellow silk scarf I got her in the hotel gift shop.

There was even a hatter at work in the old lodge across the way, and I had him make up a couple tall-crowned cream-colored Monarch of the Plains hats, best head cover for this country or any other, you ask me.

We had three weeks until Teethadore would be at Old Faithful, so we waited for Lucretia's trunk to come and then took a stage over that way, stopping at Hot Springs and taking the waters. Lucretia all jammed into her lady duds was not happy. She said she'd had no idea how much she was putting up with before.

It was the rump end of the season here at Old Faithful, the days warm and sunny, some frost at night, but up this high winter didn't blow in, it just shut its jaws.

There were boardwalks laid over the fissured travertine where the hot water seeped, and we were walking the morning after we had got there when I looked up ahead and froze in angry horror. Some fool in a straw boater and a celluloid collar was over by a little tree, poking a grizzly cub with his furled umbrella.

His wife—found out later that they was newlyweds—was laughing and all entertained.

I wondered where the mother was. I didn't have a gun big enough to do the job, but it didn't matter, there was a sudden roaring grunt and she came round a bump of travertine—grizzlies are a lot faster than horses—and the dude took about two steps and she was on him, tearing his chest open so deep his lungs and heart was torn completely out.

The woman was screaming and running and the bear took about two steps after her and then she went back to her cub and they took off.

A couple lodge hands with rifles come running over, both so damn scared that they was levering cartridges out as they ran. The bears were long gone anyway, and the woman was slumped in a heap on the boardwalk. Some other folk come by with a stretcher and put her on it and hauled her up to the lodge.

"Gaddamned fool got what he deserved," I said, real low so I wouldn't be heard. Fool. Idiot.

I looked round the basin at the green trees and the ghostly white marl from the geysers. I'd been through here first in '72, and there was a railroad spur right to the lodge now. I guess I showed sadness in my face, Lucretia come and put her arms around me and said, "It was beautiful then, but it's gone, Luther."

"We were both young together," I said. "I look forward to some sedate and ordinary, dull life. So far we have been through a war, a typhoon, Washington, D.C., and other petty diversions. I told you turnips? I don't want to raise turnips. I want to raise potatoes. Turnips stick up above the damn ground. Forward and pushy. Potatoes stay buried. I vote for the meeker vegetable."

The lodge was all in a huzzah as there hadn't ever been a mauling by a bear. All the guests was crowded into one of the big dining rooms while the manager flannel-mouthed away about this unheard of crime, first time ever, no idea where this rogue animal came from.

A feller slammed in past us, caroming off the doorjamb, and his slouch hat was pulled down so low that I couldn't see him. He had poured quite a little Panther Sweat down his gullet, he reeked like a busted still.

"Twarn't the bar's goddamned fault, ya lily-livered fish-backed weasel-hearted pomaded fop!" said the stranger. "Yer stupid unbaked bridegroom got his guts tore out 'cause he was a-pokin' a cub in a tree! He worked hard to get hisself killed! I kin see better brains in mule's asses!"

"It's Buffalo Jones," I says, delighted. "What he's doin' here I do not know."

Buffalo was wearing a floor-length wolfskin coat and yellow boots. He looked sorter like a big hairy mushroom with yeller feet.

"Mr. Jones," said the manager, "thank you for your advice, but if you wouldn't mind . . ."

"I mind, ya posy-smelling carny-barker," roared Jones. "I told you not to leave the damn garbage out but ya did so the guests could see some goddamned bears. Ya satisfied now?"

Buffalo had run out of steam and he turned right around and was marching in the direction of the saloon and he glanced at me and stopped and turned and looked hard.

"Wherever they sold ya that goddamned mask a Luther Kelly go take it back, he's a lots uglier and they orter give a bottle of stink out with the mask they want to fool his friends."

Buffalo squinted hard at Lucretia, who was laughing into the back of her hand.

"Pretty lady," he said. "Them men your momma warned you about? He's it. He's all of 'em."

"My wife," I said, for the first time.

Buffalo went from comic to courtly so fast I couldn't see the damn blur. He bowed to Lucretia and offered her his arm and said, "Let us go somewheres quiet and never mind him. I'll call the sheriff my own self."

We took Buffalo up to our suite and sent for drinks and seegars. We talked of old friends, Washakie finally dying, when it was sure he'd outlive us all, this and that.

"Buffalo here has been trying to cross buffalo with cattle for thirty years. Soon as he can get a live calf out of it he's in business."

"That's about right," said Buffalo. "I don't like giving up. It means having to think of something new to do."

I asked what he was doin' here, and he said he was a consultant. I asked what he was doin' with a job the name of which he probably can't even spell, and dressed like a dustmop for it at that.

There was a knock at the door and when I opened it the manager came in, oozing oil, and said, "You are needed, Mr. Jones."

Buffalo motioned for us to come and we follered along, tramping the full length of the downstairs and out the back, where I heard the sounds a boar grizzly makes when it wants to eat the world.

Buffalo took a lantern and walked out to the dark. A huge bear hung by one foot from a Douglas fir well bent—I thought that Buffalo had set the record for size on snares. A steel cable hung down and the bear hung from it, clawing the air and time to time curling up and biting the cable.

"They needed a discouragement consultant," said Buffalo, peeling off his coat. He picked up a ten-foot lodgepole with a whittled grip and walked over to the bear and proceeded to beat on it like the damn thing was a dirty rug and Easter was next Sunday.

Buffalo pounded on that thousand-pound critter for a good long time and the bear's growls were getting thinner and not near so convincing. Then they flat turned to bawls.

Buffalo stepped over to the fir and pulled on something and the bear slid down to earth. The cable come off the foot. The bear sat up.

"And don't come back ya son of a bitch!" yelled Buffalo, running at the bear and waving the club.

The grizzly gave a squeal of pure terror and run as fast as it could go, off into the night.

"You just got to know how to talk to 'em," said Buffalo, with his hands spread wide. "It's easy, if you just know how to talk to 'em."

23

Teethadore wasn't planning on a great long hunt—just two weeks. Hardly time to render even a single species extinct, but the cares of office weighed on him and how would it look if he was up here shooting the last of the mountain boomers and the Swiss invaded us or something?

I waved to Lucretia and she waved back and Buffalo Jones stood behind her looking innocent—he was a gent and she would have a good time. There was much yet to see on day rides wasn't all covered with sandwich wrappers and beer bottles. There's a funny thing Americans do: they think if it's beautiful throwing garbage on it makes it even purtier.

Teethadore had a camp set up big enough for a cavalry division including a Professor of Taxidermy who would tenderly care for the heads and hides of them things Teddy and his fellers shot. There was a feller named Burroughs who was a "naturalist" who shot everything that flew, hopped, crawled, scratched, whistled, tweeted, growled, roared, or just sat there picking at itself.

We were to leave in the morning, all animal matter in miles having been done right in. Teddy seemed happy to see me, clapped me on the back and said he'd brung me a present.

My eyes narrowed some.

He'd had this made up custom, he said.

Cold drops of sweat poured down my spine.

So he hands me a package all fancy wrapped says "Tiffany" on it and I looked it over careful trying to spot the trigger that would set off the bomb that would leave me hairless and without eyelashes for months. Didn't seem to be one. I opened the package, pointing as much of it as I could at Teddy and inside wrapped in black velvet was a custom hunting knife in a silver sheath looked a lot like something you'd give a Bulgarian field marshal in gratitude over having lost only half the army 'fore he got to the war.

"Jesus," I said, picking it up, "is there a poodle and a yacht to go with this thing?"

Teethadore was hurt. He always took his rifles and shotguns down to Tiffany's to have fancy engraving and such put on 'em. He'd take an eight-pound shotgun in and triple the weight and wonder why he shot under everything flew past.

"I appreciate your efforts, Kelly," said Teddy.

"Ain't made any yet," I pointed out. "Now what poor critter minding its own business up there are you set on exterminating?"

"Hunting is manly and puts us in touch with our forebears."

"Your forebears would have starved or fallen off cliffs," I said. "Ain't none of you survived till they invented eyeglasses."

I was getting dangerous, and he knew it. I knew a lot more about Kettle Hill and the glorious Rough Riders than he'd like let out. There was about two dozen newsmen running about, eager for a good quote.

"Ah, a word, Luther," says Teethadore, walking away from the scribbling leeches. "I have perhaps treated you unfairly from time to time. You need have no fear of further requests upon the part of the government. Prior to coming here I burned all the records . . . . . . but, you son of a bitch, if you set me up with the reporters I'll rewrite the records from memory and have you off to Ougadgeedutphu to study tribal warfare."

"Fair enough," I says.

"I wish to shoot a mountain goat," said Teddy.

"Why?" I said. "I got you three."

I shot them for him, truth to tell. The hardest part of being a guide is keeping your sights on the critter and pulling the trigger the same time the dude pulls his. It's a gift, you have to be born with it.

"The taxidermist was incompetent. Moths have wreaked havoc with my trophies."

Hard for me to understand how a feller can get so Shakespearean over a couple of bug-chewed goat heads, but Teddy was larger than life, which to me means just a freak of nature.

In the morning we set out with a pack train would've done about right for an expedition to conquer Mexico. There was six hunters and then cooks and wranglers and the goddamned journalists coming along behind like gulls behind a sardine boat.

There was two other guides, young pups who looked at me half awed and half belligerent. Second night out I dragged them off to a nice remote rock where we drank whiskey and wondered how many of these here mighty hunters we could bump off cliffs or leave as diversions to charging grizzlies. They was good boys, and we sort of mapped out our hunting.

I took Teethadore and a British feller named Plumley up high for goats. Goat hunting is easy. They are never attacked from above and are sure there ain't anything up there. So you get above them and roll a rock down and they will be in your lap in seconds. For us old farts this meant a lot of puffing and hauling to get us up top. Plumley looked like an eggplant with white sideburns and Teddy's grin was sort of frozen in pain. We snuck to the edge and looked down. There was about thirty head of goat down there.

"When we stop gasping and can see some I'll lever a rock over and then you fellers stand ready. They'll come over the top in a goatly wave."

"Grim country here," said Plumley. "Never seen anything like it."

He was used to potting tame grouse on the piss-flat moors of Scotland.

In a few minutes we had quit heaving, had some breath back, and our eyes didn't have dancing blurs on them. I tipped a big chunk of rock up on the edge, nodded, and sent it on over.

It weighed a couple hundred pounds, and it made one hell of a crash first time it hit and skidded, and then it went dead into a big spur way the hell down with the goats and sort of exploded. There was chips flying every which way, and I saw six goats fold up and fall to their deaths, casualties of flying bits of rock. The others started up as quick as they could and were bounding from hoofhold to hoofhold, I swear the damn things could get all four feet on a postage stamp.

The Anglo-American Union saw to their artillery, and I stepped back out of the line of fire and line of goat.

The goats busted over the top like popcorn jumping out a pan, and Teethadore and Plumley blazed away and they hit not one hair on one goat.

This awesome marksmanship caused me to grin wide like a shark. Teethadore was about ready to jump on over—I wouldn't have stopped him—and Plumley was looking at his rifle with deep distaste.

"Bugger all," said Plumley. I thought it a fair assessment.

I heard the three paced shots of trouble. Someone was hurt down there and any in hearing were honorbound to come to his aid.

"We'd best get down," I said. I started, leaving them to pick along behind as best they could. All I had by way of guns was a Colt, I wasn't going to treat Teddy as kindly as I had long ago.

Going down a mountain is easy, if you haven't a pack on—with a pack it's harder than going up—so I hopped and let gravity speed me along and when I got clear down to the base of the mountain I turned right toward the long high cliff the goats had been on.

I hadn't heard any more shots so I wasn't sure where the trouble was. Then I saw a circle of men up front and I come up to them to find I had committed manslaughter. A newspaperman I had found particularly obnoxious had been hit by a dead goat traveling at a fast speed, and the goat drove the scribbler into the ground sort of like a tent stake and up to the knees at that. The goat then sort of flattened the feller every which way. The mess sort of looked like a big strawberry shortcake with a dollop of hairy whipped cream on top.

"His editor will never believe this," someone said. A pretty good epitaph for a newspaperman, I thought.

Someone fat and breathless come running down the trail from the cliff, screaming that there was another one. We left the past-help newsie and went on to find yet another murder-by-goat which had been made at a sharp angle, so all was left was a wide red smear amid the scattered pencils.

These here reporters were going to be closed-coffin jobs, for sure.

I wondered if I had picked off any others. (I hadn't had such a soul-satisfying day since Moses took to the weeds.)

Teethadore and Plumley wheezed into the disaster area, and Teddy was perspiring like a longshoreman and blind from the water on his glasses. Teddy walked right up on top of the goat which was on top of the reporter and pulled off his glasses and asked questions while the blood stuck to his boots.

I folded my arms and looked. Damn, the great have a dignity unmatched by us mere mortals, I remember thinking, I hope he gets stuck there.

Plumley harrumphed for a while and then he pointed out to TR that he might better stand somewheres else and make his speech as he didn't look so very good where he was. Teddy squelched off to one side and put on his glasses and glared at the mess. How dare this son of a bitch commit such an unpleasantness! On one of TR's hunts! The nerve of the bastard, probably went to Yale! And here he was *dead* and TR couldn't even rescue him!

I was polishing my fingernails. Unarmed man drops rock off cliff, killing six mountain goats and two reporters, while the rulers of All the World That Matters blaze away, missing all.

A couple camp tenders come with some tarps and began rolling the reporter and his goat up—it would take a trained anatomist to separate the two—and behind them come some packers who was trying to keep straight faces while they loaded up the mules they was leading.

Everybody but me took their hats off while the mules with the goo went by. Since I had managed this I sort of thought it would be ill-mannered to start showing respect I didn't feel.

"There's still four trophy goats up there," I said to TR.

He sent some of the younger packers after them.

Teddy spent the afternoon expressing deepest sympathy for the families of the departed. I spent the afternoon whittling and chuckling, for it sure don't take much to amuse me.

That evening Teethadore allowed as how he would like to find one of them most fearsome carnivores, the grizzly bear. I had noticed some fresh sign down toward the little river, of a huge boar with a broke claw on his right hind foot, which was probably infected and paining him.

The bear come into camp about midnight that night, and the horses and mules went berserk out of terror and knocked down the pole corral and pulled up the picket stakes. I had my .405 Winchester and I racked six slugs into that bear before he went down. At fifty-odd, I was slowing down some and it occurred to me that many more of these situations and there'd be the one I wasn't equal to.

Poor Teddy had run out in his Union suit to shoot the bear, but when he went through the tent flap his glasses got knocked off and all he could do was beller cuss words and grope around for them. A couple other folks in the tent run right over him and his dignity was low enough now to go through a door without opening it.

When morning come and the bear was all laid out where I'd knocked him down the reporters were on him like terns on a dead whale. Clambering up top and looking at the claws and the fangs, they were damaging the coat. I didn't care much one way or another, and I took great pleasure in asking Teethadore what His Lordship's pleasure was in the way of animals for the middle of the coming night.

Teddy grated out how he would like to shoot a trophy grizzly and I said that it was impossible, this was the last one, all the ones left were about the size of Jack Russell terriers and he'd have to be content to own a trophy could fit comfortable in a washtub.

Teddy stomped off and Sir Beresford Plumley come and he was to prove himself a gentleman.

"Mr. Kelly," he said, "is it possible this trip could become even more ridiculous and fatal?"

"Dead certainty," I says. "Teethadore drags disaster behind him like a skunk does stink."

"Thought so," says Plumley. "Believe I'll repair to the lodge and stay there."

The old bird saddled a horse right smart and rode off, and I knew that I would miss him. Grains of horse sense was uncommon hard to find round here to begin with.

Teddy held a press conference with his booted foot on the bear's head, never actually *saying* he'd shot it, but his outthrust jaw was taken at face value. I sat and leaned against a tree, snickering.

The afternoon had turned off with storm clouds and the smell of snow blowing down off the Pitchstone Plateau, a good time to be out hunting for the snow would worry the game down from up high.

Teddy and I went out about three in the afternoon, taking a back trail I knew up to a saddle that was a pass from four different drainages over. Game would be moving through it like a white sale day at Marshall Field's, and if we were upwind in the right place we could pick and choose.

We hobbled and tied the horses and walked the last mile, taking up a stand in some jumbled rocks that looked down on the game trails. We sat still as rocks our own selves and the game started moving right away. There was elk in bunches, and deer in their ones and threes and once a fat black bear which Teddy scoffed at as an unworthy opponent. Then the game was still and I nudged Teddy when I saw a flash in the trees and a great boar silvertip stalked out and stood for a moment on top. He must have got the scent of us so diluted he couldn't tell where we were or which way to go to avoid us. He stood up on his hind legs and sniffed and Teddy fired, blowing off the bear's lower jaw. The animal bellered in pain and rage and Teddy shot again and again without coming near him. All I had was the Colt and to tell the truth it wasn't a lot of use to me at that moment.

Teddy wanted to run to the horses and set out, but I stopped him, saying that we'd leave him to stiffen and bleed. An hour later we went down and the horses went plumb crazy at all the bear scent, or so I thought. Well, they should have because the bear had only gone off into a screen of lodgepole and he come out, armed plenty good with those claws and mad as hell. We shot and ran and the horses bucked and I fell off, with the Colt in my hand and I scrambled up atop a big boulder and when the bear would make a lunge up I'd try to shoot down his throat and finally I hit the spine.

That bear took more killing than any other I ever saw.

I come down off the boulder and slumped against it and had a relaxing time breathing for a while, and I enjoyed the very act of it because for a moment there I thought maybe I wouldn't be doing it much longer.

Teethadore was furious. He'd made a bad shot and his guide had to finish the critter off, he'd blown off the jaw and so it was worthless for a rug for the floors of Sagamore Hill, and Teddy hadn't gotten his way which always did put him in a black pet.

"You know," I said, "it'd be safer you just went back to the capital and moved your janissaries around the globe and left this to me. Just leave me a list and I'll fill it."

He came on over, trying to control his wrath and not doing too well. I hoped to give him a fit of the apoplexy.

"You are the most insolent and insubordinate son of a bitch I have ever . . ."

"Miles says the same thing," I said. Teddy and General Miles hated each other with black hatred, for there was only one knob at the very top and they both meant to have it. Teddy was newly the President but Miles was the General of the Army, and Miles didn't think much of Teethadore's tactical genius.

"You wouldn't . . ." said TR, remembering that I knew all about Kettle Hill and Santiago.

"Depends," I said.

We left the bear for the skinners and went to our horses who were shaking like wet dogs with fear, and walked them around and got on 'em and headed for the main camp.

When we got close we ambled through a covey of scribblers and camp tenders and got off at the rope corral and stripped off our saddles and bridles and blankets and set them on the lodgepoles cut and hung for the purpose.

A young feller on a lathered horse come up the trail and I heard some shouting and saw a bunch of fingers pointed at me.

Lucretia. Something was wrong. I lassoed a big fresh horse and was pulling him to the side when the feller said Mrs. Kelly was ill and I should return right away. I threw my gear on that horse cursing the straps and rings and swung up and rode, unseeing, I didn't know or care what I rode over or what might be follering behind me.

I took care the horse didn't pull or break anything, but if the way was clear and the footing good I made the bastard stretch. He was about windblowed when I got to the hotel and I just slid off him and run inside. I was rushed down the main hall and through a couple sets of double doors where they had an infirmary, and a couple doctors were standing there looking grave.

One motioned me over to the far wall of the room.

"Mrs. Kelly has had a miscarriage and then a mild hemorrhage," he said. "It is grave, but she has much improved. Please don't excite her."

She lay propped on several pillows to ease her breathing, but she opened her eyes when I parted the curtains and I leaned over and she put her arms around my neck and just cried for a time.

"I wanted a child so," she said. "The odds were against it. But I wanted your child."

She cried herself out and then she went to sleep, the dead sleep of the exhausted. I sat there watching her and thinking on how I was a bit old to be starting a family. I knew I'd give her anything she wanted, and now I couldn't remember how it had been when I didn't know her. She'd got into every corner of my life somehow. I'd wandered to her, and the sun came up inside me.

I got into the bed, snuggling close beside her. Her sweet breath touched my face.

There were a lot of places that I wanted to take her.

And the list would sure grow in the morning.